Fiona Leitch is a novelist and screenwriter with a chequered past. She's written for footballing and motoring magazines, childbirth videos and mail order catalogues; DJ'ed at illegal raves in London, been told off by a children's TV presenter during a studio debate; and was the Australasian face of a series of TV commercials for a cleaning product. All of which has given her a thorough grounding in the ridiculous, and helped her to write funny stuff.

facebook.com/fionakleitch

instagram.com/fionaleitchauthor

Also by Fiona Leitch

The Nosey Parker Cozy Mysteries

The Cornish Wedding Murder

The Cornish Village Murder

The Perfect Cornish Murder

A Cornish Christmas Murder

A Cornish Recipe for Murder

A Cornish Seaside Murder

The Cornish Campsite Murder

The Cornish Castle Murder

The Cornish Christmas Pantomime Murder

The Cornish Honeymoon Murder

The Cornish Halloween Murder

THE CORNISH HALLOWEEN MURDER

A Nosey Parker Cozy Mystery

FIONA LEITCH

ONE MORE CHAPTER

One More Chapter
a division of HarperCollins*Publishers* Ltd
1 London Bridge Street
London SE1 9GF
www.harpercollins.co.uk
HarperCollins*Publishers*
Macken House, 39/40 Mayor Street Upper,
Dublin 1, D01 C9W8 Ireland

First published by HarperCollins*Publishers* Ltd 2026
1

A catalogue record for this book is available from the British Library
ISBN: 978-0-00-885384-6

Printed and bound in the UK using 100% renewable electricity
by CPI Group (UK) Ltd

FSC www.fsc.org
MIX
Paper | Supporting responsible forestry
FSC® C013604

To the late and much missed Sir Terry Pratchett. Your influence on my writing lives on in Shirley, who is becoming more like Nanny Ogg with every book.

Chapter One

'She's chained herself to what?' I couldn't keep the exasperation out of my voice as I listened to the rather more amused one at the other end of the phone line. 'Okay, I'm on my way…'

I was right in the middle of preparing for a buffet I was catering that evening for the Penstowan Chamber of Commerce. It was their annual general meeting, held (against everyone's better judgement) in a private room at the Market Arms, which seemed to always end in either a punch-up or a drunken karaoke session. So the current Chair, my old friend Tony Penhaligon, had decided to lay on food, to keep everyone in a good mood and hopefully line people's stomachs enough to soak up the alcohol. Whether that would stop Louisa Tremayne belting out 'I Will Survive' was anyone's guess. Louisa owned the nail bar and beauty salon on Pike Street and always had a thing or two to say for herself. Having heard her caterwauling on several memorable occasions I had to concede it was worth a shot.

I took a tray of sausage rolls out of the oven – despite spending several years honing my culinary skills at catering college, I seem to have spent a large proportion of the following years making sausage rolls, vol au vents, and sandwiches – and left them under a mesh cloche to cool. I took off my apron and whistled for Germaine, my fluffy white Pomeranian, who was curled up next to the radiator. She lifted her head sleepily to look at me.

'Walkies!' I said brightly. She gave me a withering look. 'Yes, I know it's cold out there. But I need to go on a rescue mission, and I'm not leaving you on your own with a plate of sausage rolls nearby.' Because that dog loved pastry and pork sausage meat even more than most of my buffet customers did.

I bundled myself into my coat and picked up the dog lead. It was late October, which in the UK can mean temperatures in the high teens or in single figures, and today it was 11°C – not freezing by any means, but cold enough, especially as we'd had something of a heat wave in September. I picked up the reluctant pooch and carried her outside, locking the front door behind me.

'I'm not carrying you all the way there,' I said, ignoring her pleading look as I set her down. She gave a resigned sniff, and together we trotted down the road, down the hill, where the trees that lined the road formed a leafy canopy of browns and golds overhead, and onwards into town.

St Ann's convent had been built just outside Penstowan

some time in the early 1800s by a prominent local industrialist, which practically made it a new-build compared to other convents and monasteries. It had supposedly been built to show his devotion to God, but local gossip claimed it had actually been created as a convenient way to dispose of his troublesome, confirmed spinster sister, who refused to marry or toe the line and behave the way society expected an unmarriageable (for that read 'over the age of twenty-five') woman from a good family to behave. The adjoining cottage hospital had been added a hundred years later; there had been plenty of room, the land belonging to the convent stretching on all sides for a considerable number of hectares. However, both buildings had fallen into disrepair in the 90s, and the nuns had joined a convent somewhere in Kent. The local council had slapped a compulsory purchase order on the land around them, in order to build houses on the surrounding fields. The original buildings, meanwhile, were left to rot, until a developer bought them. And that was when the trouble started.

I heard the protestors before I saw them. Cries of 'Stop the developers!' mingled with the screech of seagulls, and someone somewhere had one of those loud-hailer things.

'What do we want?'

'More GPs!'

'When do we want them?'

'Now!'

I couldn't disagree with their sentiments, but I wasn't sure that standing in a street in Penstowan was going to help the NHS with their recruitment and funding crisis. I turned a corner and found myself face to face with the small crowd (although pretty big for Penstowan), clutching banners and arguing with the good-natured police officers who'd been deployed to stop any trouble.

'All right, Chrissie?' I said, to the cheerful black PC who was watching the goings-on with a bemused look on her face. She'd moved to Penstowan a few years back, swapping South London for Cornwall just like I'd done after I left the Met. I'd suffered a little from culture shock when I'd moved back, having been away from Penstowan for twenty years (apart from visits to see my mum and dad); I couldn't imagine the culture shock a native London bobby must've gone through, moving from a place where muggings and street robberies were an everyday occurrence, to somewhere you were more likely to be assaulted by a stray sheep.

'Hi ya. Come to bail out your mum?'

'Yup. Thanks for calling me, although if she does it again you can just go ahead and throw her in the slammer.'

She laughed and led me over to where a couple of other officers, PC Brett Something (I'd never got his surname and, as he clearly didn't like me very much, I was too scared to ask what it was) and Old Davey, who was officially PC Trelawney but no one called him that, stood in front of a bulldozer. Davey saw me and nodded.

'All right, Jodie? Come to get your mum? She's a live wire, ain't she?' he said, trying and failing to keep the look of admiration off his face.

'Don't encourage her,' I said. 'Where is she?'

Brett and Davey stood back and revealed my mum, chained to the wheel of the bulldozer. Next to her, also chained, was her best friend and fellow political firebrand, Jocasta.

'Hello, love,' said Mum. 'Come to join us? Did you bring a cushion? My bum's getting numb, sitting here. Bloody cold this ground is.' She shifted. 'I think I sat on a pile of wet leaves. It feels like there's something stuck to my nethers.'

'Of course she hasn't,' said Jocasta. 'She's come to talk you into giving yourself up, haven't you? Once a puppet of the establishment, always a puppet of the establishment.'

'Oi!' I said. 'I'm not a puppet. You can sit there all day for all I care.' I started to turn away, but Mum called out to me.

'No!' I turned back, trying not to smile. 'No, I mean, I reckon we've made our point, don't you, Jocasta?' Mum gestured to a group of workmen standing nearby. 'We've stopped them working, haven't we? It'll be getting dark soon, so there's no point in them starting anything now. They'll pack up and go home for the day once we've gone.'

'Hmm,' said Jocasta, managing to pack a whole lot of betrayal into that one syllable.

'Oh good, you're here,' said Daisy, my teenage daughter, appearing next to me. She handed me the placard she was holding and I automatically took it without thinking. 'My arm's starting to ache.' She bent down to make a fuss of Germaine. 'Have you come to join the protest, Germaine? Who's a good little agitator, then? You are!'

I swung the placard round to examine it. No more flats! Medical centre NOW! it read in bold letters. I sighed.

'I don't disagree with any of that,' I said, 'but you need to be picketing the town hall. The council are the ones who gave them planning permission, after all.'

'Oh don't you worry about that,' said Daisy, an evil glint in her eye. 'There's a council meeting next week…'

'As long as Nana doesn't chain herself to the planning committee,' I said. Next to me PC Brett cleared his throat.

'If you could be getting your mother and her friends away from the bulldozer now—' he said, in an officious tone.

'Friends? There's only her and Jocasta—'

'Hello!' called a voice from the other side of the bulldozer. I groaned.

'You've not got Bob involved in this too?' I said. Bob was Mum's new beau; they'd been 'stepping out', as he put it, since Christmas. He was a lovely man, but he was a bit older than Mum, and not quite as fit and healthy as she was.

'Of course he's involved. He was the one who got us the chain and the padlock.' Well, he did own a hardware store. I walked round to the other side of the bulldozer.

'Poor Bob, don't let her lead you astray! You shouldn't be sitting out here in the cold.'

'No, I reckon you might be right about that, love, seeing

as I lost all feeling in my right leg about twenty minutes ago…'

That was all I needed to persuade Mum that she'd done her duty and it was time to come home before she developed piles, put Bob in hospital, or got herself arrested. Chrissie was about to come off duty, so she offered to give Mum, Bob and Jocasta a lift back to mine after she clocked off – it was cold and all uphill – much to Brett's ill-disguised disgust. But it was a good idea as it was a surefire way to make sure the disruptive pensioners stopped making a nuisance of themselves.

'I'm not supposed to take sides,' said Chrissie, dunking a biscuit into her tea, 'but I have to agree with you.' We were sitting in the kitchen – me, Mum, Daisy, Jocasta, Bob and Chrissie – having a brew and a chat. 'A new medical centre would be better for the town than another housing development. I've only been here a few years and I can't believe the amount of new houses they've built! I know we need them, but we could do with more doctors and another dentist, too.'

'It just makes so much more sense,' agreed Jocasta. 'We're not even saying they can't build any houses. They could still pull down the old convent building or convert it into flats. But the cottage hospital building isn't in that bad condition. Why can't they refurbish and reopen it?

God knows we need more medical facilities in the town, especially with all the new people moving here.'

Mum scoffed. 'I wouldn't want to live in that old convent.'

'Why not?' I asked. 'It's a beautiful old building. If they did it sympathetically—'

'Ha! Nothing to do with anaesthetics—'

Daisy and I looked at each other. 'She means aesthetics,' I said.

'It's got more to do with the fact that building is full o' ghosts.' Having delivered her portentous warning, Mum sat back with a satisfied air and dunked a Rich Tea biscuit into her brew.

'Ghosts?' asked Bob, looking at her in awe. Bless him, he was well loved up over my mum. 'You seen 'em, have you, Shirl?'

'What, the ghostly figures of a load of old nuns, floating along the corridors?' asked Daisy, who I suspected was not taking this entirely seriously. 'Why would nuns be scary anyway? I've seen *The Sound of Music*.'

I shuddered. 'Oh God, just imagine moving in and having to listen to some ghostly Sister singing "doe a deer" all night.' Daisy and Chrissie sniggered.

'Yeah, ghostly singing nuns might be annoying but they'd be harmless,' said Chrissie.

Jocasta shook her head. 'You're kidding, aren't you? You lot obviously never went to a convent school. I did, and let me tell you the sisters were terrifying. And a bit too handy with a ruler over the knuckles, too. They turned me into the atheist I am today.'

'It's none of that,' said Mum. 'Ooh, get me! "Nun" of that, d'you get it? No, I'm talking about what went on in that convent, and in that hospital too. Them were dark days. Don't you remember, Bob?'

'When are we talking about? Because I have trouble remembering what I had for breakfast.' He was joking, but he clearly didn't know what Mum was going on about.

'It was a home for unmarried mothers,' said Mum. I rolled my eyes.

'There's nothing wrong with being an unmarried mother,' I said.

'No, I know there ain't,' said Mum. 'But when I was a teenager it was thought of as a scandal if a girl wound up with a baby, and no father around. God knows, a girl can't get herself pregnant, can she? And yet no one said anything about the boy what got her that way.'

'So what went on at this hospital, then?' asked Daisy, leaning forward to take another biscuit.

'The girls' families would drop them off, about the time they started to show,' said Mum. 'They'd leave them with the nuns until they'd had their babies, and then… Well, not all the girls wanted to give their babies up, but like I said, it were frowned upon if an unmarried young woman had a baby. Sometimes the family would come and collect them, and the child would be brought up by the grandparents – probably plenty of kids out there with a much older "big sister" who was actually their mum.'

'Just like that storyline in Eastenders,' said Bob, and we all nodded.

'You ain't my muvva!' screeched Daisy.

'I AM your muvva!' said Chrissie, and they laughed. But I didn't.

'What happened to the girls whose families didn't want to bring up their babies?' I asked. Mum looked solemn.

'The nuns would arrange for the babies to be adopted,' she said. 'Even when the girls wanted to keep them.'

Daisy and Chrissie now looked horrified. Jocasta smiled at them sympathetically.

'You two are both too young to know what it was like back then for women,' she said. 'Especially young women. We have equal rights now – or almost equal, anyway – but back then, we were treated like second-class citizens a lot of the time.'

'That's terrible,' said Daisy, shocked. 'When was this?'

'I don't remember when they opened the hospital,' said Mum, 'but this was back in the 60s. It were all very well for them to talk about miniskirts and free love and burning their bras, and it might've been different in places like London where they were all a bit more sophisticated and that, but outside the cities it was the girls what suffered.' We were all silent for a moment, apart from Germaine who, under the table, decided to fart and yawn simultaneously, in a way which somehow managed to be cute.

'More tea?' I asked, standing up, but Mum still had a bombshell to drop.

'I made friends with this girl who was staying there,' she said. 'Must've been 1967, 68? I was fifteen or sixteen. I'd left school and I got a job at the old greengrocers on Plough Road – you must remember that, Bob? It were before they built that stupid one-way system, when you could still drive down there rather than having to go all round the houses like you do now.' Bob nodded. 'She came in, asking for directions to the nearest train station. I must've looked at her like she was an alien, because I thought everyone must know there wasn't a station anywhere near here – used to be one at Launceston, but that got closed a couple of years earlier, thanks to Dr Beeching and his cuts. When I told her that, she looked like she was going to burst into tears, so I took her out the back and made her a cup of tea, like you do, and she told me they were going to take her baby from her.'

'Poor girl,' I said. I could only imagine the heartbreak of having your child forcibly removed from you, and it was enough to make me feel the sting of tears in my own eyes. 'Did she get away?'

'Not that day, no.' Mum suddenly grinned. 'I persuaded my boss to let me do the deliveries to the convent after that. He was only too glad really, he said the nuns gave him the willies. Dot, her name was. She used to meet me in the kitchen when I brought the fruit and veg, and we talked about how she could get away and where she could go. She ended up giving birth there – we thought it was probably the safest thing to do – and then a couple of nights later I helped her climb out of a window with her baby. I hid her at the shop until the morning, and then got them both on a bus to Barnstaple so she could get the train back up country.'

'Wow!' I said, looking at my mum in admiration. I used to take the mickey out of her for being a bit bonkers, and wind her up by calling her an old biddy, but my mum was actually completely brilliant; a maverick with an enormous heart and a great sense of mischief. 'Do you know what happened to her?'

'Yes, we wrote to each other for a few years, although we did lose touch in the end. I know that she ended up in Derby, where she pretended she was a widow so the neighbours wouldn't talk about her, although I'm sure they all guessed what had happened – she was very young to be a widow. A few years after that she met a nice bloke and told him exactly what had happened, and he didn't care. Married her and looked after her little boy like he was his own.' Mum grinned again. 'I got into a lot of trouble, though.'

'Did you? What happened?' Daisy leaned forward again, but this time it was to listen to her grandmother, not take a biscuit.

'I'd been putting money aside to give Dot, to pay for her escape,' said Mum. 'But when it came down to it, there wasn't enough. So I might've stuck my hand in the till and nicked a couple of quid, to cover her train fare and a couple of nights in a boarding house. Might've given her a bit of food to keep her going, too…'

'You didn't! Wow, Nana, you're a badass, a real rebel.' Daisy held up a hand and Mum high-fived her.

'Boss found out and sacked me. When your great-grandad found out, he was going to give me a right telling off, only your great-grandmother stopped him,' said Mum. 'She said, "Bert, you go to church every Sunday and sit there in your finest, giving it all that about being a Christian and doing good deeds, but you've not helped a soul in need your whole life. Your daughter helped a poor young woman what had been taken advantage of, and kept a baby with its mother. You should be proud." I can't say as he was proud, but he kept his mouth shut.'

I laughed. 'Good old Nana. I can just imagine her doing that.' The women in my family all had very strong opinions on what was right and wrong, and the current generation of them was exactly the same.

Chrissie looked at her watch. 'Well, thank you for the tea, and for sharing your criminal history with me, Shirley. I think the statute of limitations has probably passed now though, so I won't be arresting you.' She stood up. 'Don't tell Nathan, but if I caught you doing the same thing now I might pretend I hadn't seen you.'

'Yes!' hissed Daisy. 'I knew you were a badass too, despite the uniform.'

Chrissie laughed and jokingly wagged a finger at my daughter. 'Don't think that gives you carte blanche to go back to that building site and be a nuisance, though. I'd better be off.'

'Oh God, look at the time!' I said. 'I've got the blasted

Chamber of Commerce thing in an hour and a half, and I've got vol au vent cases to fill. Everybody out of the kitchen!' I looked down at my feet. 'And that includes you, Germaine.'

Chapter Two

'Got any more sausage rolls?'

We were in the back room of the Market Arms, overseeing the buffet. The pub had been decorated ready for Halloween and was festooned with glow-in-the-dark skeletons, shiny purple bats, and plastic pumpkins of a violently orange hue. A mannequin dressed as a witch, complete with a pointy black hat that was starting to look a bit floppy and an old broomstick that wouldn't have taken the weight of any except the most undernourished old crone, loitered suspiciously in a corner. Fake cobwebs festooned the corners. At least I assumed they were fake; they could have been real, the result of an inefficient cleaner. They were in my house, anyway. The decor didn't feel entirely appropriate for a Chamber of Commerce meeting, but then the Penstowan Chamber could be pretty inappropriate themselves at times, so maybe it was just as well.

I slapped Nathan's hand away from the plate before he could grab one.

'Honestly, you're worse than Germaine. They're not for you.' He gave me a mournful puppy-dog look, so I gave in. 'Oh, go on then. Just one.'

'You know I deserve it,' he said, swallowing a mouthful. 'There's not many husbands who'd get home from work and then come out and give their wives a hand with their evening job.'

'It's okay,' I said, rolling my eyes, 'I've already put in your nomination for Husband of the Year.'

'You have? Oh great, I'll go home then…' Nathan turned to walk away, but then laughed and grabbed me. I let him kiss me on the cheek and then pulled away.

'I'm working!'

'No one's watching, they're too busy fighting over the pork pies.'

'I don't think it's pies they're fighting over,' I said, condensing what remained of two plates of sandwiches into one. As it was a buffet I wasn't serving anyone, but I liked to keep the display looking nice and not as if a plague of West Country locusts had swarmed all over it, stripping it of anything containing sausage meat (not many vegans in the Penstowan Chamber of Commerce) and just leaving behind sad piles of crumbs and the odd lettuce leaf that had found its way onto their plates. Buffets ain't about health food, are they?

'It did get a bit heated, didn't it?' Nathan leant against the bar and watched the franchise owner of a local mini-market dive for the last cheese straw before the bloke who ran one of the tourist tat shops overlooking the beach could get it. 'I was trying to listen in to the meeting from the bar, but I couldn't make out what they were saying.' He sipped at his pint of lager. 'And to be honest, up until the point the shouting started, it was dead boring.'

'Lots of complaints about St Ann's,' I said.

'Really? I'd have thought they'd be behind it,' said Nathan, surprised. 'More residents means more business, surely.'

'I think it was more about protestors getting in everyone's way. The lack of policing was mentioned…'

'Huh! They do know how many officers are stationed in Penstowan, don't they? Unless they expect me to drop any murder enquiries and take Matt and Sunil down there with me.'

'What murder enquiries?' I'm ashamed to admit I perked up a bit at that. Nathan laughed.

'Sorry, don't get over-excited. There's the hit-and-run on the back road near Camelford – no cameras, no witnesses, no one dobbing in their friend or neighbour with a damaged car, so no leads. That's been going on for months now, and I don't think we'll get any further. And then there was that kid who OD'd. We're still looking for whoever supplied him, but it's just a wall of silence.'

'Oh,' I said, trying not to sound disappointed because that would make me look like a monster. 'I thought maybe something new had come up.'

'Nope. The residents of Penstowan and the surrounding

areas can sleep soundly in their beds tonight,' said Nathan. He nodded towards something, or someone, as it turned out, behind me. 'Here's the man who'll know.'

I turned around to see Tony, my oldest friend in the whole world, coming up behind me.

'Lovely buffet as always, Nosey,' he said. I groaned.

'I thought we'd stopped using our childhood nicknames, Snot Face.'

He laughed. 'Yeah, sorry. Although I thought you two would be sitting here talking about the shenanigans from earlier and wondering what it was all about.' He grinned. 'Being nosey, in other words.'

'Okay, yeah. Busted,' I admitted. 'Go on then, spill the beans.'

'St Ann's, innit? All those unwashed troublemakers getting in everyone's way.'

'Oi!' I said indignantly, but he was smirking. 'You obviously know my mother was involved.'

'Shirley, God bless her, her ears'll be burning tonight. Although of course no one could say too much about her, because Bob's boy Greg's a member of the chamber and he were here.'

'Of course,' said Nathan, grinning hugely. 'They daren't say anything nasty about his future stepmum.'

'Stepmum? Get outta here,' I said. 'It took Bob eight years to ask her out. He'll be in his grave before he plucks up the courage to propose.'

'Oh, you never know…' teased Tony. 'Anyway, that weren't all they were saying about it. Gerry Hughes – you know him, runs the AdventureLand farm park – he were saying his brother's working on the development. Proper freaked out, he is.'

'Freaked out? By what, a group of pensioners with placards?' I scoffed. Tony shook his head and looked serious.

'Nah, of course not. He said stuff keeps going missing—'

Nathan scoffed this time. 'Thefts, on a building site? Whatever next. My uncle Bob was a builder—' I snorted and he gave a resigned sigh '—yeah, yeah, Bob the builder, I know… He built an extension on his house and I don't think he paid for ninety per cent of the materials.'

'I don't mean theft,' said Tony, ominously. He must've been taking lessons from my mum. 'Just stuff going missing.' Nathan and I obviously looked like we still didn't know what he was going on about, because he continued. 'He said they've been demolishing some of the internal walls in the old convent building. He stopped for a tea break, and when he went back the mallet he was using wasn't there.'

'Someone moved it,' suggested Nathan.

'But there weren't no one about,' said Tony. 'And then the next day it shows up again, somewhere else in the building.'

'Okay…' I said, doubtfully. I hadn't expected a load of beefy builders to be superstitious or easily scared, but what did I know?

'It don't sound that bad, now I say it out loud,' admitted

Tony. 'But he reckoned the place just feels eerie. He said it felt like he was being watched.'

'Probably by the foreman, to make sure he doesn't misplace his mallet again,' I muttered, and Nathan laughed. Tony threw up his hands in defeat.

'I give up. It does sound daft now, but Gerry had the hair on the back of me neck standing up.'

'If Gerry's brother or anyone else working on the site has any issues with tools going missing, tell them to report it,' said Nathan. 'It's still theft at the end of the day.'

'Not if the stuff keeps turning up again,' I pointed out, but he rolled his eyes at me and I realised he was trying to change the subject and discourage Tony from gossiping about it. Good luck with that, I thought. I might have the nickname 'Nosey', but as far as I could see I wasn't the only one who liked to stick their beak into other people's business and then have a good natter about it.

We packed up the leftovers – not that there were many – and then headed outside to Gwyneth, my trusty (but slightly rusty) van. The Market Arms' car park was tiny, having been built in the days when the main form of transport would have been horse and cart, both of which would've been housed in the coach house behind the pub, but that had long ago been sold off and turned into a couple of flats. I had to go backwards and forwards several times, executing a ten-point turn (instead of the usual three-point one) in order to get around a ridiculously big but suspiciously clean truck – you know the type, normally called something like the Ford Gigantosaur or the Nissan

Wolverine, beloved by people who say they need it for its 4 x 4 capabilities but who never use it for anything more challenging than the school run – which was parked at an angle and taking up three spaces. As I finally managed to reverse around the Toyota Over-Compensating-for-Something and out into the street, I looked up at the skyline. It was almost eleven o'clock, and overhead stars punctuated the darkness. There was a faint glow over the sea from the almost-full moon; it was waxing gibbous, or "waxing gibbons" as my mum had once mistakenly said and never been allowed to live it down (my imagination had gone into overdrive with that one, imagining a bunch of hairy monkeys sitting around doing their bikini lines), with the full moon just a couple of nights away. Luckily for the local constabulary it would be too early for Halloween; luckily, because the full moon always seems to bring out the worst, or at least the unpredictable, in people. Throw Halloween into the mix and it can be chaos, even in a small town like Penstowan. Silhouetted against the night sky were the outlines of houses, some with lights still in their windows, and, in the distance, St Botolph's church, the iron cross at the top of the steeple glinting in the moonlight. It was starkly beautiful. But there was another light, somewhere I hadn't expected to see one.

'Look!' I said, stopping the van and pointing, but just then a couple of people leaving the pub crossed the road noisily in front of us, distracting me and drawing my eyes to them.

'What?' asked Nathan, his gaze following my finger.

I looked back, but the light wasn't there. Maybe I'd imagined it.

'Oh – nothing. I think I was just seeing things that aren't there.'

But I couldn't shake the feeling that for a few seconds I had seen it; a light on, in one of the windows of the old abandoned convent.

The next morning I came downstairs to find Mum bustling about in the kitchen. Although she lived in the granny annexe we'd had purpose-built for her (which included a small but fully equipped kitchen), when it came to making anything more substantial than a cup of tea she always seemed to be floating around using my pots and pans, my food, and my electricity.

'Morning, love,' she said, taking my butter and my strawberry jam from the fridge, which she then proceeded to spread on my bread, which had just popped up from my toaster.

'Morning. Nice of you to make me breakfast,' I said, putting down the empty mugs I was holding (from the early morning cups of tea I had earlier taken up for me and Nathan to drink in bed) and reaching for a slice. She slapped my hand away.

'Get your own,' she said, which struck me as advice she would've done well to heed herself, but I didn't push it.

'I need feeding up this morning, I've got a long day ahead of me.'

'More protesting?' asked Nathan. He'd followed me into the kitchen, already dressed and keen to get his own breakfast before heading off to work.

Mum shook her head hastily. 'Nah, not today. Bob's got an appointment with the podiatrist in Exeter this morning, so I'm going with him.'

'Aah, how sweet,' I said. 'You can hold hands while he gets his bunions looked at.'

Mum ignored me. 'And then we're going to have a mooch around the shops, and have lunch out. Which reminds me—' she turned to look at me '—I won't be needing dinner tonight.'

'Bold of you to assume I was going to make you any,' I said, but the fact was I always made enough for Mum to have some, even when she said she'd sort herself out, and she always ended up eating it. But we had to do this little dance every time so she still felt 'independent'. She absolutely was still independent, she was just too bloody lazy to cook.

Nathan poured granola into a couple of bowls, added a splash of milk, and topped them with fresh raspberries and a handful of blueberries. He handed me a bowl. 'Eat,' he said. 'Leave your mother's toast alone.'

'It's my toast,' I grumbled half-heartedly, but despite the fact that hot buttered toast with strawberry jam smells absolutely amazing, I actually feel better eating something a bit more healthy for breakfast. Which is much easier when someone else has made it for you.

We all tucked in, with Germaine sitting patiently next to Mum, waiting and hoping against hope that today would be the day when we finally gave in and gave that poor, neglected dog a whole piece of toast to herself (today was in fact not the day).

'Ooh, hot buttered toast,' said Daisy, sniffing the air as she appeared. I laughed.

'If you want some you'd better join Germaine,' I said.

'I might just make some myself,' she said, reaching down to make a fuss of the dog, whose eyes still never left Mum's plate. 'Germaine! You're such a scavenger!'

As she dropped a couple of slices of bread into the toaster I looked at her properly, finally noticing what she was wearing.

'Hang on! It's not even nine o'clock and you're fully dressed?' I asked, apparently flabbergasted. 'What's happening? I thought it was half term this week?'

'Oh, ha ha,' she said. 'If you must know, I've got a busy day today.'

'Not you as well?' I sighed. 'Everyone's busy apart from me. All I've got planned today is sitting around, reading a good book and eating chocolate.'

'Sounds awful,' said Nathan, finishing his granola.

'It's not easy having a good time,' I said. 'Even smiling makes your face ache after a while.' He laughed and stood up, bending down to kiss me on the forehead.

'You can always come and help us go through the hours

and hours of CCTV footage Sunil's dug up for that hit-and-run,' he said.

'I thought you said there wasn't any?'

'Not in the actual accident location, no, but you know that was never going to stop Sunil. So in the absence of any other leads whatsoever he apparently had a dig around last night and found cameras on the roads surrounding it.' He clearly wasn't looking forward to the prospect. 'Hours and hours of footage of deserted country roads at night…'

'I'll stick with my book and my chocolate, thank you.'

Nathan gave me another kiss and left for work. I turned back to Daisy.

'So what are you up to, then? Are you going back to the demonstration outside St Ann's?'

'Er – no. Nana will have to represent the Parker family today.'

'She's not going.'

'Isn't she? I mean, aren't you, Nana? I thought you told Jocasta yesterday that you'd be there again today?'

'Yeah, well…' Mum looked uncomfortable. 'It were proper cold out there, chained to that bulldozer, weren't it? And damp. And poor Bob, he's too old to be doing that sort of thing really. We did our bit yesterday, I reckon.'

'Hmm… Jocasta's not going to be happy,' I said. 'She thinks you two are her comrades in arms, and you're deserting her.'

'If you're that bothered, you go,' said Daisy, and Germaine yapped in agreement, although it didn't mean anything because she adored Daisy and tended to agree with whatever she said. 'I can't do it today, Joe's taking me to the Witchcraft Museum in Boscastle.'

'Joe's taking you there?' I was disappointed. 'If you wanted to go, I'd have taken you. I love that museum.'

'Joe wanted to go as well,' she said. 'His new material's about the historical oppression of women and he wants to get some inspiration.' Joe was a rap artist with a career that was on the up, although I wasn't sure that trajectory would continue if he started rhyming about witches rather than b*tches, which seemed to be what most rappers sang about. Although I couldn't deny it sounded like a vast improvement, and one I heartily approved of.

'Sounds like his new album's going to be a right bundle of laughs,' murmured Mum. I shook my head discouragingly at her.

'No, no, fair play to him, it's better than singing about hoes in da club and all that shizzle,' I said, grinning as Daisy fought to stop herself dying of absolute cringe.

'Whatever you do, do not say that sort of thing in front of Joe when he gets here,' she ordered me.

'What, you don't want him to know how cool your mum is?' I teased.

'That's one way of looking at it…'

'I haven't been to the Witchcraft Museum in years,' mused Mum. 'Have they still got those rocks there, you know, the ones shaped like—'

'Yes,' I said quickly.

'Shaped just like a lady's—'

'Yep, still got it.'

'And there's another one that looks just like a bloke's—'

'Yep, they've still got that one too,' I interrupted, eager to not get into a discussion with her about rudely-shaped pebbles. 'You should take your camera, sweetheart. NOT to take pictures of rocks shaped like genitals,' I said hastily, as Mum opened her mouth to say something, a mischievous grin on her face, 'but because there's loads of interesting stuff there and it might give Joe some ideas for cover art, if they still have covers these days, what with everything being streamed online.'

'Yeah, I'm going to,' said Daisy.

'You could get some good photos to add to your portfolio,' said Mum. Daisy glared at her. 'You know, the one you were putting together for your university applications.'

'Yeah…'

'Okay,' I said, looking from one of them to the other, 'what's going on?'

'Dunno what you mean,' said Mum, innocently.

'Why are you glaring at your grandmother?' I asked. Daisy groaned.

'Nana, you said you wouldn't say anything.'

'I didn't! I haven't!'

'Come on, one of you spill or I'll set the dog on you,' I said firmly. Germaine chose that moment to yawn and look as unthreatening as possible.

'It's about university,' said Daisy. 'I was thinking I might take a gap year.'

'Oh, okay.' But I could tell there was more to it than that.

'Or actually, I might not go at all…' Daisy looked at me, as if waiting for an explosion.

'Oh, okay.' I stood up and went over to her, giving her a little squeeze. 'Why didn't you just say that?'

'I know you wanted me to go—'

'Woah woah woah, I was just happy for you to go if you wanted to,' I corrected her. 'You know that I'll never tell you what to do. Other than to wash the dishes or make a cup of tea.'

'You don't mind if I don't get a degree?'

'What, like the degree I've got? Oh that's right…' I smiled. 'Plenty of people don't go to uni, and they still manage to earn a living and have a good life. Nathan didn't go, either. In fact I think I know more people who don't have a degree than ones who do.'

'Oh, right – good.' Daisy seemed nonplussed that I wasn't annoyed. 'I thought you were keen for me to be the first one from our family to go.'

'Sweetheart, the only thing I want you to do is be happy. If that means going to uni, great. If it means staying here in Penstowan with your mum for ever, that's even better…' I grabbed her for a cuddle. 'Give Mummy a kiss, stay with me for ever…' I gave a maniacal laugh, puckering my lips for a big wet kiss. She shrieked and pulled away, fighting me off.

'Get off, you mad woman! All right, all right, I'll go to university!' We all laughed and I took the opportunity to nick her last half slice of toast.

'See, I told you to just tell her,' said Mum, and I nodded.

'As much as I hate to ever admit Nana's right, she often is,' I said. 'You can tell me anything.'

Breakfast out of the way, Joe turned up – he'd borrowed his mum's Nissan Micra, which didn't fit the image of a bad boy rapper but definitely reflected a thoughtful young musician writing about the oppression of women – and whisked Daisy off to Boscastle. Then Bob turned up, driving his new fancy SUV – it wasn't quite as big as the massive one we'd had trouble manoeuvring around in the pub car park the night before, but it wasn't far off. The Parker women are all quite short – Daisy's the tallest of us now at a lofty 5'4" – and I had to laugh as I watched my five-foot-nothing mum hauling herself up into the passenger seat.

Finally alone, I turned to Germaine. 'Looks like it's just you and me, kid.' Germaine didn't look all that enthused by the prospect of spending quality time alone with me, but beggars couldn't be choosers.

As I'd told Nathan, I had absolutely no plans for the day other than pottering around the house, reading my book, drinking tea and eating chocolate. But you know what they say about the best laid plans of mice and men…

My phone rang. I was surprised (and a little alarmed) to see it was Jocasta calling me.

'Hi, Jocasta,' I said, warily. 'How are you this morning?'

'I'm fine,' she said. 'Is everything all right with Shirley? Only I've been calling her and she won't pick up.'

I cursed my mother; she was obviously avoiding her friend, not wanting to admit that she wasn't going to turn up at St Ann's this morning. I'm not above lying for my loved ones in the right circumstances, but I wasn't going to do it today; served her right for being a coward.

'Mum's fine,' I said. 'She must be out of mobile range at the moment. Bob's got an appointment in Exeter and she's going along for moral support.'

Jocasta sighed. 'I knew it. She's a fair-weather protestor. I just wish she'd at least turned up this morning, what with the news people coming.'

'News people?'

'Yes, we've got a film crew from BBC Spotlight coming down, and someone from the local paper, too. I was hoping to have a big crowd here.' She went quiet for a moment, and I had the horrible feeling I knew what she was going to say next. 'Are you busy…?'

So that was how I found myself (and the dog) standing outside the St Ann's building site, clutching a banner with a bemused look on my face, wrapped up in a scarf and woolly hat and dreaming of my nice warm house and my nice comfy armchair.

'I'm only staying until the TV people have been,' I told Jocasta, but she airily batted my words away with a hand.

'We'll see…' I couldn't blame Mum for bailing out and not telling her, she could be quite scary when the mood took her.

'Jodie?'

I turned round to see Donna, an old schoolfriend and owner of the Captain's Table fish and chip shop, of which we were frequent customers. 'I thought it was you. What you doing here?'

I thought it was probably fairly obvious what I was doing, seeing as I was holding a blooming great placard saying 'NO to developers! YES to GPs!' on it, but it would've been facetious to point that out.

'Oh, you know, lending my support to the cause,' I said. 'How are you?'

'Worried about my Liam,' she said, and I (somewhat uncharitably) thought, not again, because Liam had got himself mixed up in some nasty business a few years ago and had ended up in hospital after a brutal beating. She must've read my mind because she quickly added, 'Oh no, nothing like that! He's finished his degree and he's back from uni now, and he's doing a bit of labouring to earn some money while he looks for a proper job.' A passing workman – because our little crowd hadn't been big enough to stop the burly building contractors from cracking on with their work today – gave her a look. 'Not that this isn't a proper job! It's just not a proper job for someone with a politics degree…'

'What's worrying you?' I asked, eager for her to get on with it.

'This place – it's not right,' she said, vaguely. 'I – actually, let me go and find him, he can tell you himself.'

'I'm not a careers adviser,' I said light-heartedly, not wanting to get mixed up in the Fossett family's drama, but it was too late. She'd already hurried off to the caravan that was parked on one corner of the site, which looked to be serving as a break room for the workers.

'And this is Jodie, our local police hero,' said Jocasta,

leading a young woman engulfed in a puffer jacket with 'BBC' on the breast over to me.

'Ex-police hero,' I said. I could just imagine Nathan's reaction if I was all over that evening's Spotlight news programme, claiming to be a police officer. I pulled my scarf further up over my face, trying to dissuade further interaction.

'She got a commendation for bravery when she served in the Met,' said Jocasta.

'Really? That's impressive,' said the young woman. 'If we could interview you and Jodie, Mrs—'

'It's Ms, and it's Jocasta. Yes, I think that would be a good idea.'

'Would it?' I asked, bewildered. A bloke who had the air of a technician – you know what I mean, he looked like the sort of person who knew his HDMI cables from his, um, other type of cables – came over and started fiddling about with lapel microphones and muttering about the light. And then Donna came back with Liam, who looked extremely reluctant to be there.

'Tell Jodie what you told me,' she said.

'Oh Mum…' he started, but she shook her head.

'Don't "Oh Mum" me, you were proper freaked out a minute ago. You said you were getting too scared to work here much longer.' Liam looked like he would've welcomed a sinkhole opening beneath his feet at that moment, while the young woman – the reporter – who had been discussing something with the techie dude, pricked up her ears.

'What's bothering you, Liam?' I asked, sympathetically.

He looked ready to leg it, but one look at his mum stopped him. He gave a resigned shake of the head.

'I dunno, it'll sound really silly when I say it out loud…'

'Try it,' I said. 'And even if it does sound silly, I promise I won't laugh.'

'There's these dolls,' he said, and I almost did a double take because I didn't know what I'd been expecting him to say, but it definitely hadn't been that.

'Dolls?'

'I told you it sounds stupid.'

'No no, go on. Dolls can be right creepy, can't they? My mum bought me a Tiny Tears when I was little – you know those old baby dollies that cry and pee their nappies?' Liam looked mystified, and I guessed Donna and her husband hadn't bought him one when he was a kid. 'Anyway, it used to just cry at random moments, even when I wasn't playing with it. Scared the bejesus out of me. I've never liked dolls since.'

'They're not that sort of doll. They're, like, made of rags – not a rag doll as such but, like, a bunch of dirty old rags bundled up into a sort of vaguely human form. They're all misshapen and they have these kind of grotesque faces —' Liam pulled a face, as if to demonstrate. 'They're a bit like voodoo dolls, I suppose, only there's no pins sticking in them or anything.'

'I see,' I said. I didn't, but I had a vague recollection of seeing that same type of doll somewhere. 'Where did you find these dolls?'

'That's what makes it so creepy,' said Liam. 'We've been

knocking down some of the internal stud walls in the convent, so we can reconfigure the interior layout.' I nodded, thinking of the builder Tony had told us about the night before, whose mallet had mysteriously disappeared one day only to reappear the next. 'We found the first one hidden in a room up on the first floor. It looked like it had been walled up in there for years.'

I shivered. That did sound a bit eerie.

'You said "the first one". How many have you found?'

'I know of five, so far,' said Liam. 'Everyone just laughed at the first one, but now people are starting to get a bit freaked out.'

'I'm sorry, I couldn't help overhearing,' the reporter butted in. 'I'm Letitia Burke, from BBC Spotlight. Could you tell me more about these dolls?'

'What the bloody hell are you doing here?' came a gruff and extremely pissed-off voice from behind us. 'Get that bloody camera out of the way! This is my land and I want you off it now.'

We all turned round. A tall, well-built man in his fifties, with a scowl that somehow seemed to cover not just his face but his entire body, stood there glowering at us.

'Ah, Mr Devlin,' said Letitia Burke. 'You're the developer, is that right?'

'It is, and that's the only answer you'll be getting out of me today.' Devlin angrily shoved the technician and the cameraman out of the way. 'Go on, bugger off!'

'Mr Devlin—' started the reporter, but he was having none of it.

'This is private property, and all of you are trespassing.' He turned to Liam, who shrank away from him. 'Get back to work, I'm not paying you to gossip.'

'We're from the BBC—' Burke wasn't backing down, I'll give her that, but she was never going to impress the angry property developer by invoking the name of our state broadcaster.

'I don't care if you're from the BBC, the NHS, the BMI or MFI, get off of my land, now!'

Chapter Three

To be fair we weren't on his land, we were outside the perimeter of the building site, but I decided that discretion was our best course of action here and suggested we move further away, out onto the pavement. From here the diminutive size of the crowd of protesters was even more obvious. I felt sorry for Jocasta; the protest had been her idea, after taking the more legal route – lodging objections at the planning stage, and turning up to complain in person at council meetings – had failed. As far as I knew a lot of people in Penstowan were on her side, as we desperately needed more GPs in the area, but I wasn't sure that turning the old maternity hospital into a medical centre would've solved that problem anyway; it had taken almost a year to recruit a new GP at our local surgery to replace one that was retiring.

'There were more people here yesterday,' Jocasta told

Letitia Burke. 'Don't let the size of the crowd fool you, nobody wants this development to go ahead.'

'There was definitely a bigger crowd,' I agreed, although I wasn't sure 'nobody' wanted the development to happen. There were plenty of families living in Penstowan with adult children who currently couldn't afford to leave home, and if there were going to be some so-called 'affordable' flats and houses being built and set aside for local people (as had been agreed in the planning stages), then they'd probably be all for it. 'But people have got stuff to do, haven't they? Jobs to go to and that.'

The reporter smiled. 'Don't worry, we can shoot it so the size of the crowd isn't too noticeable. This is just the kind of campaign we like to get behind.'

So we stood and let ourselves be interviewed – although I made sure it was mostly Jocasta who did the talking – and then I handed my banner over to someone else, as Germaine was getting bored and she was less skilled at not showing it than I was.

'Jodie, do you have a minute?' Letitia had followed me down the road and called out to me. I groaned to myself. Would no one leave me alone to go home and read my book?

'Yes, of course. What can I do for you?' I forced myself to stop and smile at her.

'I couldn't help overhearing what that young man was saying to you before,' she said. 'You remember, about the dolls?'

'Oh, yeah.' I looked back to see if I could see Liam, but

he was obviously back at work. 'I'm sorry but I don't really know what that was all about. Mr Devlin appeared before I could get to the bottom of it.'

'Right…' She looked at me, like she didn't quite believe I didn't know more than I was letting on. 'You've helped the police on a few occasions, haven't you? I knew I recognised the name.'

I laughed. 'Don't tell me I'm famous.'

'Ha! Infamous, more like. Which is actually far more interesting, from a journalistic viewpoint anyway. Do you think that's why he came to you? For help, maybe?'

'Nah, his mum's an old schoolfriend, that's all,' I said, but damn it, maybe she was right. Maybe Liam was genuinely scared by whatever was going on, and Donna, knowing my background (recent as well as our schooldays), had thought I was the right person to go to. That familiar itch – that tingle when I felt, when I knew, that something wasn't right – had started in my brain. I wasn't going to be able to let this go, was I? Not until I'd spoken to Liam again, anyway.

I shrugged and walked on, leaving the reporter staring after me, although hopefully she'd turned away by the time I skidded on a slick of wet leaves on the pavement and nearly went head over heels. Germaine, of course, had a lower centre of gravity and trotted straight to Rowe's café without incident, where we discovered that the whole town had gone Halloween mad. I narrowly avoided a pile of pumpkins haunting the doorway, bumping my head on a spider dangling from a thread above it. I yelped before I could stop myself, even though I knew it wasn't real. At least I hoped it wasn't. I recovered just enough to make it to the counter and order a tea for me and a puppuccino for her (they'd recently started serving all manner of doggy delights, and Germaine was now hooked). But I was still so out of sorts I didn't even look at the cakes on offer until I was standing right in front of the till and, under pressure, had to just order a fruit scone with jam and butter.

'Can I tempt you into trying one of our new pumpkin spice lattes?' asked the woman behind the counter.

'What? Oh dear God, no.' I grimaced, and she did too, in sympathy.

'I don't blame you,' she said in a low voice. 'Bloody horrible, they are. The boss wanted to try and cash in on all this Halloween and "Fall" nonsense, so I had to ask.'

We sat down with our respective pick-me-ups and drifted into deep thought (I did, anyway – Germaine just drifted into deep whipped cream). Although I hadn't seen these dolls, I had some mental image of what Liam could've been talking about. As my phone pinged with a message, I had an idea. The text was from Daisy, which was a very handy coincidence.

Found the rocks Nana was talking about! Followed by a photo. Yes, it really did look like a man's you-know-what.

Glad you're having a good time, I typed back. ***Do they still have those creepy voodoo doll thingies there?***

There was a pause as she read my reply, then a row of dancing dots.

Yes! They're sooo creepy! Then another pause, and then—

'Bingo,' I whispered, looking at the photograph she'd just uploaded. Under the table, Germaine lifted her head with a quizzical little noise. 'It's fine, Germaine, it just means I can send Donna a photo and get her to ask Liam if they look like this.'

But I didn't need to do that, because just then the door of the café opened and Devlin walked in. He looked less angry than when I'd last seen him, but more fed up. I looked away, hoping he wouldn't notice me or remember that I'd been a protestor.

'Do you mind if I join you?' I looked up and there he was, holding a mug of tea. Bugger. There were loads of other tables free, so he clearly wanted to talk to me.

I resisted the urge to say what I wanted to say ('Yes, actually, I do mind') and gestured to the chair opposite me with a tight smile.

He sat down. 'Sorry I had a bit of a go at you back there,' he said, looking genuinely contrite.

'That's okay,' I said. Awkward. 'I know you've got a job to do…' Why was I making excuses for him? He was rude, and he'd been quite threatening.

He shook his head. 'No excuse. But the last year has been very stressful, getting planning permission and everything. I thought once we started building, that would be the easy part almost, but…'

'People want doctors,' I said, simply. 'They don't think we need more houses.'

'The protestors? Oh, yeah, they're certainly making life difficult. But it's not them that's the problem.' He folded his hands on the table in front of him. 'What was Liam Fossett talking to you about?'

'Oh, nothing really...' I wasn't sure what to say. I didn't want to get him into trouble or anything.

'He told you about the dolls, didn't he?' Devlin stared at me. I didn't answer. 'It's fine. Well, it's not fine, but one of the other blokes told me you're some sort of private detective. Is that right?'

'Well... sort of.' I mean, no, I wasn't really, but I had proved useful in quite a few cases, as Letitia Burke had alluded to.

'Can you find out who's been leaving these around my site, then?' He pulled out his phone, looked something up, and then held it out for me to take. On screen there was a photo of a doll, not quite the same as the one Daisy had just sent me from the Witchcraft Museum, but near enough. 'Scroll through, there are more.'

I flicked through the photographs. The dolls were just as Liam had said: old and raggedy, with expressions that were blank but all the more menacing because of it. 'Liam said there were five,' I said, still scrolling, 'but there's more than that here.'

'I found the first one,' said Devlin. 'I thought it was weird but I expected it to be a one-off, so I didn't worry about keeping it quiet. But after more turned up and the lads started freaking out I tried to play it down. I started taking them home when I could before too many of the lads could see them. You wouldn't believe a bunch of big strong blokes could be terrified of a couple of daft dolls, but they are. Even I was, when I found the first one.'

'I've seen dolls like this before,' I said. 'Not out in the wild, as it were. At the Witchcraft Museum.'

Devlin nodded. 'That's what I thought they were. Witchcraft.'

'If you're worried about them, why not go to the police?' I asked. 'If you think someone's been sneaking onto the building site and putting them there, that's breaking and entering, isn't it? Or vandalism.' Devlin didn't say anything. 'Aah, I see. You think someone's been planting them, but you're also worried they've been there for years and you've disturbed something.'

'I don't believe in witches,' said Devlin, but that wasn't the same as actually disagreeing with what I'd said. I nodded.

'Fair enough. And I suppose if you went to the police, word could get out about the dolls and you'd get even more negative publicity over the development. Who'd want to buy an apartment in a haunted convent?'

'That had crossed my mind,' the developer admitted.

'Okay. Well, the first thing the police would normally ask in a case like this is, can you think of anyone you've upset? But it looks like you've pissed off half of Penstowan.'

'I know.' Devlin shook his head. 'I don't understand it. We need more housing around here, especially for local people. All I'm trying to do is make a couple of abandoned old buildings useful again. I know some people wanted a medical centre, but the council or the NHS or whoever weren't willing to spend the money on developing one. I'm not a charity. If my business doesn't make a profit then I can't employ anyone.'

'Yeah, I know. So the other thing we'd normally ask is who has access to the site?'

'My workers, obviously, but they'd have to be bloody lucky to plant something without anyone else noticing.'

'They couldn't sneak back at night?' I asked, remembering the light I thought I'd seen the night before.

'No, the gate into the site is padlocked shut, and there's only two of us with keys.'

'You and who else?'

'My foreman, Ken. But it ain't him. I've worked with Ken for years and there's no way he'd do anything like this.' Devlin gave a short laugh. 'He don't have the imagination, for one thing.'

'Yeah, whoever came up with the doll idea has definitely watched one too many horror movies,' I said.

'So will you look into it for me?' Devlin pressed. 'I can pay you whatever the going rate is.'

I had been wondering how exactly I could find out who was behind the dolls, but the words 'pay you' and 'going rate' made me immediately gird my loins and decide that I would find a way. What can I say? Catering work is always a bit patchy in the winter.

'Okay. I'll do what I can.' I sipped my tea to give myself time to think. What should my first move be? 'Can you get me one of those dolls? It would probably help if I could work out where they came from in the first place.'

'Jesus Christ Almighty!' Nathan almost jumped out of his skin as he entered the kitchen. Devlin had been as good as his word and, not long after I'd got back from town, he'd brought round a whole box full of dolls. I'd taken them out to have a good look, lining them up in the order they'd been discovered (as far as Devlin could remember). So there was now what looked like the world's least inviting dollies' tea party going on on the kitchen table.

'Sorry, babe,' I said, hastily going over and calming him with a kiss.

'Please tell me this is not the start of some weird Etsy shop,' he said. 'I could see Jocasta selling this sort of stuff, but not you.'

'You don't think I'm in touch with my inner Earth goddess?' I teased.

'I think your inner Earth goddess would be cleaner and less spooky…' He picked up one of the dolls and sniffed it, grimacing. 'Oh God, they smell as well.'

'You'd smell too if you'd been bricked up behind a wall for years.' I picked up another one, which looked even more the worse for wear than the one he'd chosen. It felt damp, and was covered in mildew.

He looked at me in amazement. 'What the hell? Where did you get them from?'

'The builders working on St Ann's have been finding them, all over the site,' I said, putting the doll down and wiping my hands on my jeans. 'The developer, Tommy Devlin, has asked me to look into it.' I tried not to sound too pleased with myself, but of course Nathan picked up on it.

'Oh wow, have you got your own case?' He smiled, throwing the doll down and pulling me into his arms. 'Has he actually taken you on, or are you just sticking your nose in?'

'Bloody cheek!' I said. 'He's asked me. He's even paying me.'

'Wow. He must be desperate.' I tried to pull away in mock-anger, but he laughed and squeezed me tighter before leaning in to kiss me. He let go. 'I'm joking, babe. That's great. It'll – you know what, I was actually about to say, "It'll keep you out of mischief", but of course it won't.'

'It'll keep me out of your hair, though,' I said. 'My next big catering job isn't for another two weeks, so I'd have been sniffing round your hit-and-run otherwise.'

He laughed. 'If your mum was here she'd say that sounds like a euphemism.' He wrinkled his nose. 'Can we get those things out of the kitchen? I don't think I'll be able to eat with them watching me.'

'Not very hygienic either,' I said. I started to pile the dolls back into the box, and then stopped, looking at the one in my hand.

'Don't tell me you've had a breakthrough already?' asked Nathan, incredulously.

'I don't know…' I picked up another doll and turned it

over in my hands, then reached for another. 'See this one?' I held up the one that had caught my attention. 'Look at its face.'

'Do I have to?' He really did not like those dolls…

'Don't be a wuss, she's not going to hex you or anything.'

'How did we go from calling it "it" to "she"?' Nathan shuddered. I nudged him.

'You big jessie! Look at this one – actually look at her, not squinting in case she gives you the evil eye or something.'

He sighed and took a proper look, his face clearing. 'Oh yeah, I see what you mean – she's – it's not like the others, is it? It's got quite a nice face, under all the dirt.'

'Exactly. And the material her dress is made out of is pretty, where it's not all worn away. This looks like the sort of doll a little girl would've loved years ago.' I put her – it – down on the table and pulled another doll out of the box. 'Now this one, well, it's barely even got a face, has it? It's just a blank bit of fabric with crosses for eyes and a thin line of stitching for the mouth. Which is what makes it so disturbing, I think.'

'Lack of emotion or expression can be quite menacing,' agreed Nathan. 'It's why the Daleks are so scary.'

'Yes! That's it, exactly.' I turned the doll over in my hands. 'That's not the only difference, either.'

'No? What else is there?'

'That first one, although it looks handmade like the others, it looks to me like more time and care's been put into it. Look at this one – it's a bit wonky, and all lumpy. Although,' I mused, 'that might just be because it's old and whatever it's stuffed with has started to break down.'

'That first one's lumpy, too,' said Nathan, 'but it's still a better shape. It looks more… human, I suppose.'

'It looks like a toy made for a child to play with,' I said. 'The others look like they should have pins sticking out of them.'

'Like the ones at the Witchcraft Museum,' said Nathan. I looked at him in surprise.

'When did you go to the Witchcraft Museum?' I asked. 'I love that place! Why does everyone keep going without me?'

He laughed. 'Keep your pointy hat on, babe. I haven't been, but they had a break in at Halloween last year and some of their exhibits got nicked. I'm sure I told you about it at the time. Nothing that valuable – they left the office computer, for starters – but I remember seeing some photos of dolls like these.'

'Oh yeah, I vaguely remember now,' I said. 'And someone stole their voodoo dolls?' I looked down at the one in my hand. Could it have come from there?

'Yeah, only a couple, though, not a whole box full. We never found who did it, but the owners reckoned it was some local kids having a laugh, daring each other to go in and take something on Halloween night.' He grinned. 'The owners said they were going to put signs up around the village saying the stolen items were all cursed, and a terrible accident would befall whoever had taken them. They got everything back by Guy Fawkes night.'

I laughed. 'Serves 'em right.'

'So anyway, what does any of that mean? That they were made by different people?'

I shrugged. 'I dunno, it's early days yet. Still, worth noting.' I dumped both dolls back in the box with their sisters – why did I keep making them sound human? – and handed it to him. 'Can you put these somewhere Germaine —' the poor animal was exhausted after our trip into town, and was sleeping it off next to the radiator '—can't have a go at them?'

'Yep,' said Nathan. 'And somewhere we don't have to look at the ugly little things.'

'Don't say that!' I hissed. 'You'll upset them…'

I washed my hands thoroughly, still feeling the clamminess of the dolls on my hands. The dirt and mildew on some of them did suggest they were quite old, but were they really? How long would it take for them to have got that damp, even being left on a building site in the cold? We'd had a lot of rain recently – it was that time of year – which would probably have accelerated the growth of any mould on them. But even then they would have to have been left on the site for a while; surely they wouldn't be that damp and dirty if someone – a builder or labourer, maybe – had been sneaking them into place every few days, which Devlin had told me was pretty much the rate they were being found.

I shook my head in frustration, but I was being daft; it was far too early in the investigation to know anything for certain yet. All I did know was that I was hungry, Nathan would be wanting dinner soon as well, and Daisy and Joe would be back in a bit, too.

I took some leftover potatoes and assorted veg from the fridge. Bubble and Squeak would be the perfect way to use it up, served with sausages and a fried egg. I mashed up the cold potatoes, then chopped up some bok choy that I'd bought for a stir-fry that hadn't happened. Traditionally Bubble and Squeak is made with cabbage, but the leafy part of the Asian greens would work just as well. I had a large carrot which was on the way out, so I peeled and grated it, then sliced up half a red onion (I'd used the other half on a pizza) and chopped up a bit of cooked broccoli that was floating about in a Tupperware container. All of the veg went into the mashed potato and got mixed together.

I put the oven on for the sausages – I'd normally cook them under the grill, but when you're doing Bubble and Squeak it needs a little bit of attention, so it was much easier to pop them in the oven and forget about them – and then dumped my potato and veg mixture into a hot oiled frying pan. I let the bottom go brown and crispy before turning it over and mashing it all into itself, patting it down so the new bottom (if you know what I mean) could go brown and crispy as well. I repeated this over and over, so the Bubble and Squeak would be a gorgeous combination of soft potato and crispy bits.

'Oh wow, that smells amazing,' said Joe, as he and Daisy bustled in, both of them bundled up in puffer jackets and beanie hats. Germaine had managed to sleep through Nathan's return, but she couldn't ignore Daisy or Joe, who she'd come to love almost as much as her young mistress.

'All right, Joe? You staying for dinner?' asked Nathan, coming downstairs, now out of his smart work suit and clad in trackie bottoms and a sweatshirt.

'If that's okay…?'

'You know she likes to feed people,' said Daisy, and I laughed.

'I do. I even got some vegan sausages for you,' I said. Joe smiled broadly.

'Oh Mrs W, you're the best,' he gushed. Daisy rolled her eyes.

'Kiss arse.'

'Thank you, Joe. I'm glad you appreciate me, even if my own daughter doesn't,' I said. Cue more eye rolling. 'And how many times? It's Jodie.'

'I do appreciate you, Mum,' said Daisy. 'I even bought you a present.' She held out a bag with the museum's logo printed on it. 'Not saying you're a witch or anything.' Germaine barked. 'Although you have got a familiar.'

'And a third nipple,' said Nathan, dodging out of my reach before I could belt him. Cheeky sod.

'I shall rise above that remark,' I said. I took the bag

from Daisy and reached in, laughing as I drew out my gift. I held it up for Nathan to see.

'Oh good,' he said, mildly. 'Another doll…'

Chapter Four

I slept like a log that night despite the presence in the house of the demonic dollies, although I did have some very weird dreams, none of which I could quite remember in the morning. The only thing I did remember was a room with a cot in it, filled with the sound of a baby crying. That's Daisy, I thought in my dream, and I went over and lifted her up, cuddling her close to my heart. Only when I looked down at the infant at my breast I realised it wasn't my beautiful baby girl at all, it was one of those bloody dolls. And then I'd woken up.

Nathan had tossed and turned all night next to me, and he looked bleary-eyed as he reached out to turn the alarm off.

'Stay there,' I said, kissing him. 'I'll bring you up a cup of tea while you give yourself time to wake up.'

'Wife of the Year,' he murmured dozily. I nudged him.

'Don't go back to sleep!'

I climbed out of bed, stopping to wrap myself up in the big fluffy dressing gown I'd bought last winter, and then headed out onto the landing. The door to Daisy's room was ajar a little, so I gave a low whistle and then waited. I heard the bed creak and then the pitter patter of tiny paws as Germaine, who had spent ninety-five per cent of her nights since we'd adopted her sleeping next to Daisy, despite our supposedly strict (but in reality completely ignored) 'no dogs on beds' rule, jumped down from her comfy spot and joined me.

'Morning, sweetheart,' I whispered. She followed me down the stairs to the kitchen and went straight to the back door. I didn't blame her; I need a wee first thing as well. I let her out into the garden, flicked the kettle on and then paid a visit to the downstairs loo (I wasn't going to join Germaine outside). As I waited for the water to boil I thought over the events of the day before and wondered where my investigation was going to go from here.

My first port of call, I thought, should be talking to Liam and some of the other workers, particularly those who had found dolls. I grabbed a notepad from the drawer, the one I normally make my shopping lists on, and began to jot thoughts down.

Who found each doll? Has one person found more than others – could they actually be the person planting them?

That was supposing the dolls were being planted now, rather than having been left walled up years ago. I shivered.

Now that was a disturbing thought. Why would someone have done that?

Talk to the Witchcraft Museum about dolls.

They would be able to tell me when or why someone might use a doll (or nine, as I currently had sitting in a box in the dining room). They might even be able to tell me if the dolls really were as old as they looked, maybe even who made them. If there were still people practising witchcraft locally, they would surely be in touch with them? It would be helpful if they were, because other than Jocasta, who was more of a New Age hippy than a witch (although she did still have a touch of the Earth Mother about her), I didn't know anyone who was a Wiccan or Pagan or whatever they called themselves. I mean, there was that shop in town that sold witchy jewellery and stuff like that – you know the sort of shop I mean, full of cheap crystals and incense burners and dream catchers, pentagram pendants and weird-smelling candles, and statues of Buddha and Shiva and black cats, like a pick 'n' mix of spirituality – and the woman who ran it, Cynthia, had long black hair, Celtic symbol tattoos, and she loved a clanky silver bracelet or six… but I got the impression that with her it was more of a fashion thing than her actually being Wiccan. Forty years ago she'd have been a Goth teenager with a crush on Robert Smith and a Sisters of Mercy album on her record player.

If someone is planting these dolls, why?

If I could answer the why (and the how), it would lead me to the who. I smiled to myself; that sounded like something my dad would've said. He'd been dead, what, thirteen years now? And I was still taking advice from the late Chief Inspector Eddie Parker.

I poured hot water into two mugs and left the tea to brew for a moment while I let Germaine back in. It was cold out there this morning, and she'd got her business sorted out in double quick time.

Why would someone plant the dolls? The most obvious answer was to scare the builders, and the most obvious hypothetical answer to the follow-up question – why would you want to scare the builders – was to stop them working. I already knew there was a lot of opposition to the development, so it wasn't much of a stretch to think that anything untoward happening on site must be connected. I knew that Jocasta and her small but dedicated band of protesters (dedicated apart from Mum and Daisy) had tried all the legal routes to stop it. Would they move on to illegal ones? As Nathan had said, he could imagine Jocasta with those dolls – out of everyone I knew, she was the one whose 'vibe' they fitted the most – but I couldn't imagine her climbing over the locked gates onto the site to plant them. Not because I couldn't imagine her breaking in (I totally could), but I doubted she could physically climb over them. I could see her taking a pair of bolt cutters out of the capacious tote bag she habitually had slung over her shoulder and snipping off the padlock, but that hadn't happened; Devlin had said there'd been no signs of forced entry.

I fished out the tea bags and took the mugs upstairs, a plan forming in my head. Nathan had begun to nod off again, so I put the mugs down and gently leaned over to kiss him. He murmured and then his eyes fluttered open again.

'Bugger,' he said.

'That's a fine way to greet your wife when she kisses you,' I said. He laughed, struggling to sit up.

'No, I mean I must've fallen asleep again.' He yawned as if to prove his point.

'I felt you tossing and turning last night,' I said, climbing back into my side of the bed. 'Couldn't sleep?'

'I kept having nightmares,' he said. 'I kept waking up afterwards and then it took me a while to fall asleep again, and then I'd have another nightmare and wake up again, on and on…'

'What were you dreaming about?' I asked, sipping my tea. 'You worried about anything?'

'No.' He picked up his own mug, not looking at me. I grinned.

'You dream about those dolls?'

'No! Well,' he admitted, 'I might've done…'

'I did too,' I said. 'I'll stick them in the van when I'm dressed. I think we'll sleep better without them in the house.'

After a quick kiss and cuddle which the dog attempted to get in the middle of (she'd wolfed down her breakfast and padded back upstairs while we were drinking our tea), we both got up and got ready for the day. Nathan, of course, had to go to work, and I had a destination in mind today: Boscastle. It was a shame, I thought, that Daisy had only been there the day before, as we could've gone together; as much as she'd enjoyed it, it wasn't a huge museum and she probably wouldn't be particularly keen to go back again quite so soon. I could take Germaine for company, although maybe that would be a bad idea – I hadn't had a dog last time I went, so I had no idea how dog-friendly it was.

Daisy was making the most of it being a school holiday and having a lie-in. I kissed Nathan goodbye and waved him off to work like a proper Fifties housewife, and then went and prodded my recumbent daughter. She was already awake but lying in bed, scrolling on her phone. Germaine, having ruined my snuggle time with Nathan, had made her way back to Daisy's room and was lying with her nose hooked over Daisy's arm, looking for all the world as if she was perusing her Instagram feed.

'I'm glad the dog looks so happy with you,' I said, 'because I need you to dog sit today.'

'That's fine,' said Daisy. 'I'm only going over to Jade's so I can take her with me, or Jade can come here. Don't forget I've got drum practice this evening, though. I can't miss that, I'm already in Jocasta's bad books for missing the protest yesterday.'

'I'll be back in plenty of time for that. No Joe today?'

'No, he's got a Zoom with his record company and he needs to work on a song for them. He's in a bit of a tizz about it.' Joe had told us at dinner last night that he was working on a new direction in his music – away from rap and more towards 'spoken word pop', as he called it – and I got the impression he was quite nervous about the record company's reaction. She pushed Germaine's nose out of the way. 'Germaine, you're fogging up my phone screen with your heavy breathing…'

I left her to it and headed back downstairs to where Mum was (once again) helping herself to my breakfast materials. I could ask Mum if she wants to come, I thought, but then I remembered the conversation about the rude rocks the day before and hesitated. I needn't have worried, though.

'Four slices of toast this morning?' I asked, suddenly noticing her plate. 'Maybe you should've had dinner last night after all.'

'They're not all for me,' she said haughtily. I stared at her for a moment and then it hit me. My jaw physically dropped. 'Don't stand there with your mouth open,' she admonished me. 'You look like a goldfish.'

I snapped my mouth shut, and then opened it again. 'Don't tell me Bob stayed over for a night of passion?' I looked at her, feeling a little incredulous but also thinking, good for her, because she'd been on her own a long time now and I knew how much she missed my dad. 'Oh my God, Shirley Parker, are you actually blushing?'

'Why should I blush? Believe it or not, love, I ain't a virgin.' Mum stared at me defiantly for a second, and then we both got the giggles.

'Stop it…' I gasped. 'No, really, did he stay over? I didn't think he had it in him.'

'He didn't,' said Mum, and we both giggled even harder. 'Shush, stop it, he'll hear us!'

'Sorry,' I said, struggling to stop laughing.

'He just stayed over for a cuddle,' said Mum, getting herself under control. 'At his age that's about all he can muster.' We both snorted again. 'Should've gone for a toy boy instead.' She peered at me, anxiously. 'You don't mind, do you?'

'What? Of course not. I'm happy for you, Mum.'

'You know he could never replace Dad.'

'I know.' I smiled and gave her a hug, almost causing her to drop her toast (well, hers and Bob's). 'I mean it, I'm happy for you. He's a lovely bloke.'

'Thank you.' She smiled and then pulled a face. 'He snores even louder than your dad, though.'

'I think that's a case of the pot calling the kettle black,' I said, remembering how loud my mum's own snoring was. That was part of the reason we'd built a whole annex for her and not just added another bedroom – so we could be as far away from her nighttime nasal symphonies as possible. 'Anyway, I've got stuff to do so I'll leave you two lovebirds to it…'

'You're not too old to get a clout round the earhole, you know,' said Mum, but I could tell she was happy. Love truly is a many splendoured thing.

I carried the box of dolls out to Gwyneth, my trusty

rusty van, and I'd just clambered into the driver's seat when my phone rang. Debbie.

'Hi ya, Deb,' I answered, pulling my seatbelt across my chest. 'How are you?'

'Fine,' she said. There was an edge to her voice that meant she clearly wasn't fine. 'Are you busy?'

'I'm off to the Witchcraft Museum in Boscastle,' I said. 'Do you want to come, or are you working today?' She was a nurse at the local GP surgery.

'I took a couple of days off so I could spend time with the kids over the holidays,' she said, 'but they've both told me they "have plans", so I'm at a loose end.' Hmm, I thought. Maybe that was why she wasn't fine.

'Come with me, then,' I said. 'It's a nice drive, the museum's fun, and we can have lunch somewhere afterwards. I can swing by and pick you up…'

So I had company on my trip, after all. Debbie steadfastly insisted that she was absolutely fine, until I made the mistake of asking her what her two children, Matilda and George, were up to. Matilda, or Tilly, was a couple of years younger than Daisy and obsessed with clothes and make-up. George was a couple of years younger again – thirteen or fourteen – and into football and video games. Daisy had once described them as 'boringly heteronormative' (I'd been trying to convince her to keep Tilly company one day while Debbie had an appointment to go to and her husband, Callum, had been away for work), which had made me roll my eyes at the time, but she wasn't wrong; Tilly liked 'girl stuff' and George liked 'boy stuff'.

'Tilly's gone shopping to Exeter with a group of friends,' said Debbie. 'She had more make-up on just to get on the bus than I do on a night out. They all wear too much make-up these days.' I nodded, although I was thinking, *My Daisy doesn't…* But no one wants a smug friend at a time like that. 'And George – he's got friendly with this kid whose family live on a farm out by Hatherleigh. Callum dropped him off there on his way to work. Apparently he's going to spend the day with this Riley kid pretending to be a farmer.' She sounded quite disgusted by it.

'Well,' I said, carefully, 'that's good, isn't it? He's out getting some exercise and fresh air. You were worried that he was spending too much time on his X-Box.'

'You know what farmers do?' she asked, and I shook my head even though I'd grown up in the countryside and had a pretty good idea. 'They shoot rabbits.'

'Aah…'

'George and Riley are going to be striding around with rifles, shooting stuff.'

'Not on their own, surely?' If that was the case I could see why she was worried. Young teenage boys and guns do not mix well, in my experience.

'No, of course not, I wouldn't have let him go otherwise. Riley's dad's going to be supervising them.' She sighed. 'I was going to take him and Tilly to the Eden Project, like we did the other year, when they have all the Halloween craft stuff going on. But they'd rather hang out with their mates.'

So that was the issue. I looked away from the road (but just for a moment – the roads round that way are very twisty) and smiled gently at her. 'Debs, they're growing up. It's natural. Would you've wanted to go out with your mum at Tilly's age?'

'No, probably not. But George—' Her voice gave a little break.

'Oh, sweetheart.' As luck would have it there was a lay-by up ahead, so I pulled into it and turned off the engine. I turned to face her. 'Being a mum is simultaneously the best thing in the world and the worst, isn't it?'

She nodded, her eyes filling with tears. 'I just thought they'd need me for a bit longer.'

I reached out and hugged her, which wasn't easy with our seatbelts on. 'They do still need you! They always will. I still need my mum.' I could feel my own eyes getting watery, because I felt exactly the same way every time we talked about Daisy going to university. When she'd told me that she was thinking of not going, I'd felt such a rush of relief go through me; I'd have her for a bit longer. But one day she'd still leave me. I gulped. 'We lose our kids over and over again, don't we? When they're babies they're our whole world and we're theirs. And then they start to get independent and they go off to school, and we have to get used to them not being with us all the time. I mean, even though I was working, I still had her with me whenever I was home. And you just start to get used to that, and then they grow up a bit more and start hanging out with their friends, not with you. And then after that they leave home…' I wiped my eyes and looked at Debbie, who did the same. We both gave laughs that were also half sobs. 'Bloody hell, woman, state of us!'

'You started it,' she said.

'No I didn't! Giving me all that guff about George wandering around the countryside with a shotgun—'

She guffawed. 'I just hope he doesn't shoot Riley's dad. He did say he didn't like the idea of killing anything.'

'He's a good lad, he'll have loads of fun and then come home and tell you about it,' I said. 'And in the meantime you and me'll have fun too.'

'Yes, you're right.' She gave a big snotty snivel and went to wipe her nose on her sleeve.

'Tissues in the glove box!' I said quickly, and she smiled gratefully. 'Do you think…' I started carefully. 'Do you think you could be perimenopausal?'

'Hmm…'

'Let me put it this way: you definitely are. You're acting just like I was before I went on HRT.' I started the engine up and pulled the van out of the lay-by. 'And let me put it another way: in the olden days they'd have said you were in your witch phase…'

Chapter Five

The road into Boscastle wound round and down, into the valley that (usually) shelters the small seaside town from the worst of the elements. I say 'usually', because it was that exact topography which had exacerbated the terrible flood that had almost destroyed the place in 2004. I could still remember watching it, unbelieving, on the news at my old home in London. After days of torrential rain, the Valency – the small river that flowed through the centre of the village – had risen almost seven feet in the space of one hour, bursting its banks. Thousands of tons of water had been channelled into the valley, the force of it carrying away rocks and debris which had smashed into and demolished the village's bridges. There was a visitors' car park at the beginning of the valley, and vehicles left there had been swept away downstream by the raging torrent where they'd formed a churning bottleneck against the harbour wall, forcing the water back up river towards the village, before finally ending up in the sea. And not just cars; caravans, boats, and even buildings had been ripped away and thrown into the ocean. The violence of Mother Nature had been on full display that day. It was sheer luck that no one had died.

I parked the van in the visitors' car park and we got out, following the river down on foot. Every time I'd been here since that fatal day I'd imagined how it must've felt to see the water rising so quickly, churning into a destructive force. It was almost impossible to equate that torrent with the gently flowing waters beside us.

Boscastle is a pretty place, full of gorgeous stone cottages, shops selling Cornish trinkets to tourists, and little cafés where, on warm days, you can sit outside and enjoy your traditional cream tea. It was cold and quite blustery that day – far too cold to sit outside – but the sun was out, sparkling on the rippling waves of the river and shining on the bus load of elderly (but hardy) tourists who had arrived at the same time as we had.

We passed an ice-cream parlour which was (unsurprisingly) not exactly doing a roaring trade, a couple of art galleries with their windows full of watercolours of boats, blue and green sea glass sun catchers, and figurines of Cornish piskies – cute, but typical tourist wares – and a shop that sold surf gear in the summer and walking gear in the winter. They *were* doing a roaring trade, mostly in woolly hats. I wished I'd brought my own; my ears were starting to go numb in the cold wind.

The Witchcraft Museum was set back a little way from

the river. It was only a small building – a two-storey, whitewashed stone cottage, adjoining another, single-storey cottage which was owned and run by the National Trust as a café. Once upon a time it would probably have been a fisherman's cottage, or maybe even two or three fisherman's cottages. But now it was home to a surprisingly large and beautifully curated collection of occult artefacts.

There was a small garden area out the front – usually no more than a few pots and planters – but a big iron cauldron had been placed there, no doubt in honour of the season. Fiery orange witch hazel had been planted around it to represent flames, and ivy grew out of it, trailing over the sides like green smoke. A couple of black-clad mannequins were in attendance, their haggard faces squinting at the cauldron. One gripped a poison bottle, while the other was poised to add a plastic frog to whatever magic potion they were cooking up.

'Go on,' said Debbie, waving her arm at them. 'You need three witches to make a coven.' I laughed and joined them, pretending to sniff the potion as Debbie took a photo. 'Oh yes, you make a very convincing hag.'

'Er – thanks?'

We paid the entrance fee and made our way around the exhibits. Debbie stopped at a glass case and admired a couple of witches' diadems, gold-coloured tiaras decorated with crescent moons and stars.

'Ooh, I love that one,' she cooed. 'I could just see myself in that, popping down to Lidl's for some milk.'

'There's a matching ceremonial blood-letting dagger to

go with it,' I said. 'Handy if someone's trying to take thirteen items through the "twelve items or less" till.'

'I like the long red dress she's wearing, too.' She nodded to a photograph of a woman in the same display, wearing the aforementioned red dress and diadem. She had long, velvety black hair and a cleavage a grown man could've got lost in. It felt vaguely Seventies porn movie.

'Callum would have a coronary if you turned up in that,' I said, thinking of her husband, an absolute sweetheart who adored her but who was quite staid (certainly compared to Debbie). 'You'd scare the life out of him.' She laughed.

'Maybe so, but I think he'd still enjoy it.'

We moved on, past a glassed-in shelf unit which held a display of interesting rocks. Debbie stopped again.

'Oh my God!' she squealed. I knew what she'd seen without her saying anything.

'I know.'

'That rock's shaped just like a—'

'Yep.'

'And the one underneath it looks like—'

'Yes, they were used in fertility rituals,' I said. 'Moving on…'

We moved on. Past the life-size diorama of a witch's kitchen, complete with old crone (mannequin, not real life) sitting at the battered wooden table, measuring out herbs and various other special ingredients from glass jars into a pestle and mortar. The first time I'd come here I'd only seen her out of the corner of my eye and she'd given me quite a shock, as I'd thought she was a real person. Past the display of brightly coloured and beautifully illustrated tarot cards. We made our way up the stairs to the first floor, which had suitably creaky wooden floorboards and was lined with more glass display cabinets. In one corner a larger-than-life-sized humanoid figure, dressed in green velvet robes and topped with a goat's head, boasting magnificent horns and a long, glossy beard, stood guard over the occult treasures.

'Niiiice…' said Debbie, giving it a wide berth. 'My mum had a pair of curtains like that. Green velvet, I mean, not covered in goat horns.'

'This is what I'm interested in,' I said, gazing into the long display case on the left-hand side of the room.

Inside was a collection of dolls, or 'poppets', as the accompanying signs described them. Some had been made with more obvious care than others: one was knitted, with brown curly woollen hair, a pullover and embroidered eyes, the mouth a bright red line of stitches. A small photograph of a woman, also with brown hair, was pinned to its chest. Another was a cloth doll, wearing a nurse's uniform – a red dress, with a white apron bearing a red cross over it, and a matching head scarf. The only thing that wasn't uniform was the iron nail piercing its stomach.

'Ouch,' said Debbie. 'Oh, that's sad, listen to this! "The case of the pregnant nurse…. A drunken Saturday night in 1941 ended in a witch's spell to cause a miscarriage. This type of poppet was used to good effect to end unwanted pregnancies."'

'Ouch indeed,' I said. 'Some of these are quite gruesome,

aren't they?' I pointed to another knitted one, this time of a female Army sergeant in full uniform with a noose around its neck. 'Apparently this sergeant was a little too hard on the new recruits, so they got their own back by casting a spell with this doll. They say she suffered a fate worse than death.'

'They always say that,' mused Debbie. 'What do they mean, though? What fate is worse than death?'

'Being sat in the middle seat between Piers Morgan and Katie Hopkins on a twelve-hour alcohol-free flight?' We both shuddered. 'Doesn't bear thinking about, does it? You'd be begging for Death's sweet embrace after twenty minutes.'

'It would be less painful,' she agreed. 'So anyway, do any of these look like your dolls?' I'd told her about the sinister poppets found on the building site on the way there.

'Not quite…' I ran my eyes over the display. Some of them really were disturbing, like the naked and relatively lifelike doll with its limbs bound together and needles piercing the heart (to end an affair at the office). Another, a large doll in a black dress and white lace apron and petticoat, clutching a small silver tankard, looked pretty menacing, but the sign next to it surprised me. 'Oh!' I said. 'They're not all cursed. This one was for protection.'

Debbie leant in and read the text beneath it. 'Poppet of an old woman found in a chimney in a cottage in Padstow. Before that, she was the guardian of a pub in Bodmin.' She turned to me. 'Your dolls were found in the walls of the convent. Maybe Devlin and his builders have been reading them all wrong. Maybe they're not there to scare them off, maybe they were put there years ago for protection.'

'Maybe, but protecting who from what?'

'Well, to protect the nuns, obviously,' said Debbie. 'Protecting them from, I dunno… temptations of the flesh? Singing about the hills being alive with the sound of music?'

I'd decanted a couple of the convent dolls from the box into my bag. I reached in and pulled one out, comparing it next to the ones in the glass cabinet. 'Yeah… I don't know, they still look menacing to me.'

'So does the old woman one,' Debbie pointed out, and I couldn't disagree. All of them proper gave me the willies.

'Let's go and ask the woman downstairs if she knows anything about these,' I said. I took one last look at the display case, trying not to look at the marked and disfigured baby doll, which really was enough to keep you up at night, and then headed back downstairs.

We wound our way back to where we'd come in, where two middle-aged women were sitting and taking the entrance fee from visitors. It had been almost empty when we'd got there, but there was a crowd of people waiting to come in now; it was nearly Halloween, and I supposed interest in the museum must pick up around this time, despite it being out of season. We waited for the queue to dissipate, and then approached the counter.

'Hi,' I said, 'I wonder if you could help me?' I put the doll in my hand on the countertop, and they gave me an alarmed look. 'Oh, sorry, this is mine, I haven't pinched it from the display or anything.' They both relaxed. 'I was wondering if you could tell me anything about it?'

One of the women reached out and picked it up, examining it carefully. 'Hmm... Where did this come from?'

'I – I'm looking into it for a client,' I said, not sure how much to say. I didn't want to give away that it came from Devlin's redevelopment. 'They're renovating a house and they found this behind one of the walls.'

'Old house, is it?' asked the woman.

'About two hundred years old, maybe two hundred and fifty,' I said. 'He – they were worried that it meant the house had been cursed.'

The two women exchanged looks, and then seemed to reach a consensus.

'No, I wouldn't say that, would you, Eileen?'

'No, I wouldn't.' Eileen – the woman holding the doll – smiled. 'Dolls tucked away inside houses were usually put there for protection. Although it was found inside a wall, you say?'

'Yes, I think so.'

'That's slightly unusual, if that is the case. They were usually put up chimneys, or sometimes next to the door or window lintel. Points of entry, you see.'

'Points of entry?' asked Debbie. 'You mean they were medieval burglar alarms?'

Eileen laughed. 'No, they weren't meant as protection against burglars. Two hundred years ago a big dog was the preferred method of protection against them. These were here to stop a witch getting in.'

'A witch? Wow…' I said. 'This one must've been protecting against a very powerful witch, because there's loads of them.'

Both women frowned. 'How many?' asked the one who wasn't Eileen.

'Nine.'

'Nine?!'

'So far…' The two women looked slightly alarmed by this. 'It's a large building,' I explained. 'More of a manor house kind of thing.'

'A convent,' said Debbie, and I rolled my eyes because if the women had watched BBC Spotlight the night before they'd know exactly where we were talking about.

'This sort of thing was normally peasant magic,' said Eileen. 'As far as I know, dolls like this are usually only found in cottages. Although others have been found in stately homes, but they were aimed at one person, not the whole building, and they weren't normally for protection, either.'

'They were curses?' I asked, and both women nodded. 'But these don't have pins or anything sticking in them.'

'They could've fallen out at some point while they were in the wall,' suggested Debbie.

'Possibly,' agreed Eileen.

'Okay, so we're not sure what they were put there for,' I said. 'Do you have any idea when they could've been put there? What sort of time period were people using them in?'

Not-Eileen laughed. 'You're saying when "were" they used, but people still use them now. They have done for years. There's a mangled Barbie doll upstairs that was found at Bournemouth University just five years ago. Did you see the knitted army sergeant? That's from the Fifties. But,' she said, taking the doll from the other woman and looking it over, 'I would say these are fairly new. They're dirty and they smell of damp, but I don't think they're that old. Forty, fifty years old, at most.' She handed the doll back to me.

'Thanks,' I said. 'So what should I tell my client to do?'

Eileen and her colleague looked at each other, thoughtfully.

'They've found a lot of these dolls, have they?' asked Eileen. I nodded. 'Then I'd tell him to put them back…'

'Why would she tell us to put them back?'

Debbie and I were sitting in a café a little further back up the river, warming ourselves up with hot chocolate and cake. The pumpkin spice latte craze had yet to hit Boscastle, for which we were very thankful, and the only Halloween-esque touch was the owner's beautiful black cat, curled up by the log burner.

'To carry on protecting the building from something,' I said.

'From what?'

'No idea,' I admitted. 'But if that's what they were put

there for, going by the number of them that Devlin and his team have found, there is or was something very very bad out to hurt the residents of that convent.'

'The devil?' asked Debbie, looking incredulous. 'Surely not. They were nuns, for God's sake – no pun intended. They might well have believed in the devil, but they'd have seen him off through prayer, not witchcraft.'

'You'd have thought so,' I said, finishing a mouthful of millionaire shortbread. 'Didn't nuns get excommunicated if they were found practising witchcraft? The church would've linked anything occult or witchy to devil worship.'

'The nuns at my school told us we'd go to hell for smoking the devil's lettuce and taking the Lord's name in vain,' said Debbie, 'both of which I did regularly in my teens, so I'm stuffed. I can't see them taking witchcraft lightly.'

'No.' I sat back in my chair, musing. 'Of course it all depends on who put them there, and when. Most of them were tucked into wall cavities. Who'd have access to that?'

'Builders,' said Debbie, scooping the last dregs of hot chocolate froth from her glass with a long spoon.

'But not the ones who originally built the convent,' I said, 'because that woman didn't think they were old enough for that. They certainly don't look two hundred years old, do they? Just going by the way they're dressed.'

'There must've been renovations at some point,' said Debbie. 'Maybe they put up new internal walls to change the layout. Maybe they had an influx of nuns after *The*

Sound of Music came out and needed somewhere to put them all.'

'Yeah, maybe. They might just have needed repairs or insulation or something.' I shook my head. 'It's frustrating. The builders working on site now have access, although they'd have to be very careful not to get spotted planting a doll by one of their co-workers, but the dolls are too old. They even smell old.'

'They smell like my nana's house,' agreed Debbie. I nodded.

'I know what you mean. And charity shops – they always have that smell, too. Musty and slightly sweet. And of course we still don't really know if they were put there for protection or as a curse,' I continued, 'because that Eileen and the other woman, they didn't look quite as sure about it when we told them where they were found.'

'No.' Debbie patted her lips with a serviette, missing a spot of froth on the end of her nose. 'So, what have we learnt from this visit?'

'Not a lot.' I sighed. 'I was hoping they'd have some idea who might've made them, at least, but they reckoned there were loads of people round here at one time or another who believed in witches and curses, and any one of them could've been capable of making a doll. I mean, I couldn't – sewing on a button and stitching wonky turn-ups is about my limit. But women of my mum's age would probably be able to cobble something together. They used to teach girls how to sew at school, didn't they? My mum used to make her own clothes when she was younger.'

'Same with my mum,' said Debbie. 'I did try to make a dress for Tilly after watching The Great British Sewing Bee on the telly, but it came out looking like a giant tea bag. Dressmaking is not my forte. I'm much better at dress shopping.'

'Devlin assumed whoever put them there had something to do with the opposition to his development,' I said. 'Which was a reasonable assumption to make, given the protestors outside the site. But the dolls are too old for it to be linked, aren't they?'

'So what are you going to tell him?'

'I don't know,' I admitted. 'But what can I tell him? To stop all work on the site in case it disturbs some evil spirit that's only been held at bay all these years by some demonic-looking Poundshop Barbies?'

'Not really…'

'No. I think all he can really do is ignore them. Unless he can find a way to wall them back up in the new layout…' I grinned at Debbie. 'It could be a feature. He could mention it in the sales pamphlets: A development of spacious two-bedroom apartments with open-plan living, ensuite bathroom, and your very own hand-planted spooky voodoo doll. They'll be flying off the market!'

Chapter Six

We drove back to Penstowan. I dropped Debbie off at her house and then headed down to St Ann's, where a slightly larger crowd of protestors had formed today. I parked the van and wandered over, spotting Jocasta in the crowd.

'Shame this lot weren't here yesterday,' I said, nodding at the rabble behind her. She sniffed.

'Huh! Only here because they saw it on Spotlight and are hoping to get on the telly themselves.' She said it loudly enough for those closest to hear, then lowered her voice. 'I did contact ITV West Country and tell them the BBC had beaten them to the scoop but I was happy to give them a follow-up, so fingers crossed we'll be on the other side later…'

I wasn't sure the cutthroat world of local news worked quite like that, but I just smiled and left her to her protest.

As I stepped inside the tall wire fence that surrounded the site, a loud voice called out to me.

'Oi! You can't come in here, this is a building site!' I looked over and there was a beefy-looking man in a high-vis vest glaring at me.

'I'm here to see Mr Devlin,' I called back.

'Oh yeah?'

'Yeah. Tell him Jodie's here.' I reached into my pocket and pulled out my card wallet. 'The investigator.'

'Oh – right.' The man backed off and went to find Devlin. I was very glad that he hadn't insisted on inspecting the credentials I was holding out for him, as they consisted of a Tesco Club Card, a Co-op membership card, and a Rowe's Bakery coffee stamp card, among others. I might be loyal to an awful lot of shops but I'm not an official PI.

'Jodie! That was quick.' Tommy Devlin arrived next to me holding a hard hat. He held it out to me. 'Safety regs. Let's talk.'

I popped the hat on – it felt absurdly big on me, so I tucked my hair in it to pad it out a bit – and followed him across the site to the caravan I'd spotted the day before. There was a young man sitting inside looking at his mobile phone. He looked up, a guilty expression on his face.

'Sorry, Boss, I just had a message from the bank—' he started. Devlin just held the door open for him and waited for him to leave.

I sat down.

'Tea?' offered Devlin, but going by the state of the

caravan I didn't think the mugs would be particularly hygienic, so I shook my head. 'So, what have you got for me?'

'Not a lot yet,' I admitted. 'I've spoken to an expert on poppets – witch dolls—' Devlin nodded '—and they think that is definitely what they are.'

'Who's this expert?' asked Devlin. 'Not that weird bird who runs the witchy candle shop?'

'The woman who runs that shop, Cynthia?' I said, slightly stressing the word woman in an admittedly very mild reproach at his sexist use of the word bird. 'No, not her. Anyway, long story short, we think these dolls were probably put there for protection, rather than as a curse or warning.' I had absolutely no idea if that was true, but as the person who'd put them there wasn't around to ask – was maybe not even still alive – my guess was as good as anyone else's. And anyway, I didn't believe in curses.

Devlin exhaled gratefully (don't ask me how an outward breath can sound grateful, but it definitely can). 'Well, that's something,' he said. 'I don't mind admitting it did put the wind up me a bit when I found the first one.'

'Yeah, I can imagine.' I didn't mention that both Nathan and I had dreamt about those blasted dolls the night before. 'Anyway, the upshot of that is you're probably safe to just ignore them.'

'Good. I mean, I was going to ignore them anyway, in as much as I'm not stopping work on the site, but…' Devlin hesitated.

'But you'd still like to know a bit more about them, just in case?' I said. He nodded.

'Yeah. I'm thinking it would be good to know their background, in case this gets out.' He gestured out of the window. 'There's plenty of people out there who are just looking for a way to get this build shut down, and if not to then put buyers off by telling them the land's cursed or haunted or whatever. Not that it should get out. No one else knows outside of my team.' But even he didn't look convinced by that. I scoffed.

'You think none of your lads have gone home and told their wives or—' I thought about Liam Fossett '—their mums about these spooky dolls that keep turning up?'

'Yeah, that's what I'm worried about.' Devlin looked at me, clearly uncomfortable with that thought. 'Can you keep digging, then? Just see what else you can find out?'

'Of course. I'd rather not leave it there either, but they tell me I'm nosier than most people.' I took a notebook and pen out of my bag. I could always take notes on my phone, but I'm old school; I'll always reach for a pen before I try and type stuff onto that little phone screen. 'I just need to go over a few things, then. So it was you who found the first doll. When was that?'

'Yeah, that was about a week into the project. So… about six weeks ago?' Devlin thought hard. 'Yeah, just over six weeks ago. It was in one of the little bedrooms on the first floor, one of the old nuns' quarters. According to the plans there were originally five large bedrooms up there, and then some time in the 50s three of them got divided up into smaller rooms, like cells, almost. A couple didn't even have proper windows.'

'Can you remember exactly where you found the doll?'

'I can do better than that,' said Devlin. 'I can show you.'

We left the caravan. I followed him across the site, through the yard which must've once been the car park for the hospital building, and around the side of the old convent. Instead of going in through the front entrance, which was surrounded by scaffolding, we walked through the gardens that wrapped around one side to the back. It was quiet here, away from the noise of the demonstrators (not that they were a particularly noisy bunch). There was a brick wall along the back, which had once led to a kitchen garden where the nuns had no doubt grown a few fruit and vegetable crops, but all that grew there now was a Nineties housing estate, a row of houses backing onto it.

The garden we stood in was overgrown. The nuns would have kept it spick and span, mown and pruned and flower beds weeded, although I couldn't guess what they would've used it for. Croquet? BBQs? Topless sunbathing? It wasn't sunny enough for that today, but I didn't think it would be in the summer, either, surrounded as it was by trees, including a gnarled old oak and a skeletal weeping willow in one corner, the ground around it smothered with fallen leaves. It felt dark and damp, and the atmosphere felt melancholy and sad.

'So it was stuffed inside a fireplace,' said Devlin, leading me inside, past a heavy wooden door and up a wide staircase, which creaked ominously. The air inside was full of dust and echoed to the sound of men at work on the floor above. 'It was in one of the nicer rooms, still tiny but it had the original fireplace and a window in it.' He stopped in a doorway that led into a wide expanse of floorboards and bare bricks. 'We've taken the dividing wall down now, but it was in there.'

I went inside and walked over to the old fireplace. It was a large cast-iron one, surrounded by blue/green ceramic tiles. It must've looked very grand and out of place when the room had been divided into such a tiny space, but in its original setting it would've been beautiful.

'In the fireplace? Like, up the chimney?' I said, bending down to peer up it. I don't know why, it wasn't like there was much chance of another one being up there. I sneezed as a shower of soot floated down and tickled my nose. The hiding place tied in with the doll being there for protection; the ladies at the museum had said they were placed at points of entry, which included chimneys. Although looking at the size of the convent chimneys, witches back then must've been pretty skinny. Santa would've had no chance. I straightened up and made a note in my pad as Devlin joined me.

'Yeah, up there. It came loose as I was dragging the old metal bedstead out and accidentally banged it against the wall. It gave me a bit of a turn at first, because it looked proper eerie – all dusty, and there was soot on it too from when fires had been lit in the past,' he said. 'Although when I dusted it off it wasn't actually that bad. It looked like a little girl's rag doll.' He pulled out his phone and scrolled through the photos. 'This one.' It was the doll made with the pretty (but dirty and worn) fabric, the one I'd thought had been made with more care than the others.

'Oh yes, that one.' I made another note. 'Was anyone else with you when you found it?'

'No, it was just me. We had such a lot to do, just clearing all the crap out – they'd left behind a load of old furniture, not just bedsteads but old wardrobes and chests of drawers, and it looked like squatters had been in there at some point. I had the lads going through the whole building, dragging everything out to the skip.'

'Did you show it to anyone else?'

'Yeah, of course I did. After the initial shock I wasn't that worried about it, I just thought it was weird, so I took it downstairs and showed Ken, my foreman – the bloke who shouted at you earlier. He just laughed and said we should put it in the caravan, give the lads a fright when they came in for their tea.' He smiled ruefully. 'Only they all got spooked by it and made us take it away.'

'Can I ask why you didn't throw it in the skip?'

Devlin gave an unexpected laugh. 'Ken did. And then at the end of the day I took it out and stuck it back in the caravan, as a wind-up. He's always first in, so I knew he'd be the one to find it. When he came in the next morning he almost shi – he almost soiled hisself. I threw it back in the skip and then later on he climbed in and got it and stuck it on the passenger seat of my van.'

I smiled. 'That's like the story I heard about some bloke's girlfriend reading The Exorcist. She was so freaked out she threw the book in the sea. But then he found another copy in a charity shop, bought it and soaked it in a bucket of water and put it her on bedside table, like it had come back to haunt her.'

Devlin laughed again. 'That's just evil. My missus would divorce me if I did that to her.'

'And quite right, too,' I said. 'So you kept the doll so Ken wouldn't be able to prank you again?'

'Well, eventually. It did go back and forth a couple more times first until it weren't funny anymore, and then I just forgot to chuck it away.'

'You mean you were keeping hold of it so you could scare him again when he wasn't expecting it?' I said, and Devlin grinned.

'Guilty as charged. Although I did also think I might give it to my daughter. She's into weird stuff like that.'

'But you didn't,' I said, thinking, *I'm not sure I'd be giving a child of mine a doll I'd found shoved up a chimney.* But hey, different parenting styles and all that.

'No, I thought better of it. It's a bit mouldy, ain't it? I kept it, and then about a week after that we found the next one,' said Devlin. 'One of the lads found it inside a wall.'

'Inside the wall?'

'Yeah, back in the little cell rooms again. They'd been partitioned off, like I said. Just stud walls, easy enough to knock down.'

'Assume I don't know what a stud wall is, exactly…'

Devlin smiled. 'Why would you? Come with me.'

We went back out onto the landing and up another flight

of stairs, to where a couple of builders were hard at work. They looked up as we entered, giving me the once-over and obviously wondering who I was, but they didn't speak.

'All right, lads?' I asked, and they nodded.

'We've taken down the old stud walls in here,' said Devlin, 'and because it's now one really big room again we're putting another one up to divide it in two. Dean,' he said to one of the builders, 'show Jodie what you're doing.' Dean looked puzzled but he just nodded and waved me over.

'We're putting up a new stud wall, to change the floor plan,' he said. 'We build the frame first – a couple of vertical timbers, one screwed into the floor, one on the ceiling, and then between those we fix upright timbers – the "studs". Couple of noggins between each one—' he spotted my puzzled expression '—short pieces of wood slotted in between the uprights to brace them and keep them stable. And then we screw sheets of plasterboard onto both sides of the frame to give you the wall. You ever watched Grand Designs or one of them home renovation shows? You'll have seen them on there.'

'Oh yeah, I know what you mean,' I said, picturing it. I turned to Devlin. 'So your boy ripped off the plasterboard and it was inside that?'

Devlin nodded. 'Resting on a noggin.' He slapped Dean on the back. 'We'll leave you to it.'

'A poppet on a noggin,' I murmured, noting it down. I was learning all sorts of new words today. 'Who found it?' I asked, following him out of the room.

'One of the labourers, Simon. Good lad, I've not used him before but I wanted to employ as many local lads as possible on this one.'

'To try and appease the angry natives? Good plan,' I said, although it hadn't entirely worked. 'And Simon brought it to you?'

'Well, no,' said Devlin. 'He gave this bloodcurdling shriek – I thought the daft bugger had shot himself with a nail gun or something, but it was just this bloody doll.' He shuddered. 'I don't blame him really. He was up there all on his own, and it was in one of the darkest rooms in the whole building.'

'He was knocking down a wall in the dark?' I asked in disbelief. That would surely go against Health and Safety regulations, never mind me in my ridiculously large hard hat.

'No, course not. He had a work lamp – one of those big temporary lights on a stand? LED, really bright. But in a room like that it just threw a load of shadows and made the dark corners look even darker.' He shuddered. God, he really was still spooked, despite me telling him not to be.

'They're just dolls,' I said. 'Probably for protection, remember?'

'Yeah – yeah, of course. It's just that…' He hesitated.

'Go on. Look, if you're worried about something, that's what I'm here for.'

'This'll sound really stupid.'

'So what if it does? I'm not going to tell anyone.'

Devlin looked around, as if making sure no one would

overhear us, but there was just the two of us standing at the top of the staircase. When he spoke I felt goosebumps on my skin, even under my thick jacket. 'I sometimes think I can hear a baby crying…'

I left Devlin inside the convent. He'd decided to gather all of his workers together and tell them what I'd told him about the dolls – that they were most likely put there years ago as protection – so they could stop freaking out about them and carry on with the build. I hoped for his sake it worked, and for my sake that I was right and that they weren't actually an omen of ill fortune. Superstitious nonsense, I told myself. As for him hearing the sound of a baby crying, well, that was either someone outside with an unhappy child – never mind the fact that I couldn't hear any noise from the road where we stood, or that the whole convent felt eerily quiet inside, the atmosphere almost suffocating, somehow – or his imagination, no doubt working overtime because of the dolls. But I hurried down the stairs and out of the building nonetheless, keen to be outside.

Being out in the fresh air again didn't shake my unease, and as I crossed the overgrown lawn again I had the intense feeling that I was being watched. I stopped and turned to look back at the convent, scrutinising every window, but there was no one there. I did think for a moment that I'd caught a glimpse of movement from the tiny window right at the top, in what must've been an attic room, but it was just a cloud moving across the sky and letting a flash of sunlight through to sparkle on the glass.

I was sure that was all it was…

I hastened around to the front of the site again, left my hard hat with one of the builders, and headed home.

Chapter Seven

'So,' said Nathan, as we cleared up after dinner that night, 'have you solved the mystery of the creepy dolls yet?'

'More or less,' I said, although really I felt like it was weighing most heavily on the 'less' side.

Nathan threw down his tea towel and pulled me in for a hug. 'It was a sad day for the force's case closure rates when you left, Mrs Withers.'

'I had to leave, I was making you look bad, Mr Parker,' I said, and he laughed.

'Nah, you made me look good.' He kissed me. 'At least we'll sleep better tonight now you've got rid of those horrible dolls.'

'Yeah…'

He pulled back and looked at me. 'Babe…'

'They're not in the house,' I said quickly. 'They're in the back of Gwyneth. I took them down to the museum earlier and the people who work there told me what they could, but Devlin still wants to know more about them.' He looked at me again, an eyebrow raised. 'Okay, not just Devlin, I do too. There's something weird about the whole thing that I just can't put my finger on.'

'Those dolls are weird, full stop. What are you thinking?'

I put the kettle on for tea and sat down at the kitchen table, Nathan following suit. 'The women at the museum said these dolls are used for curses, just like voodoo dolls, but also often for protection, and that kind of fits in with where they've been turning up.'

'Kind of?'

'The first one was up a chimney, which is your classic witch entry point,' I said, attempting to sound knowledgeable. Nathan grinned and nodded.

'Classic, yeah. Known for it, they are.'

'Shut your handsome face, you. But the others were actually walled up, which is apparently unusual, and there's been nine of them so far, which is also not normal—'

'I can't believe you're using the word "normal" in connection to these dolls in any way,' said Nathan.

'You know what I mean. The dolls are – or were – normally found up the chimneys of small cottages, or maybe a pub. The woman at the museum called them "peasant magic", which means they weren't normally found in big houses, because the owners would've been richer and better educated, and therefore less superstitious.'

'Hmm...' said Nathan. 'A convent isn't a big house as such, though, is it?'

'True, but can you imagine nuns believing in witches? As Debbie said – I took her with me – nuns might believe in the devil, because you can't really have God without his opposite number, but they'd defeat him with prayers and exorcisms, wouldn't they? Not dolls.'

'No, that's true…' Nathan stood up and put tea bags in a couple of mugs as the kettle came to the boil. 'So how do you think they ended up in the walls? When was the convent built?'

'Eighteen hundred and something. But at least some of the dolls were found inside stud walls which were put up later, in the Fifties, to create more bedrooms for the nuns.' I frowned. 'Although that doesn't tie in with the other thing the woman at the museum said.'

'Which was…?'

'She reckoned the dolls looked around fifty years old at the absolute maximum. And I have to say I agree with her, looking at the fabric – some of it's just got that sort of Seventies vibe, you know? The colours are faded, but two of them look like they used to be brown or orange, which don't strike me as Fifties colours. Although I'm not basing that on anything other than watching repeats of The Sweeney with my dad and laughing at the clothes. If the dolls were put there when the walls went up, that was seventy years ago, not fifty.'

'The museum woman could be wrong,' Nathan pointed out. 'Like you said, you're not really basing the age on anything concrete. So they could've been put there when the stud walls went up.'

'Yeah, I suppose you're right… So even if we have some idea when they were put there, we still don't know why,' I said. 'Or by who.'

'No,' said Nathan. 'Shame you can't talk to someone who used to live there, but there's "nun" of them left.' I groaned. 'D'you get it? "Nun"?'

'Oh great, you're into puns as well now. Just don't make it a habit…'

That evening as we sat in front of the telly I cracked open my laptop and started researching. Mum had joined us, as she often did, and as usual she'd dived for the remote control. But Nathan had got there before her and had put some daft sci-fi movie on. Mum gave a dissatisfied harrumph but didn't say anything.

'You'll like this one, babe,' he said to me. 'It's about warrior nuns in space. It feels kinda apt, bearing in mind what you're working on.'

'Sounds brilliant,' I said.

'Are you being sarky?'

'Just a tad.'

'Not my kind of thing either,' said Mum.

'Yeah, but that's just because Bradley Walsh isn't in it,' teased Nathan.

'No, it's all over with Brad now,' I said. 'He's been usurped by Bob.' I looked over at my mum and, God bless her, she was all red in the face again. Shirley Parker blushing, twice in one day! Would wonders never cease?

Nathan obviously noticed, but as he's a much nicer person than me he immediately stopped teasing her. 'Bob's a lovely fella,' he said. 'Which is just as well, because if anyone upsets my mother-in-law they'll feel the full force of the law.'

Mum giggled. 'Oh, you! You're a sweetheart.' She settled herself down in her armchair. 'Come on, then. Bring on the space nuns.'

Back to my research, conducted to the unholy combined background noises of surprisingly attractive women of the cloth kicking butt and zapping bad guys with lasers while reciting the Lord's Prayer. It was quite surreal, and more than a little distracting, but eventually I found what I was looking for.

St Ann's, as everyone in town already knew (everyone who'd been in my year at St Botolph's Primary School, anyway, as we'd done a class project on the history of the town), had been built in 1846, as part of the Oxford Movement – a theological movement begun by high-church members of the Church of England. What that actually meant, I wasn't sure – I wouldn't know a 'high-church' member if they slapped me round the face with a religious tract – but the movement developed into 'Anglo-Catholicism'. I wasn't sure what that meant, either, what with me being a heathen, but the upshot was that the convent of St Ann's was Anglican, rather than Roman

Catholic. And that was rather handy, as I had an 'in' with the Anglicans…

I went out into the kitchen (so as not to disturb Nathan and Mum, who were both riveted by the film) and dialled a number on my mobile.

'Hello, do you have a moment to talk about Jesus?' I asked. At the other end of the call Carmen laughed.

'Hang on, that's my line!' she said. 'Don't tell me I've finally converted you?'

'Nope, still going to hell,' I said, and she laughed again.

'You're not going to hell. I think God can recognise good people, even if they never come along to watch one of their closest friends perform a service on a Sunday morning…'

'Yeah, yeah, if I come to your wedding does that count?' Carmen was engaged to Tony, who I'd known since our first day at the aforementioned St Botolph's school. And now his fiancée was the vicar at St Botolph's Church.

'As long as you promise not to do the catering,' said Carmen. 'You know I love your cooking, but you seem to have an unfortunate effect on weddings.' I couldn't deny it; I'd met Nathan after I'd catered Tony's last wedding, where let's just say nothing exactly went to plan – not for Tony, or his bride-to-be, or his ex-wife. I sincerely hoped that it would be third time lucky for him.

'I can't really deny that,' I said. Even my own wedding had been interrupted by murder. 'Anyway, do you know anything about St Ann's?'

'The old convent? No. It got closed down years before I

even got here. Is this about the development?' She sounded concerned. 'I heard about Shirley getting arrested…'

'She didn't get arrested,' I said, 'she just made a bloody nuisance of herself.'

'You sound quite proud of that.'

'Well, she's had plenty of practice… Nah, I am proud of her. But it's not that. There's a… a delicate situation that I'm investigating, and I was looking for some background on who lived there, what they got up to, why it closed, all that sort of thing.'

'Hmm… The parish records might have what you're looking for.'

I'd never even heard of them. 'Really? How can I get hold of them?'

'I can go through them with you, they're in the church office. Most of them are computerised now, of course, and some of the older ones are on microfiche, but the really old ones are in boxes in the crypt.'

I shivered. But of course they'd be in the crypt. Just to add to the creepy factor.

Carmen was still talking. 'Come over to the church in the morning and we can have a look.'

The next day I wrapped up warm and drove over to St Botolph's. The sunshine of the day before had disappeared, to be replaced by a thick fog that had drifted in overnight from the sea. The van's headlights seemed to illuminate rather than penetrate the pale grey patches of floating mist that obscured hedgerows and twists in the roads, but I'd driven this winding route many times and could almost have done it with my eyes shut. Almost.

On the passenger seat next to me, Germaine whined. She didn't like the fog. She normally enjoyed car journeys, particularly in the summer when I let her have the window down, but this nasty grey stuff was spoiling her view.

'I know, sweetheart,' I said. 'I don't like it either.' I was already going under the speed limit, but I slowed down even more as we approached a hairpin bend; you never knew who could be coming around the corner from the other direction, although most of the accidents along this stretch of road happened in the summer. They were usually caused by holidaymakers who were unfamiliar with the road and took the bend too fast, or locals stuck behind more cautious tourists, who got impatient with them crawling along slowly and overtook where they shouldn't have.

I was relieved when we reached the church. I parked up and let Germaine out, after having strong words with her about not going off after any rabbits or birds or whatever in the graveyard, as this was not the season to go dancing about around graves. I shivered, but she just cocked her head and looked at me as if I was mad. No self-respecting Pomeranian would choose to go racing across a fog-bound graveyard when there was a house nearby, invitingly lit up against the dark and promising doggy treats. She'd been here many times before and knew Carmen was a soft touch when it came to all creatures great and small.

Carmen had opened the door at the sound of the van. She stood in the doorway, outlined in a halo of electric light, smiling. She looked for a moment like one of the lesser-known saints, if saints wore bright pink chunky jumpers over their dog collars.

'Morning!' I called, getting a Tupperware container out of Gwyneth and heading over.

'Come in, come in!' she said, stepping back to make way for me and the dog. 'I hate this damp fog.' She eyed the container. 'Is that…?'

I held it out to her. 'Something to go with our tea. A new recipe I'm trying out – pumpkin spice cupcakes. I'm still trying to decide what I'm making for the do on Saturday.'

'Ooh, yummy,' she said, taking the container and leading the way into the kitchen. 'I'm surprised you went with pumpkin spice, it's very… American.'

'Yeah, it's everywhere at the moment so I thought, if you can't beat 'em, join 'em. Anyway it's not actually pumpkin spice, it's pumpkin with cinnamon and ginger.' I shrugged off my coat and scarf and draped them over a kitchen chair. 'I'm not sure if I like them or not, so I'll be pleased to hear what you think of them.'

Carmen flicked the kettle on – I noted that she already had two mugs and the canister of tea bags out – as I sat down.

'So, what are you looking for?' she asked, once the tea was ready and we were both sitting at the table, the open Tupperware container of cupcakes in front of us. She reached for one now and inspected the cream cheese frosting for a second before biting into it.

'I'm not actually sure,' I admitted. 'I'm hoping I'll know it when I see it. If I see it.'

She swallowed her mouthful of cake. 'Oh, that's good,' she said. 'The cupcake, not you not knowing what you're after.'

'Hmm,' I said, tasting my own cupcake. 'I don't know, I think I used too much ginger.'

'Anyway, I had a little look last night after I spoke to you,' said Carmen. 'The convent closed in 1982. Nothing sinister – because I'm assuming that's what you're looking for? They just ran out of nuns.'

I laughed. 'Ran out of nuns?'

'You know what I mean. Fewer young women signing their lives away to God.' She crossed herself and looked upwards. 'No offence, Boss.'

'None taken,' I said, in a booming voice.

'I couldn't be a nun,' she said, taking another bite of cupcake. 'Saying no to pleasures of the flesh.'

'Well, I mean, you are with Tony so that's almost the same thing…'

'Ha! How dare you. If I wasn't a woman of the cloth and therefore bound to celibacy until marriage, I'd tell you exactly how wrong you are.' She smirked.

'I'm shocked. Does the Bishop know?'

'Why, do you think he'd want to?' We both laughed. 'Anyway, back to the matter in hand before I incriminate myself—'

'Too late.'

'The convent started winding down in 1981 and closed for good in 1982. The church moved the few remaining nuns to another convent in Kent. St Mary's. I've been there, actually, it's a beautiful place, not far from where I grew up. Even back then, St Ann's was in need of repair, and the powers that be obviously thought it wasn't financially worth it just for a handful of sisters.'

'A shame for the ones who had been there a long time,' I said, finishing my cupcake. The flavour was growing on me.

'Yes, several of them were getting on a bit and had probably been at the convent since they signed up.'

'What about the hospital? Did that close at the same time?'

'Yes, although that had been winding down for rather longer, I think.' Carmen wrinkled her nose in distaste. 'I'm surprised it lasted as long as it did, to be honest. I thought all the homes for unmarried mothers would've died out by then.'

'I don't know, back when I was at school I remember people going on about single mums like they were the scourge of society,' I said, musing. 'I remember someone's older sister getting pregnant, and everyone was like, "Silly girl, getting herself up the duff", but even then I thought it weren't like she did it to herself, was it?'

'No,' said Carmen. 'The man can always walk away, but the woman's literally left holding the baby. The woman always ends up carrying the responsibility for something they both did, but she's the one who gets called names.'

'Seems like it's the wrong way round to me,' I said.

'Absolutely. So yes, the hospital officially shut its doors on September 12th, 1982, two months before the last of the sisters moved out.'

'What happened to the people who worked there? Or was it just nuns?'

'No idea. I can't imagine it was solely nuns – they'd have needed someone medically trained on the staff, surely, in case something went wrong during labour. But that might be in the microfiche records, or the ones in the crypt. There was a big push several vicars ago to get all the old records scanned in, but I'm not sure how far they got. The parish council keep talking about digitising them all, but I honestly don't think we need half of them.' She finished her cupcake and stood up, brushing crumbs off her jumper. 'Right, shall we go and see what we can find?'

We took our mugs of tea over to the church, stopping to wrap ourselves up in our coats first. St Botolph's was a beautiful church and I always felt at peace there, despite being a self-confessed heathen; Nathan and I had got married there (although that hadn't been the plan), and my dad was buried in the graveyard. But today, with the thick fog, the church seemed to be floating in and out of focus, a blurred shape in the distance. As we crossed the churchyard Germaine yapped and trotted off in front of us, disappearing for a moment in the mist before stopping to sniff at different bushes and to pounce on a couple of yellow weeds (she had a real thing about yellow flowers). 'Don't go too far!' I called. She stopped again and, turning back to look at me defiantly, sidled up to a grave. I knew exactly what she was about to do. 'No, Germaine!' I shouted, horrified. 'Not there!' But as usual she completely ignored me and peed up the carved angel that stood guard over whoever was buried there's eternal rest. 'Oh my God…'

Carmen laughed. 'Don't worry about it. I'm sure old…' – she went over and peered at the stone plaque beneath the angel – 'old Harold Penhaligon doesn't mind.'

'Penhaligon? That'll be one of your future in-laws Germaine's just desecrated,' I pointed out. 'Well, future dead in-laws.'

'As long as she doesn't pee on my living mother-in-law-to-be I don't care.' Carmen bent down and ruffled Germaine's furry head. 'Although Brenda loves Germaine because she's a good girl, oh yes she is, so I think she'd forgive you. Oh yes she would!'

'You need to have a baby,' I said in mock disgust. Carmen gave me an enigmatic smile but didn't say anything. I gaped at her. 'Holy crap, are you pregnant?'

'What?' Carmen looked horrified. 'No, of course not! There's a few members of the parish council who are already less than impressed with me because I don't have a penis like a proper vicar. If I got pregnant out of wedlock I seriously think they'd burn me as a witch. Tony and I haven't actually, you know, done that. Things have got a bit heavy but we have to wait until we're married before we can go the whole hog.' She grimaced. 'Did I really just use "whole hog" as a euphemism for having sex? That sounds horrible.'

'You mean, before you make luuurve,' I drawled, and she laughed. 'So what was that smile about, then?'

'Just that we were discussing it last night, after I told him I was looking up the old maternity hospital records. Basically the minute that ring's on my finger I want to be making babies.' She sighed. 'We're both getting on, which is fine for him but my child-bearing days are rapidly coming to an end.'

'You better hurry up and set a date, then.' At our feet, Germaine whined; the poor animal hadn't had a fuss made of her for at least twenty seconds and she was starting to feel neglected and unloved. 'Failing that, get a dog...'

The parish office was in a small room set off to one side of the church. Stone-lined and with two high windows letting in a draught, it was nearly as cold in there as it was outside. Two desks had been crammed inside, and there was a row of filing cabinets along one wall: generic black veneered office furniture from the Nineties, probably from Ikea or somewhere similar. A huge printer sat on a wobbly-looking trolley, sharing an extension lead with a kettle and a surprisingly fancy coffee machine – one of those pod ones – which looked incongruous in its newness next to all the old stuff.

Carmen noticed me looking at it. 'Present from Tony,' she said. 'I think it was old floor stock from the shop. I didn't have the heart to tell him I prefer using the kettle.'

One of the desks was served by a very old PC and a wooden dining chair, but the other had a proper padded office chair on casters in what looked like black leather. A much more modern laptop sat on that desk. Carmen pulled out the office chair and sat on it, opening the laptop.

'I saved all the stuff I found, if you want me to print it out?' she asked. 'If the printer's working, that is. It always needs me to replace the magenta. Always.'

'Thank you, although I might not really need it. The exact dates of the convent and hospital closure might come in handy, but other than that… I still don't really know what I'm looking for.'

'Can I ask what it is you're working on?'

I realised I hadn't told her about the dolls, so I quickly nipped back out to the van to get one. Walking through the graveyard on my own, through the fog which had thickened even more since we'd arrived, sent my senses (and my overactive imagination) spinning; it felt for all the world like the mist was full of moving shapes, and whispers on the light breeze – the spirits of the dear departed who now called St Botolph's their home. I shivered and told myself to stop being an idiot.

Back inside the office, the electric heater was on and the temperature felt a lot better than it had, even with a small furry dog sitting in front of it and absorbing most of the warmth. I held the doll behind my back. This one had a rather fetching muddy purple dress, although 'burial shroud' might have been a better description.

'So, Carmen,' I said, in my best Al Pacino gangster voice,

'say hello to my little friend!' I pulled the poppet out and threw it to her. She shrieked and scooted the chair out of the way, not even attempting to catch it. I laughed and (eventually) so did she.

'Ruddy Nora,' she said, gasping for breath, 'what on earth is that?' She bent down to pick it up off the stone floor. 'Oh dear God…' She studied it, turning it over and then back to look at its face. 'That's probably the most disturbing doll I've ever seen, and I had an older cousin with a collection of Cabbage Patch Kids.' She shuddered and handed it back to me, wiping her hand on her black trousers. 'It's filthy, too. And smelly.'

'You don't like it? Oh no, I got you one for Christmas.' I laughed and told her how Devlin had been finding these dolls all over the convent.

'So you want to know who planted them, and why?'

'Yeah. I was hoping the records might tell me when, at least.' I told her the museum ladies had thought the dolls were fifty years old, maybe, but no more. 'But Devlin said the last time any work was done on the convent, when the partition walls were put up, was in the Fifties. So that's too long ago.'

'Yes… Can I have a look again?' She held her hand out and I passed the doll back. She studied it again and then nodded. 'When I moved into the vicarage there were curtains just like that over the whole house. Reverend Thomas was here, ooh, in the early Eighties, so he was vicar here for about forty years and I don't think he ever decorated. So that material could be forty years old, or maybe a bit more. They were in good condition, just really old-fashioned. I gave them to the charity shop.' She set the doll down on the desk. 'So, now my heartbeat's returned to normal, what do you want to look at?'

'The history of the convent, I suppose,' I said. 'The recent history, anyway. So the dates of any renovations in the last fifty or so years, if there were any. And anything else that kind of leaps out at us.'

'Riiight…' said Carmen.

'I know it's a bit vague, but I don't have anything much to go on,' I said. She nodded.

'Well, at least those things should be easy to find. There's a folder for the church with details of building work in it – dates, invoices, that kind of thing – so there's probably something similar for the convent.' She took a bunch of keys from the desk drawer, then stood up, walked over to one of the filing cabinets, and unlocked it. 'Why don't you take a look through all this lot, while I see what I can find in the database?'

'Sounds like a plan,' I said. I opened the top drawer and flicked through the folders, but they were all to do with the church itself and various other bits of parish stuff. The next drawer yielded more of the same, until I got right to the back, where a lone file named St Ann's had been tucked in behind the others.

I pulled it out and scanned the contents. Lots of invoices and bills, mostly for things like electricity and heating oil but also a few repairs and general purchases for hospital supplies, lightbulbs, and miscellaneous everyday items like that. I put it back and tried the bottom drawer. This one appeared to be dedicated to the convent and hospital, although it didn't go that far back. More bills; the latest I could find, for repairs to the hospital's industrial-sized washing machine, dated August 1976, and the earliest being an invoice from a gardener from 1958, for pruning the trees in the convent's apple orchard which, going by the hand-drawn map of the works undertaken that accompanied it, didn't exist anymore – it was now the site of the housing estate that had been built around 2001. The church had been selling off pieces of the land long before Devlin had got his hands on it.

I found one that referred to the renovation the developer had told me about, where some of the larger rooms had been sectioned off into small cells for the nuns, but it just confirmed that the stud walls had indeed been put up in 1953, by a building company that – after a quick search on my phone – I could see no longer existed. There was a name on the invoice – William Bradshaw – and I supposed that I could ask him if he or one of his workforce had put the dolls inside the walls at the time, but it was seventy-three years ago, and the chances of him still being alive today were slim. And even if he was, would he remember them?

'Found anything?' asked Carmen. I sighed.

'Nothing helpful,' I said. 'But then I don't really know what I was expecting. Are there any records of hospital staff? Or patients? Or the nuns who lived at the convent?'

'Yes,' said Carmen. 'I think they're in a box in the crypt.'

Of COURSE they're in the crypt, I thought. 'But I don't

really think I can let you have those, not without a warrant. Or at least a good reason…'

'No, fair enough,' I said. 'Confidentiality and all that. It's probably not relevant anyway.'

Carmen got up and made her way over to the printer, which had kicked into reluctant life and was creaking its way through a couple of pages of print. She gathered them up and handed them to me. 'That's all the stuff I could find. I don't know how much of that you already knew but I thought it might be handy to have it all in black and white.'

'Thanks,' I said, glancing down at it. 'I think I might have to accept defeat and tell Devlin there's no real way of knowing who planted the dolls so he should just ignore them. It's all superstitious old wives' tales anyway, isn't it?'

We walked back to the vicarage and had another cup of tea and a cupcake (the flavour was growing on me, but I'd definitely used too much ginger and made a note to use less if I made them again), then Germaine and I thanked Carmen for her help and clambered back into the van. As we drove home I thought over what we'd discovered, which was – not much. I'd just decided to tell Devlin that I'd hit a dead end and that he should put the whole thing behind him and carry on, when he rang. I pulled over to answer.

'I was just on my way to see you,' I said, cheerfully.

'Good,' he said, and the tone of his voice made my cheerful mood instantly evaporate. 'Because there's something you need to see.'

Chapter Eight

'You were right to call us, Mr Devlin,' said Nathan, staring up at the wooden ceiling beam above our heads. Tommy Devlin grunted.

'I didn't want to,' he admitted, 'but Jodie said I should. I didn't expect the boss to turn up though.'

'Perks of hiring an investigator who's married to the local DCI,' I said. 'It was one thing when it was just the dolls, but this – this means the situation has escalated, doesn't it?'

'This' was a length of rope, flung over a low wooden beam and tied. Into a noose. I shivered. In some respects it wasn't as eerie as the witch dolls, but its message was a lot clearer. And the gloom of the shadowy attic room made it even more obviously menacing.

'When did you discover the noose?' asked Nathan, taking a couple of photographs of it.

'About forty minutes ago. I got straight on the blower to Jodie, and she got on to you.'

'When did you last come up here?' Nathan lowered the phone and looked at him. 'Because I'm assuming the noose wasn't here then.'

'Yesterday, I think? Or the day before. I weren't planning on touching this room until next week, but we've got ahead of schedule so I thought I'd get one of the lads up here to start measuring up. I came up here to have a look at what needed doing, but other stuff came up so I left it.'

'And no one else has been up here?' asked Nathan. 'As far as you know?'

'As far as I know, no one.'

'Well,' I said, shining the torch on my mobile phone on the floor, 'someone's been up here. Footprints in the dust, see?'

'They could be ours,' said Nathan, but I shook my head.

'Nope. They're too big for me, and you're wearing smart shoes – the soles are smooth. You can see, there, the pattern of the tread in the dust. Whoever it was was wearing trainers, or maybe work boots. Possibly like the ones you're wearing, Mr Devlin, only they're too small to be yours.'

'So someone with feet smaller than a size eleven, bigger than a size…?'

'Five,' I said.

'Wearing trainers or boots,' finished Devlin. 'So that's more or less everyone on site.'

'Yeah, but at least we can rule out a ghost or mid-twentieth-century witch,' I said. Nathan laughed.

'Oh good, we might've had trouble arresting either of those,' he said.

'So you'll be able to arrest whoever did this?' demanded Devlin. 'You'll investigate it? Discreetly, I hope.'

Nathan and I exchanged looks. 'We'll be extremely discreet,' said Nathan. 'Because there's not really anything we can do about it, officially.' Devlin opened his mouth to protest. 'There's been no actual crime committed here, Mr Devlin, except possibly trespass, although if it's someone working on site then it's not even that. This could be dismissed as a prank.'

'But you said it was good that I'd called you!'

'Yes, because now we'll have it on file, and if anything else happens—'

'"Anything else"? Like what?' Devlin was annoyed. 'What has to happen before you take it seriously?'

'I am taking it seriously,' said Nathan firmly. 'Which is why we log this, and the incidents with the dolls, and that way if it does turn out that someone is targeting you or the build then we will have a firm case against them.'

'And he did say "officially",' I pointed out. 'I'll keep looking into it. I'd hit a bit of a wall with the dolls – no pun intended – but this gives us more to work on.'

'How? We still don't know who did it,' said Devlin.

'No, but we'll be able to narrow it down,' I said. 'We know the noose wasn't there the last time you came up here. So someone's been able to sneak up here and put it up some time between then and about an hour ago. That could be someone who's working here, because although they'd have to be careful not to be seen, access would have been easy. Or maybe someone could have broken in overnight and done it?'

'The fence around the site is locked,' said Devlin. 'There's no sign of a break-in.'

'Could someone have climbed over?' asked Nathan.

'I don't know – maybe…'

Nathan looked at his watch. 'I'm sorry I can't do anything more at this point,' he said, 'but Jodie will keep looking and she'll keep me updated.' He held out a hand to shake and after a brief hesitation Devlin took it. 'You wanted to keep this quiet, didn't you? So this is probably the best way to go about it.'

'Yeah, I suppose so.'

I followed Nathan out of the room and down the first flight of stairs.

'You can't blame him for not being happy,' I said. 'First the dolls and now this. Someone really doesn't want him here.' I almost walked into him as he stopped at the top of the next flight of stairs down. 'Woah, look out, babe.'

'Can you hear that?' Nathan was still, listening.

'Hear what?'

He looked around and then gave me a brief smile. 'Nothing. Sorry. What were you saying?'

'That someone wants Devlin out of here,' I said, following him down the rest of the stairs. 'Don't you think?'

'I don't know. It could still just be a prank. How does the noose fit in with the dolls? Even if you can work out when the noose got there, you still don't know when or how the dolls did.' He stopped again, in the doorway out to the garden. 'You really can't hear that?'

I stopped, the hairs on the back of my neck tingling. I listened hard. There was something, right on the edge of hearing, but I couldn't make out what it was. 'It's just noise from out in the street, isn't it?' To be fair, it could genuinely have been that – it was mid-afternoon, so mums and dads would be walking to the nearby school, possibly with their younger children, to pick their kids up. But as soon as I thought that I remembered it was half term; no school run today. I shivered.

'Got time for a cuppa somewhere?' I asked, keen to get away from the convent and into somewhere warm.

'Sorry babe, not really. I only came because Devlin said you were with him, otherwise I'd have sent a uniform.' We crossed the garden and walked around to the main gate, where Nathan handed in his hard hat. He glanced around and then bent down to give me a discreet kiss. 'I'll see you at home. Be careful, yeah? And don't bring any more spooky dolls home…'

I watched him leave and then spotted Devlin heading for the caravan. I followed him over.

'Oh good, you're still here,' he said. 'I made a list of all the lads who found dolls, like you asked for. Although I don't know how much use it'll be now.'

He left me to go through the list. I made a cup of tea, grimacing at the brown tannin stains on the mug (there's a school of thought that says these stains, particularly in a teapot, add to the flavour of the tea, but they put me off –

although admittedly not enough to stop me using a builder's mug in a hot beverage emergency), and settled myself down on the lumpy sofa at one end of the caravan.

I skimmed the list. Had anyone found more than one doll? That could possibly be suspicious… But no. All nine poppets had been found by different people, including the first one found by Tommy Devlin himself. One of them had even been found by the person who'd first alerted me to the strange goings-on: Liam Fossett. Maybe I should go and talk to him.

I put my hard hat back on, finished my tea, and went outside to look for Liam, but the first person I came across was Ken, the foreman. He was standing by the fence, watching the small group of hardy protestors gathered outside, but he turned to look at me as I approached.

'They're getting smaller,' I said, gesturing to the crowd. Today there were only about six of them. I couldn't see Jocasta but she was probably around somewhere.

'Yeah, the cold weather's seen them off,' grunted Ken. 'I dunno what they reckon they'll achieve, coming out here and making a nuisance of themselves. Council've granted us permission so we ain't doing anything wrong.'

'No,' I said, not wanting to get into a discussion about the rights and wrongs of building apartments instead of a medical centre. I wasn't even sure which side I was on, because truth be told Penstowan needed both. 'Can I ask you some questions? You found one of the dolls, didn't you?'

'Yeah, I did. Gave me a bit of a turn at first.' He laughed.

'Tommy tell you about me putting one of 'em in his car? He gives it all that "big man" stuff but he screamed like a schoolgirl when he saw it.'

I grinned. 'He did tell me, but he left out the bit about him screaming.' We watched the crowd again for a moment. 'The one you found, can you tell me what happened?'

He frowned. 'Not much to tell. I was tearing down a stud wall and there it was.'

'It was tucked inside the wall?' This tallied with what Devlin had told me before – about finding a poppet on a noggin. Which I still thought was an awesome turn of phrase. Ken nodded. 'So let me get this straight. The wall's untouched, you pull off the plasterboard, and there's a doll underneath staring back at you?'

'Yeah.' Ken hesitated. 'Well, actually, no. Some of the board was already off, because we'd started on it the day before but we didn't get very far before clocking-off time.'

'Right…' I said, feeling like maybe, at last, I was heading for some kind of breakthrough. 'So could someone have stuffed the doll inside there after that bit of board had been taken off, ready for you to find it the next day when you went back to work on it?'

Ken looked thoughtful. 'I dunno. Maybe… It was tucked quite a way in, but yeah, maybe, if they used a broom or something to push it inside.'

'Would there have been a broom lying around nearby?'

'Yeah, we often need to sweep up, especially while we're in the demolition phase.'

'Okay… Do you know who worked in that section the

day before you found it? Or could someone have gone in there the next day before you got there?'

'It's one of the easier jobs, so we get the newer lads doing it,' said Ken. 'So it would've been Liam, Kai, Simon, or Shaggy.'

'Shaggy?'

'Yeah, we all call him that because he's a surfer, he looks like Shaggy out of Scooby Doo. Ah, what's his real name…' Ken clicked his fingers. 'Lewis. It would've been one of them four, or maybe a couple of them, I dunno. I tell 'em what to do but I don't babysit 'em.'

'Right.' I inspected the list again, and sure enough all four of the men were on there. 'I need a chat with all of them. Can you point me in their direction?'

Ken sent me back to the convent building. This time, however, I went in through the front entrance, squeezing between scaffolding, where I followed the sound of music (not *THE Sound of Music*, which would have been more apt, but the sound of a radio) into the grand main hall, through a small arched doorway on the right, and down some steep stone steps into a cold, musty basement. The ghosts of a thousand fictional horror movie victims cried out to me, but they were soon drowned out by the sound of good-natured banter and the radio DJ introducing 'Shake It Off' by Taylor Swift.

'I'm looking for Shaggy,' I said, as I came upon a couple of young men stacking loose bricks into a pile and shovelling up other assorted bits of debris. The question was rhetorical, however, because it was quite obvious who

Shaggy was. He did indeed look like a typical surf dude, with chin-length wavy (shaggy) hair and the faded remains of a summer tan, evidence of long days spent catching the waves on Penstowan beach.

'That's me,' he said, giving me a cheerful but quizzical smile. 'What can I do for you?'

'I just wanted to ask you some questions about these dolls everyone's been finding, all over the site,' I said.

'Not "all over" the site,' said Shaggy's companion. I frowned. 'You said "all over", but it's only been in the convent. Nothing in the other building.'

'I didn't realise work had started in there,' I said.

'It hasn't, not properly, but we have been clearing stuff out,' he said.

'What do you want to know?' Shaggy rested his chin on the handle of the broom he was holding.

'You found a doll, didn't you?' His name was on the list Devlin had given me, along with the other three labourers Ken had mentioned. 'Where was it?'

'Inside one of the stud walls, up on the first floor. I pulled the plasterboard off and it was behind there.'

'Was the wall in one piece when you started working on it? Or had someone else already pulled some of the board off?'

Shaggy's companion looked at me shrewdly. 'Are you suggesting that someone here planted those dolls?'

'What's your name?' I asked.

'Kai.' That was handy; he was on my list of people to talk to.

'I'm not suggesting anything at the moment, Kai,' I said, 'I'm simply trying to establish the facts.'

'I told you someone here was doing it,' said Kai to Shaggy. 'I reckon they stuffed it in there and poked it behind the remaining plasterboard with a broom.' Shaggy looked down at the broom he was holding in surprise, as if expecting to see a poppet on the end of it.

'Nah, they couldn't have done,' he said. He looked at me. 'Have you seen these dolls? They're, like, really old and dirty.'

'They're dirty, but that doesn't mean they're old,' insisted Kai, and I found myself nodding. He was right. I still thought the material was old, but that didn't necessarily mean the dolls themselves were. Did it?

'So some of the board had already been removed, and someone could have had access to the cavity behind it?' I asked, making sure.

'Yeah, I suppose so,' said Shaggy doubtfully, while Kai answered, 'Yes,' much more forcefully.

'You found one as well, didn't you?' I asked Kai.

'Yeah, the day after he found his,' he said. 'Same thing: inside a stud wall. We hadn't started taking it down, but there was a hole in the plasterboard which looked like it had probably been there a while, big enough to get your hand in.'

'Big enough to get a doll in, you mean,' I said, and he nodded. 'What about the other dolls? Do you know if they were found in the same kind of situation?'

'I don't know about all of them,' said Kai, 'but the ones I do know about were.'

'Right,' I said. This had turned out to be a very interesting conversation. Interesting and, hopefully, illuminating. If either of them had been responsible for planting the doll Ken had found – which had been my original reason for coming to talk to them – then I doubted they would've mentioned that the plasterboard had been damaged or removed when they'd found theirs. 'Thanks for your time, lads, you've been really helpful.'

I left them to it and climbed back up the stairs, grateful to leave the oppressive air of the basement. It was fine with two strapping young men in residence, bright work lights on and Heart FM playing loudly, but I could only imagine what it would be like down there on your own, in the darkness, almost silent but for the thump of your own heartbeat. And again, there was that sound, the one that I could almost but not quite hear. The one that sounded a bit like a baby crying, but was doubtless in reality just the wind blowing around the building site.

I drove home, glad to get away from both the cold and the gloom of the convent. It was easy to shrug it off now, standing in my lovely warm kitchen, with my lovely fluffy dog (who had been quite happy to stay shut safely inside the van gnawing on a dried pig's ear – one of her favourite but most revolting treats – while I braved the builders).

Easy to shrug off that feeling of sadness and despair that seemed to permeate the walls of the place, but which was probably just my imagination working overtime.

I tipped the box of dolls out onto the kitchen table. Germaine immediately gave a low growl, probably at the smell, which was bad enough to human noses so God only knew how bad they smelt to a doggy one. I picked up the doll that had been found first and examined it again.

This one, to me, felt different to the others. I'd already noted how it seemed to have been made with more care; it was a proper doll shape, and it was wearing a nice dress made from pretty flowery material while the soft body was made from a plain fabric which had probably once been pink. I turned over the hem of the dress; it was secured with a small but straight running stitch, the white thread discoloured with age and smoke. I could easily imagine a little girl playing with a doll like this, so how had it ended up tucked inside a chimney?

I put it down and picked up another. It was lumpy and misshapen, clothed in something that looked more like a sack than a dress. If I could imagine a little girl playing with the first one, then I could also easily imagine her being given nightmares by the second. The hem of this doll's dress had been left to fray, so I took it off and turned it inside out to examine the side seams, not really knowing what I was looking for; confirmation, I suppose, that this one had been made in more of a hurry than the first. The stitches here were big, with some of them coming loose, and there'd been no effort to keep the seams straight – they were positively wonky. I pulled the material taut to examine those seams more closely, as they'd been obscured by a lumpy bit of doll.

'What did I say?'

I turned round and there was Nathan standing in the doorway of the kitchen, hands on his hips. 'Literally the last thing I said…'

'You said not to bring any more spooky dolls home,' I said. 'One, these aren't "more", they're the same ones I already had, and two, this is my house and if I want to fill it with spooky dolls I will.' Germaine whined and I bent down to make a fuss of her. 'Don't worry, babykins, Mummy won't bring any more smelly old dolls home.'

'So you take note of the dog but not me,' grumbled Nathan, but he wasn't really annoyed. I trotted over to him and ruffled his hair.

'Aww, poor baby, are you feeling unloved?' I teased. He stuck out his bottom lip in a pout.

'Yes, I am. I think you should make it up to me immediately.' I laughed as he pulled me into his arms and started to show me exactly how I should be making it up to him.

'I will, but maybe not immediately,' I said. 'It's getting close to dinnertime, so this place will turn into Clapham Junction shortly.'

'Fair point,' he said, releasing me. 'You're not off the hook for ever, though.'

'Wouldn't want to be,' I said. 'Do me a favour and look at this.' I led him over to the dolls and picked up the shapeless dress, holding up the seam I'd been studying. He wrinkled his nose.

'What am I looking at?' I opened my mouth to say, A seam, but he obviously knew I was about to make some smartarse remark as he said, 'I know, it's a seam, but what about it?'

'What colour is it?'

He looked at me like I was going mad. 'What do you mean, what colour is it? It's white.'

'Pure white.'

'Yes.'

'Like, a really clean pure white.'

'Yeah, so wha— Oh, I get it…' He took the dress from me. 'The material looks old but the thread holding it all together looks brand-new.'

'That's what I was thinking.'

'Okay…' He looked thoughtful. 'Okay, but this is inside out, yeah? So the seams wouldn't have been exposed to whatever the rest of the doll was exposed to, meaning it might not have discoloured in the same way.'

'No, maybe not…' I hadn't thought of that. I picked up the doll itself and started examining the seams, but it had obviously been stitched and then turned inside out to stop the seams showing. I opened a nearby drawer – you know, the one everyone has in their kitchen that has random utensils and bits and bobs that you daren't throw out but you hardly ever use, that regularly gets stuck when someone puts the potato masher in there? That one – and took out a pair of scissors. There was a small ragged line of stitching along one of the doll's feet, probably where an opening had been left to get the stuffing in and then sewn up. I unpicked it with the scissors and started to pull out the stuffing.

'Now that doesn't look old, does it?' I said, pulling out handfuls of fluffy cotton wool. Not only was it snowy white, it was still soft and full of bounce. I reached into the head of the doll and paused as my fingers made contact with something less fluffy. The body had been quite floppy, but the head had – somehow menacingly – been firmer, and lumpier. I tugged out whatever it was and dropped it on the table, my brow clearing as I realised what it was.

'Screwed up rags,' said Nathan, poking at it. 'They must've run out of cotton wool.'

'Except they would've started by stuffing the head,' I pointed out. 'More likely they ran out of rags and went and bought the stuffing.' I picked up a piece of rag and smoothed it out. 'Not just a rag, either. Part of a T-shirt.'

'A band T-shirt,' said Nathan, holding it up and reading the lettering on another piece. '"Twenty" something.'

'Twenty One Pilots,' I said, putting my piece of rag together with his. 'Pretty certain they weren't around in the Fifties, when the walls were put up.'

'Or in the Seventies, when you thought the fabric was from.'

'I still think that's when the fabric's from,' I said. 'That's why it looks and smells old.'

'It does look like my nana's old curtains,' admitted Nathan. 'She gave me a set when I first left home. I didn't have the heart to chuck them in the bin, so I gave them to a charity shop.' He smiled ruefully. 'They're probably still there. I can't see anyone buying them.'

I facepalmed myself so hard that Nathan looked alarmed. 'Oh my God, I'm a moron. All the way through this, the answer was right there in front of my face. I should've worked it out when Debbie said it.' Nathan grabbed my hand before I could slap myself again.

'Easy, hun, you'll give yourself a red face. What should you have worked out?'

I didn't answer immediately, but instead picked up the first doll and carefully unpicked a seam that, like the first one, had been sewn along one foot. I tugged out a handful of stuffing. It too was cotton wool, but it had yellowed and lost a lot of its bounce, compacted by age. I smiled at Nathan in triumph.

'See? This stuffing's old.'

'Okay…'

I sat down at the table, exhausted by my mental exertions. 'This was the first doll they found, yeah?'

'Yeah…'

'It was inside a chimney. Whether it had been put there to guard against witches, or whether there was another reason, it was stuck up there some time in the past and left until Tommy Devlin found it and told everyone about it.'

'Okay. So it was made when?'

'No idea. But a good few years ago. Decades ago, probably. Someone, either one of the workers or maybe a protester or whatever, heard about the doll and how it had freaked out Devlin and his lads, and decided to start making and planting more dolls around the site, probably in an attempt to get the build shut down. Makes sense?'

'Yeah, it does. So these other dolls…?'

'Debbie and Carmen and now you, you all mentioned that the fabric looked like old curtains. It's just like that bit in *The Sound of Music* when Maria makes the children matching outfits. Debbie said the dolls smell like her nana's house, and you just said about giving your nana's curtains to a charity shop. I even told Debbie that's what the dolls smell like to me – a charity shop.'

Nathan looked at me and I could see he was starting to get what I was driving at, but he didn't say anything.

'So whoever decided to plant more dolls had to make them, and for that extra eerie factor they needed to look old. So they went to the nearest charity shop and—'

'Bought some old curtains!' finished Nathan. 'They made them out of old curtains! Bloody hell, I think you're right. I wondered what you were on about when you mentioned *The Sound of Music*.'

'They smell really musty, don't they? Every time I've ever bought something from a charity shop, it's had that same smell. You remember that Quicksilver hoody I bought from the Animal Rescue Centre shop? I had to wash that God knows how many times before it stopped smelling, even though it was perfectly clean.'

'Blimey,' said Nathan, impressed. I allowed myself a moment to feel smug.

'Admittedly, this is pure conjuncture at this point, but it all makes sense, doesn't it?' I asked. He nodded.

'It does. So do you think the person who made and planted these dolls is the same person who left the noose?'

'I don't know. It looked to me like all the stud walls have been demolished now, which is where they were leaving the dolls, so that might've forced a change of tactic. Or maybe they realised the dolls alone wouldn't be enough to scare Devlin off.'

'Or maybe someone else decided to join the fun,' suggested Nathan. 'The question now is, what will they do next?'

Chapter Nine

I stuck the dolls back in the van after that, wanting to forget about them and the noose (and whatever else was potentially coming Devlin's way) for the evening. Daisy helped me make dinner (prawn stir-fry with noodles) and afterwards, while she and Mum, who had graced our table with her presence again that night, cleared up, Nathan and I took Germaine for a quick walk. It was too cold to be out for long so we just did a quick circuit of the roads around ours, arm in arm as the dog trotted along off her lead, snuffling at the bushes and peeing up against the roadside electrical junction box on the corner. I snuggled into Nathan's chest as we stopped to let her do her business, warming my cold cheeks against his woolly scarf.

'Come on, Germaine,' I said, my voice muffled against him. 'Pee faster.'

Nathan laughed. 'Oh, she won't. She enjoys taking her sweet time.'

'Well, I suppose if something's worth peeing on, it's worth peeing on properly.' I pulled away and grimaced. 'My ears are so cold they're starting to sting.' Nathan smiled sympathetically, then sniggered and reached out to pull my beanie hat down over not just my ears but my eyes and the whole top half of my face, too. I grunted and pulled it back up. 'Oh, very funny. That's police brutality, that is. That's—' I stopped as I saw something in the distance, down the hill and back towards the town.

'What, me keeping my beautiful wife's cute little ears warm is abuse, is it?' he teased, and then he stopped and turned round to see what I was looking at. 'What is it?'

'I thought I saw a light on down there.'

He stared for a moment and then turned back to me. 'Well, yeah, it's the town, there's a lot of lights on down there.'

'No, not in the town – what do you take me for? In the convent.'

'You can make that out from here? In the dark?'

'Yeah. I mean, no, but see the dark bit and then that building there? With the row of lights on? That's the library. Follow it along past the pub – there – and then you've got the housing estate further on, and in between that and the pub is where the convent is. Roughly.'

'It's pitch black,' said Nathan. 'I can't see it.' Honestly, he could be infuriating at times. I sighed.

'Yes, I know it's pitch black now, but a moment ago I saw something. A light.'

'A light? In the convent?'

'Yes,' I said, but of course it had only been for a second and now I was starting to doubt myself.

'Is there even any electricity connected?' asked Nathan.

'I don't think the building is connected but there must be a generator, because Devlin's got these big work lights rigged up,' I said. 'But I don't think it was one of them. I think it was a torch or something.'

Nathan looked at me, and for a moment I thought he was going to tell me not to be daft, but of course if he'd been in the habit of talking to me like that I wouldn't have married him.

'Are you sure?'

'No.'

'Because bearing in mind what's been going on, there could be someone in there planting another noose or whatever. I could see if there's any uniform free to go and check it out.'

'Would you?' I asked, grateful that he hadn't dismissed me.

'Of course. Give me a minute.' He pulled out his phone and called the station while I whistled for Germaine, who'd finished doing her business and started heading for home without us. I caught her and clipped her lead on as Nathan disconnected the call. 'We're in luck. Uniform have just finished a call at the pub, so they're going to swing by and take a look now.'

'Oh good. Thanks, babe.'

'My pleasure. Now let's go home and warm ourselves up.'

'Mum and Daisy will still be up...'

'I meant with a hot drink! What are you like? Insatiable.'

We walked home and had just got in the door when Nathan's phone rang again. I went through to the kitchen and put the kettle on, lining up four mugs as he followed me in.

'Great, thanks... No, that's all for now. Have a good night.' He put down the phone and went to the fridge to take out some milk. 'That was the station. They went and had a look but the site's all locked up, so they didn't go in. They shone a torch around and hung about to see if anyone came out, but it's all quiet.'

'I must've imagined it,' I said. It wouldn't have been the first time. There was something about the place that played tricks on the mind.

'It might've been the headlights from a passing car reflecting on a window pane or something like that,' said Nathan. 'Anyway, we'll find out in the morning if anything else's been left for Devlin.' But neither of us could've imagined what that would be.

The alarm went off as usual the next morning, and as usual I went downstairs and made tea while Nathan got in the shower and brought it back up to drink in bed. As I sat propped up against the pillows reading my book I was disturbed by his phone ringing, and I was just about to lean over to his side of the bed and answer it when my own rang, too. I answered it as Nathan came back into the bedroom, wrapped in a towel and looking far more handsome than anyone should at that time of day.

'Hello?' I said, as Nathan answered his. We turned to look at each other as the people calling us – Tommy Devlin and, I assumed, someone at the station – spoke, our eyes widening. As my call ended I leapt out of bed and stood in front of him, listening to the tail-end of his conversation.

'I'll be there in ten.' He dropped the phone on the bed and hastily began to dry himself. 'Who was that? Devlin?'

'Yes,' I said.

'Thought so.' He pulled on a pair of boxer shorts and looked at me. 'What are you waiting for? You've got time for a quick shower if you want me to give you a lift.'

'You're letting me poke about at your crime scene?' I asked, hopefully.

'Poke about, no. Hover around with Devlin and keep him out of the way, yes.'

We got ready in super-quick time, and after knocking on Daisy's door to tell her we were both going out, we jumped in Nathan's car and drove down to the convent. DS Matt Turner, Nathan's right-hand man, and DC Sunil Bakshi, his, well, left-hand man, were both waiting outside the building site, talking to Tommy Devlin and his foreman, Ken. Both men looked white with shock. PC Chrissie was unwinding a roll of crime scene tape to mark out the perimeter. I nodded to her and then turned to Devlin.

'You okay? That must've been a shock,' I said. He nodded.

'Yeah, although it was Ken who found him.'

'Found him? I nearly tripped over him,' said the foreman. He looked shaky.

'That caravan over there,' said Nathan, nodding towards the caravan, 'is that your break room?'

'Yeah.'

'Chrissie, why don't you take Mr Devlin and Mr…?'

'Cromwell. Ken Cromwell.'

'Take Mr Devlin and Mr Cromwell for a cup of tea,' said Nathan. 'I need to take a look at the scene, and then I'll be back to talk to you both, okay?'

The two men nodded and allowed Chrissie to lead them over to the caravan. Nathan turned to me. 'I suppose you want a look at the crime scene?'

'I thought you'd never ask,' I said, fluttering my eyelashes. He grinned.

'I know how to treat a woman. I take it,' he said, addressing Matt and Sunil, 'the pathologist isn't here yet?'

'No, Guv, she's on her way but it'll take her at least twenty minutes to get here from Launceston,' said Matt.

'Good. Sunil, stay here and wait for her, and get some more uniforms down here if you can. We can't have Chrissie doing crowd control on her own.'

'Crowd control?' I said, looking around us. It was still early and so far the only other people on the scene were from nearby houses who'd heard the commotion, and a couple of the builders who'd got here early. 'What crowd?'

'You don't think the protesters will miss an opportunity like this to emphasise just how bad an idea this development is, do you?' asked Nathan, and I had to agree: Jocasta would be all over this like a rash once news got out.

Matt handed us both forensic paper overalls, to avoid contaminating the crime scene, and then led us over to the convent.

'It's a bit of a squeeze,' he said, clambering through the scaffolding around the front door. We followed suit and then stopped in the stone porch to put on our suits and shoe coverings, and pull on face masks. 'This way,' said Matt.

We entered the hall. I'd come in the side entrance a couple of times now, and it didn't really give you the scale of the building. I had come in this way the day before, but I'd been focused on finding the door down to the basement and hadn't really stopped to look around me. But now I did.

There was a wide staircase that swept down from the first floor, much grander than the back stairs I'd taken previously. Halfway up it was a landing, overlooked by what was probably an exquisite stained-glass window, only it had been covered in a translucent plastic tarpaulin to protect it from the building works. The garden at the side of the convent had been dark and gloomy, but now I understood why; the building had been angled so that the sun would shine through that window, no doubt casting a beautiful glow onto the stairs, making the colours sing. It was too dark to see it now, but in summer it would have been glorious.

That glorious light would also have illuminated the body that lay sprawled on the floor at the foot of the stairs.

'What do we have?' asked Nathan. Matt referred to his notebook.

'Male – obviously – looks to be in his late twenties, early thirties, although difficult to tell without seeing his face. Looks like he fell down the stairs and broke his neck.'

'Fell or was pushed?' I asked.

'That's the million-dollar question,' said Nathan, squatting down to look at the body. He started to go through the man's pockets. 'Do Devlin or Cromwell know who he is?'

'They said they think he's one of theirs.' Matt shrugged. 'They didn't know for certain, because they didn't want to turn him over.'

'He's dressed like a builder,' I agreed. I walked around the man, giving him a wide berth, and looked at his feet. 'Wearing trainers.'

'Could they be the ones that left footprints next to the noose?'

'Noose?' Matt looked alarmed. 'What noose?'

'There's been some shenanigans going on here for the last few weeks,' said Nathan. 'Only brought to my attention – officially – yesterday.'

'Maybe,' I said. 'I can't remember what pattern the treads had now, I didn't take that much notice. Like you, I thought we were just dealing with someone trying to stop the build.'

'Well this should do it,' said Matt, and Nathan nodded.

'Yeah, it will. For the moment, at least.' He pulled a wallet from the man's pocket, stood up and flipped it open.

'Here we go. Driver's licence. Connor Milburn. Born 14th April 1994.' I peered over his shoulder at the photo on the licence.

'I think I've seen him on site,' I said. 'I'm not certain, but I think he was in the caravan the other day when I was in there talking to Devlin.' I pointed up the stairs. 'Can we go up there?' I asked. Nathan nodded, handing the wallet to Matt, who put it in an evidence bag.

'Yep, let's go and have a look and see where he could've fallen from.'

We trod as gently as possible up the stairs, keeping to one side and avoiding touching the handrail in case we contaminated anything important. We reached the landing and both stood for a moment, surveying the area. I squatted down to examine the floor and then shivered; it felt like someone was watching over my shoulder. I turned my head to see Nathan dropping to his haunches to join me. It must've been him I'd felt. Mustn't it?

'There,' I said, pointing down to the wooden floorboards. Originally there would probably have been some kind of carpet or runner covering the landing and stairs, but that had been pulled up at some point, probably by the builders. 'There's a lot of scuff marks which could show that he tripped over something.'

'Tripped over what, though? There's nothing here.'

'No… His own feet, maybe? It does happen.'

'Yeah…' Nathan didn't sound convinced, and to be honest I wasn't, either.

'Or maybe there was a scuffle and he lost his balance –

or the person he was fighting with pushed him,' I said. 'But then there's been builders traipsing up and down these stairs for the last few weeks, which could probably also account for a lot of the scuff marks.'

'Yes,' said Nathan. 'There's not a lot to go on. If there'd been carpet that would've made a trip more likely, possibly, but...' He sighed and stood up. 'Okay, let's go and talk to your client and find out who our dead man is, and why he was here.'

'And when he was here,' I added, remembering the light I thought I'd seen last night. Maybe I hadn't imagined it after all. 'If this happened before the site was locked up for the night, how come no one found him then? And if he was here after hours, how did he get in?'

We left the convent, discarding our paper suits, and headed for the caravan. The two builders had a bit more colour in their cheeks, but they still looked shaken. Understandably.

'Thanks, Chrissie,' said Nathan, holding the door open so she could leave. 'Mr Devlin, you know Jodie obviously but I don't know if you do, Mr Cromwell?'

'We've met,' said Ken.

'Good. She's not officially part of this investigation, but as you, Mr Devlin, had already engaged her services and as she's worked with the police on previous cases as a consultant, I'm happy for her to remain while we have a chat, so long as you have no objections?' Both men shook their heads, so I sat down next to Devlin on the lumpy sofa as Nathan pulled up a battered wooden dining chair.

'First things first. My detective sergeant said you knew the deceased?'

The two men exchanged glances and then nodded.

'Yeah, he's one of our crew,' said Devlin. 'I wasn't sure at first as we didn't turn him over – we didn't want to touch anything, other than trying to find a pulse – but it looks like Connor Milburn.'

'We found his ID,' said Nathan, 'and it confirms it is Mr Milburn. Does he live locally, do you know? Will there be anyone at home waiting for him?'

'Don't think he's married,' said Ken. 'I hope not, anyway. He just moved into a place in Holsworthy.'

'It'll be in the personnel files,' said Devlin. 'My laptop's in the van, I'll look it up for you in a bit.'

'Thank you,' said Nathan. 'When did you last see him? Was he working yesterday?'

'Yes,' said Devlin, 'although I don't remember seeing him. Mind you, what with everything going on and the number of people on site, he could've sat next to me on my tea break and I wouldn't have noticed.'

Ken frowned. 'Nah, he was working but he asked me if he could leave a bit early. He said he had to take his mum to a doctor's appointment in the afternoon.'

'Did he come back?' I asked. I always try to hang back when Nathan's interviewing someone, but I can never keep my mouth shut for long.

'I weren't expecting him to, no,' said Ken. 'So I wouldn't have thought so.'

'So he definitely wasn't here when you locked up the

site for the day?' I asked. 'He couldn't have been working and slipped, and no one found him until this morning?'

Ken looked at me with something approaching disgust. 'You think I lock up without checking the site's clear first?'

'Not at all,' I said quickly. 'I'm just clarifying it, so we can absolutely rule it out.'

'I go round the whole site just before I lock up,' said Ken defensively, although God knew I wasn't accusing him of anything. 'And before that me and Tommy usually go around and check on what progress has been made, so we know what's still to be done the next day. There's no way anyone could be left on site and locked in, dead or alive.'

'Thank you for clarifying that,' said Nathan diplomatically. 'We're only asking because it will help us narrow down the time of death.'

'Of course,' said Ken, slightly mollified.

'So if Connor came back after everything had been locked up, how did he get in?' I asked. Devlin shook his head.

'No idea. The gate was still locked when you got here this morning, weren't it?' he asked Ken, who nodded. 'No sign of a break-in.'

'Why would he come back anyway?' asked Ken.

'To steal?' asked Nathan. 'I know theft can be a problem on building sites.'

Devlin shook his head vigorously. 'No. Not amongst our lot. I worked some places when I was younger where anything that wasn't nailed down was likely to go walkabout, but not here. I pay the lads a good wage and in return they don't steal from me.'

'Maybe he left something behind,' I suggested.

'Like what? The lads only bring a few tools with them at most, and it wouldn't matter if they left them behind because they'd need them the next day anyway.'

'Okay, let's leave that for the moment. What time did you get here this morning, Mr Cromwell?'

'Just after seven. Five past? Most of the lads prefer to start early so they can finish by four, so I always get here around then to open up.'

'So you open up and have a walk around the site before work starts for the day?' asked Nathan.

'Well, usually I just open up and put the kettle on, to be honest,' said Ken.

'But today you went and looked in the convent,' I said. 'Why did you do that this morning?'

Ken looked nonplussed. 'I don't know. I just – I just felt like I should have a look round. Maybe because of the noose being left yesterday.'

'You thought it might be a warning of things to come?' asked Nathan.

'No, not really. I dunno. It was more looking to see if anything else had appeared overnight. More dolls, or another noose or something.'

'That makes sense,' I said. 'So you discovered the body at what time?'

'I can tell you that,' said Devlin. 'Ken called me as soon as he found it. I was on my way here anyway so I didn't answer it, but I got a missed call.' He took out his phone and swiped it open. 'Here it is. Seven eighteen. Missed call from Ken.' He held the phone out to show me, and I nodded.

'And you locked up last night at what time?' asked Nathan.

'Twenty past five, give or take,' said Ken, and Devlin nodded in agreement.

'So the victim – Connor – must've come back some time between twenty past five last night and seven o'clock this morning,' said Nathan.

'Yeah,' said Devlin. 'Good of him to come back on site to get himself killed…'

Chapter Ten

But the question was, why had he gone back to the site at all? That was something no one could answer, not at this point, anyway. Chrissie knocked on the caravan door to tell Nathan that the pathologist had arrived, so he left to have a word with her.

I made some more tea – not that the two builders had drunk the last one – and sat down with them again.

'So what was Connor like?' I asked. They both frowned for a split second before answering.

'Nice enough bloke,' said Devlin noncommittally. 'I can't say that I really knew him.'

'Me neither,' said Ken.

'Did he get on with the other lads?' I asked. Ken hesitated, and then Devlin jumped in before he could say anything.

'We hadn't had any official complaints.'

'Official complaints? There were unofficial ones then,

were there?' It seemed to me to be an odd thing to say. The two men exchanged glances and I knew there was something they weren't telling me. 'If you know or even just think there's something that could help us find out what happened, you need to tell me or the police. It's not speaking ill of the dead, it's helping him.'

Devlin spoke. 'No—' But Ken interrupted him.

'He didn't get on that well with some of the younger lads. I think the older ones just thought he was a bit of an idiot, but younger ones, like Kai and Shaggy, he really put their backs up.'

'Why, what did he do?'

'He was an idiot,' said Devlin. He clearly wanted to end the conversation.

'People don't tend to go around killing other people because they're idiots,' I pointed out. 'Otherwise there'd be nobody left.'

'I don't really know much about it,' said Ken, 'but Kai was moaning about him being red pilled or something, whatever that means.'

'You mean he was a sexist idiot?' I asked. Even then, I thought, People don't go around killing other people because they're SEXIST idiots, because again there wouldn't be many people left… Although that was a little unfair, because there were plenty of men in my life who weren't sexist.

'Yeah, something like that. Kai said that he was a misogynist and homophobic and a load of other phobics,' said Ken.

'Kai says everyone's a phobic,' Devlin muttered.

'Maybe I need to go and talk to him,' I said, and the two men nodded, eager to get rid of me.

'He's normally here by now,' said Ken. And right on cue, there was a knock on the door. But it wasn't Kai, it was Liam.

'Sorry to interrupt – oh, hi Jodie,' he said, awkwardly.

'We're finished now,' said Devlin, and I thought, Oh, are we? 'What is it?'

'Only most of us are here now and we don't know what to do. Why are the police here?'

'I'll leave you to have a staff meeting,' I said, standing up. 'I'm assuming you'll send everyone home, but ask Nathan first if he needs to speak to anyone. And can you ask Kai and anyone else who knew Connor to come and talk to me before they go?'

Devlin nodded and I left the caravan. I walked back to the door of the convent to find Nathan and see what the pathologist had said.

PC Brett had been posted by the front door and he put out a hand to stop me entering. 'Authorised personnel only,' he said. 'No civilians.'

'I am authorised,' I said, although I wasn't entirely sure that I was. 'I've been working with the developer to – look, I don't need to justify myself to you, just get Nathan, will you?'

He sneered at me. To this day I have no idea why that man hated me so much, but he clearly did. He was just about to open his mouth, probably to tell me to bugger off, when Matt came out of the building.

'Oh, there you are,' he said, pulling down his face mask. 'Nathan sent me to find you.' I allowed myself a moment of smugness, but I didn't give Brett a superior smile or anything. Not on purpose, anyway. 'He said best go round the side entrance so you don't disturb the scene. He'll meet you there.'

I thanked Matt, gave Brett a smile (okay, it was a bit smug but I couldn't resist it any longer), and walked round the side of the building. It was still quite dark, which made the garden feel even gloomier, and I was glad to get inside. It was really something, I thought, when I'd prefer to be inside the same building as a corpse rather than outside in a garden.

I wandered around to the main hall but stopped short of the crime scene, where the pathologist had just finished her examination and the rest of her team were preparing to take the body away. Nathan looked up and saw me, had a quick word with the pathologist, and then both of them made their way over.

The pathologist gave me a brief smile as Nathan introduced me. 'We've met over a dead body before, haven't we? I thought you'd left, though?'

'She's here as a consultant,' said Nathan. 'She was already working privately on a linked investigation. Jodie has a way of being involved before we even get here.'

The pathologist laughed. 'Yes, I'd heard that. Okay, so this is what we know at the moment. The neck is broken, as are various other bones including the right clavicle, both wrists – probably from putting his hands out to save himself – and there's an open fracture of the left tibia.' I grimaced; I'd seen bones poking out of people's wounds several times when I was in uniform, and it was the one thing that made me feel queasy. 'All of which are consistent with him falling down the stairs, although whether he fell the whole length of the stairs or not is hard to tell. The stairs are wooden, but the floor is stone, and the head wound he sustained when he hit it would have finished him off if the broken neck hadn't.' The pathologist spoke very matter-of-factly, but then for her it was just another day at the office.

'And no way to tell from that if it was an accident or if he was pushed?' asked Nathan, in a tone of voice that sounded like he already knew the answer would be 'no'. But…

'From the fractures, no. But when we turned him over, his face was very red. Not what you'd expect from an hours-old corpse.'

'So what does that mean? I asked.

'I won't be able to tell for certain until I get him back to the lab, but it looks to me like he was scalded with something.'

'Scalded?' Nathan sounded as surprised as I felt. 'How? You mean someone threw hot water in his face?'

'Your guess is almost as good as mine,' she said with a smile. 'I think maybe someone had a cup of coffee or tea and threw it at him, possibly causing him to stumble. But that's conjecture at this point.'

'Where are you at on time of death?' asked Nathan.

'Now that I'm more sure of,' said the pathologist. 'It would've been bitterly cold in here overnight, particularly on this stone floor, so that will have had an affect, but I'd estimate he's been dead for eight, nine hours, give or take an hour or so each way.'

'So he must've been killed between ten o'clock and midnight last night,' I said, doing the calculation in my head.

'I'd say so. Rigor is well set in, so I can quite confidently say no later than midnight.'

'That's really helpful, thank you,' said Nathan.

We left her to pack up her things and get the body ready to be transported, although they wouldn't be able to take him until the forensics team – Robbo, Gary and Lisa, who I'd come across several times before – were satisfied they'd got everything they needed. The three of them were swathed head to foot in the white anti-contamination suits, hoods up, face masks, shoe covers and gloves on, so I only really recognised them as I already knew who they were. I could only tell them apart from each other as Robbo was tall and skinny, Gary was shorter but a lot more muscular, and Lisa was tiny, about four foot ten. Robbo looked up and saw us, so Nathan waved him over. He picked his way carefully across the floor – there were various markers indicating where blood spatters or whatever had been found, and around the body there were several floor plates, placed there to stop anyone treading on or contaminating potential evidence.

'All right, Jodie? Might've guessed you'd be lurking somewhere,' he said, pulling down his mask to display the friendly grin on his face.

'You know me. How's married life?' Robbo had wed his childhood sweetheart a few months back, and I'd done him a favour by not catering for him. As I've said before, me and weddings – even my own – have a tendency to get a bit murderous.

'Good, thanks.' Pleasantries over, he turned to Nathan. 'You'll be wanting to know what we've found. Not a lot, unfortunately. Obviously we don't need to look for a murder weapon—' he turned and waved his arm towards the stairs '—which is just as well for the killer, as they'd be a bugger to hide.'

'What are the markers for?' I asked. He grimaced.

'That's where we found the poor sod's teeth,' he said. 'The force of him hitting the floor knocked some of 'em out. They look like Turkey teeth to me.'

'Turkey teeth?' Nathan looked mystified.

'Teeth from Turkey,' I said, and Robbo nodded. 'You know, when people go abroad to get their teeth straightened or get implants because it's cheaper than getting them done here. They end up with really white teeth, the type you don't get at an NHS dentist.'

'Yeah. Looks like the white "tooth" part of the implants shattered on impact. When the doc turned him over you could see the metal rods left behind in his gums. Nasty.'

'I'd have thought they'd be stronger than that,' I said.

'Believe it or not, I've seen this happen before,' said

Robbo. 'Car accident. Because the implants are more rigid than normal teeth, they're more susceptible to hard knocks.'

'You learn something new every day,' said Nathan drily. 'It'd be nice to learn a bit more about who did this, though.'

'Ha, yeah… Not got much to give you there, I'm afraid. No fibres or anything around the body, or up the stairs – Lisa's been up and down them looking, but nothing. Although there was one thing – it looks like a stain on one of the stairs, about three quarters of the way up? Lisa thought it smelt of coffee, but I can't say I noticed anything. Mind you, she has this superhuman sense of smell, so I'm not doubting her. She's swabbed it, but I don't know if it's relevant.'

'It could be,' said Nathan, looking at me. 'I think she might have found where our victim fell from.'

Nathan discarded his anti-contamination suit and gloves and we walked back out to the garden. It felt like we were emerging from the dank atmosphere of death and decay into the fresh, thankfully corpse-free air, although of course I might just have been feeling hormonal and prone to poetic exaggeration. It wouldn't have been the first time.

'So, what have you discovered?' he asked.

'That our victim was not well liked,' I said. 'Which of course is just marvellous, because that gives us more suspects to rule out.'

'I really really wish, just once, we could have a victim who was loved by absolutely everybody apart from one obvious person who loathed them,' said Nathan. 'It would make my job so much easier.'

'Not so much fun, though,' I said, and he laughed.

'Oh yes, "fun". Examining someone's broken dental implants is always a laugh…' He shook his head. 'That's nasty, isn't it? I've seen some bloody horrible things in my time, like the bloke who got pushed through a window four storeys up and went through a glass conservatory roof. We found his head outside on the patio.'

'Eww.'

'Yeah. But the thing that always gets me is teeth. Don't know why.'

'Open fractures for me,' I said, shuddering. 'Bones poking out of things. Nope.'

'Good job you weren't around when they turned him over, then.'

'Yeah…'

We stood there for a moment, contemplating the frailty of the human body and the ability it had to make a really nasty mess of itself, before we both shook ourselves and returned to the matter in hand.

'Anyway, this Connor. Why did no one like him?' asked Nathan.

'Kai – one of the labourers, who I spoke to yesterday and seems like an intelligent bloke – he complained to Ken that Connor was a misogynist. Sounds like he was one of those "manosphere" types.'

'What in God's name does that mean?' Nathan looked completely bewildered.

'Ah, yeah, you're not online as much as I am, are you?

There are these social media influencers – you know what social media is, don't you?' I teased.

'Is it something to do with programmes on the wireless?' asked Nathan. He rolled his eyes. 'Cheeky mare, yes I know what social media influencers are.'

'Well basically they go around on Facebook and Twitter or whatever it's called these days, boasting about being "Alpha Males" and clenching in all their photos so their muscles look bigger – although to be honest they look more like they really need the toilet—'

Nathan burst out laughing, which echoed around the enclosed garden and made a brief shiver run down my spine. 'I know exactly the sort of bloke you're talking about.'

'Yeah, well I don't know if Connor fancied himself as one of them or if he just followed them, but that's my next port of call: talk to Kai and have a look at Connor's social media accounts.'

'Good plan,' said Nathan. 'I, meanwhile, have to go and break the news to his mum. He might have lived on his own, but she's got a house just round the corner from him. He probably still took his dirty washing round there.'

'Yeah,' I said. 'Poor woman. Even if he had some dodgy ideas, he's still left behind someone who loved him. Every parent's nightmare.'

'Yeah, I'm looking forward to it even more now, thanks. Sure you don't want to come with me?'

I was absolutely, one hundred per cent sure I didn't – I'd had to do it a lot during my time in the Metropolitan Police, and it was one duty I really didn't miss. So I gave him a kiss and headed back out to the front of the site, to see who I could find there.

Devlin had obviously finished speaking to his crew as there were only a couple of builders still hanging around. I could see Chrissie taking down people's details, so I walked over to her.

'Thank you, sir. We'll be in touch.' She dismissed the man she was talking to and turned to me. 'All right? Nathan told me to take everyone's details in case we need to contact them, but as none of them were here when the body was found he said it was okay to send them all home.'

'I suppose it's better than having them all hanging around and getting under your feet,' I said, and she nodded. I scanned the few remaining builders. 'Have you spoken to someone called Kai?'

She checked down her list of names. 'Kai, Kai, Kai… No, it doesn't look like it. Devlin made sure they all knew they were to talk to me before they left, so he should still be here.'

But it looked to me like he wasn't. I thanked her and, seeing Ken standing by the caravan smoking a cigarette, made my way over to him. He looked up as I approached and threw down the cigarette, grinding it under his boot.

'Filthy habit,' he said. 'I'd given up until today.'

'Yeah, the whole thing must've been a horrible shock for you,' I said, sympathetically. 'Can you tell me if Kai's been in yet?'

'No, he hasn't,' said Ken. 'He called me about ten

minutes ago and said he wouldn't be in today as he's not feeling well. You wanted to talk to him, didn't you?'

'Yeah, I did,' I said, thinking, He hated Connor. Connor's dead and suddenly he's not coming to work? It could be a coincidence, but it was a hell of a big one. 'Did he know what's happened?'

'No,' said Ken. 'He probably wouldn't have bothered ringing if he'd known, would he? Not like there's going to be any work going on for the foreseeable future.'

'No, I suppose not… Would you be able to give me his contact details?' I asked. 'It would be really helpful to talk to him, and if he's not well then it's probably better that it's me rather than the police calling on him.'

'Yeah, of course,' said Ken. He popped into the caravan and came back out a minute later with a scrap of paper in his hand. 'There you go. Mobile number and address. He only lives five minutes away. I'd give it a while before you go round there, though. Sounded like he'd been up all night so he might not be up to it just yet.'

'I'll be gentle on him,' I said.

I looked at my watch: it wasn't even nine o'clock yet, although it felt like it must be later, because a lot had happened over the last hour or so. My stomach was rumbling, so I walked into town and headed for the Wave View café, which overlooked the beach and was somehow, blessedly, free of Halloween nonsense, although there were plenty of posters advertising the town's Bonfire Parade. That was taking place the next day, which funnily enough was actually Halloween. I ordered scrambled eggs on toast and a cup of tea, and got to work on my phone while I waited.

I spend too much time on social media. There, I've admitted it. It's not quite an addiction, but... It draws you in, doesn't it? You think, I'll just have a quick look at what's going on in the world and then before you know it, you've spent three hours scrolling, and some of it's not particularly nice to read. I go through phases where I try really hard to cut down on my phone time, and I do feel better for it, but then I'll get sucked in again.

Connor Milburn had also been sucked in. He was on Facebook, and Instagram, and X, and on every single platform his timeline was a relentless litany of alpha male nonsense. He followed all the big 'manosphere' accounts – men who posted an endless stream of photos of themselves, tanned, muscles clenched, looking very serious as they sat at the wheel of a Lamborghini or a Porsche or some other fancy car. Their words were a constant barrage of mockery – or worse, much worse – against women. Women were stupid, vain gold-diggers whose only worth was in their looks and whether they were virgins or not. Ridiculous rants about not choosing women with a high 'body count' – I suspected the online bros were talking about a different sort of body count to the type the police took an interest in – or ones who wore too much make-up, or didn't make an effort to look feminine, who didn't want children, or had someone else's children, or who earnt a lot of money, or who earnt no money, or who wanted a career, or who were too educated – on and on it went, making you wonder if they did actually like any women, because everything they posted seemed to be aimed at impressing other men. They boasted about making six figures and how you could too if you followed their guide to investing (which looked to me like a classic pyramid scheme), about all the women they'd had and then discarded, or who they could have had if they hadn't known their own worth, about spending hours in the gym, punishing their bodies with weights. About being 'high value males' looking for wives who knew their place, which was at home, doing as they were told.

What a load of absolute toxic shite, I thought to myself. I had to drink some tea to take away the nasty taste it had left in my mouth.

And there were the conspiracy theories. There was something in the vaccines and we were all being traced by shadowy government agencies (oh the irony of them posting this stuff on the internet, on their phones or computers, all three of which were the easiest things in the world to track – no need for '5G enabled chips' in the vaccines). Or there was nothing in the vaccines and it was all just a placebo for the masses, for the sheep who blindly did what the government told them. One of them proudly proclaimed he didn't sleep with vaccinated women, which to me was proof that vaccines did have benefits, after all. I turned my phone over as the waitress brought over my scrambled eggs; I didn't want her thinking I was a fan of all this stuff. But she'd already seen it.

'That bloke talks a load of old rubbish,' she said.

'It's terrible, isn't it?' I agreed. 'And there are young men out there lapping it up.' She nodded.

'My nephew went down that rabbit hole. He had no dad, see? No proper male role models around him. That's how it happens.'

'What happened to him?'

'He moved to Dubai, because that's where all the rich young influencers live, or so he told my sister.' She chuckled. 'Silly little sod spent six months out there, got into loads of debt, and then came home with his tail between his legs. Got himself a job and a lovely girlfriend now, and he's much happier.'

'Phew, I'm glad he found his way out of it,' I said.

'Yeah, not everyone does…'

Connor had found his way out, but not of his own volition. She left me to it. I turned the phone over and checked out Connor's own posts.

Most of them were photos of himself. He obviously hadn't got the Alpha Male memo about not smiling, because in a few of his earlier pictures he had a big cheesy grin, showing off those startlingly white Turkey teeth, although in later ones he had the requisite deadly serious 'I'm a REAL man' expression down to a 'I'. He was tanned, even in his most recent picture. Had I noticed a tan on the body earlier? Difficult to say, as it had been quite dark when I'd seen him. I couldn't tell if it was out of a bottle, from a sun bed, or as a result of a trip abroad, although I was betting that if he had been somewhere for some winter sun, there'd be photos of it. Maybe he'd hankered after the lifestyle, but being a builder in Cornwall didn't give him the income for it.

He was well built, looking more muscular in his photos than he had in real (dead) life, because his poses were all very controlled, clenched, every muscle straining to make him look his best. Dead bodies tend to be less vain and more relaxed… His non-work clothes all seemed to be at least two sizes too small; trousers with very narrow legs, fitting so snugly around his groin that it seemed doubtful he'd be able to sit down (maybe that was why he was standing up in every single photo?). The buttons on his shirts strained against his pecs. It reminded me of the Incredible Hulk, at the part in his transformation just before he turns green and all his clothes rip. It couldn't have been very comfortable, and it didn't look stylish, it just looked like he was wearing a cheap, ill-fitting suit. I felt a bit guilty for thinking that; the poor bugger was dead, after all, but it made me wonder if there was any truth in what the waitress had said: lack of male role models was what made young men turn to this sort of thing. If Connor's dad was around, surely he would've gone with him when he'd bought a suit and made him get one that actually fitted?

I'd have found the whole thing – and Connor himself – completely ridiculous, if I hadn't just seen his corpse. Regardless of whatever his online persona was, he hadn't deserved to die like that.

I tucked into my scrambled eggs – murder scenes have to be pretty bad to put me off my food for long, as I've seen quite a few of them – and had almost finished when I heard the bell over the door of the café tinkle. I looked up (as an ex-copper I always like to sit where I can see the entrance and exit) and there was Tony, ordering his usual at the counter. He must've felt me looking, as he glanced over and saw me.

'Morning,' he said, coming over to join me. 'Don't normally see you in here at this time of day. You escaping for some "me" time?'

'Something like that,' I said. He obviously hadn't heard about the murder, or he'd have been pumping me for information the minute he sat down. 'Had an early start and missed breakfast.'

'Oh, something to do with your investigation?' He grinned. 'Tracking down spooky dollies. Carmen told me all about it. Any developments?'

'You could say that,' I said. 'Do you know anyone who's working on the convent?'

'The Fossett lad's got a job there, I think. Donna asked if I had anything for him, but I didn't want to give him a job in the shop, get him trained up and onboarded when he'll bugger off the minute something better comes up.'

'Something better than working at Penhaligon's department store?' I said, wide-eyed in mock astonishment. 'Surely not!'

'Yeah, all right! Retail's not everyone's cuppa tea, especially someone with a degree in Economics or whatever it was.'

'Politics,' I said. 'No, you can't blame him for wanting something a bit more exciting.'

'Poor lad will never know the adrenaline of the Christmas rush,' said Tony, shaking his head. 'Or the sheer excitement of a completed stock take.' We both laughed. 'Anyway, why you asking? You think one of the workers is behind these dolls? I thought they'd been walled up years ago?'

'That's what I originally thought, but not now…'

'Why, what's happened?'

I hesitated, but the Penstowan grapevine didn't need any help from me, they'd know all about the murder by lunchtime anyway, and probably have a bunch of theories by dinnertime to boot. Probably have solved it by the time they'd gone to bed. 'Where the dolls were found, it now looks like the walls had been damaged or demolition had already started, meaning someone could've pushed them inside the cavity recently. And then yesterday something else was found – a noose.' Tony gasped. 'And this morning…' He leaned forward, eager for more. 'This morning the foreman got to the site and found a body.'

'Bloody hell!' Tony sat back, his desire for gossip momentarily sated. 'So the dolls were a warning, and when it went unheeded they killed someone?'

'"They" killed someone? You mean the dolls?' I scoffed. 'I can just imagine them all piling in for a fight.'

'You laugh, but do you remember that Tiny Tears doll you had?' He shuddered. 'Evil, that thing was.'

'Oh yeah, that was why you peed yourself on the rug at my birthday party that time.' The waitress had just come over with Tony's bacon sandwich. She gave him a bit of side eye. 'This was a long time ago,' I explained. 'He was only about eighteen.'

'Months!' Tony interjected. 'Eighteen months!'

The waitress suppressed a giggle and walked away. Tony looked at me.

'Thanks a lot, Nosey.'

'Any time. Anyway, I don't know if the death had anything to do with the dolls – to be honest, I was so surprised by it that I didn't even think about them – but now you mention it—'

'Come on, they have to be linked, don't they? It'd be a massive coincidence if they weren't,' said Tony. He was right. Another massive coincidence on top of the other one: Kai hating the victim, and not being at work this morning when the body was found.

Could Kai have been behind the dolls? He'd certainly had theories about them, or had at least immediately cottoned on to what I was thinking when I'd spoken to him and Shaggy. If it looked like someone was starting to suspect that the dolls were recent inhabitants of the convent rather than having been walled up there years ago, then what better way to deflect that suspicion away from yourself than by being one of the first people to suggest that? It was a classic bluff. But even if he had been the one planting them, how did they relate to Connor? Had Connor even found any of the dolls? I needed to look at the list of names Devlin had given me, but I thought I'd remember a name like Connor, as it wasn't a particularly common one in Cornwall. The noose, on the other hand… The noose felt completely different to the dolls, like it had a far more sinister intent. I'd wondered if the person who'd planted the dolls, which were much more subtly menacing, would be the sort of person who would also leave the noose. A noose was a more direct, in-your-face (round-your-neck) threat. But then Connor had been pushed down the stairs, not hanged, so maybe it hadn't been meant for him anyway.

'Earth to Jodie,' said Tony.

'Oh, sorry,' I said. 'Deep in thought for a moment.'

'I could tell, there was steam coming out your ears. Who was the victim?'

'I can't tell you that until their family's been notified,' I said. I'm a gossip but I do have some standards, you know. 'I know you wouldn't deliberately let the cat out the bag, but it would be terrible if it got back to them on the grapevine rather than via the police.'

'Fair enough. Someone local, though? One of the builders, or not connected to the site?'

'My lips are sealed,' I said, proving the lie by opening my mouth and shovelling the last bit of scrambled egg in.

Chapter Eleven

I left Tony chomping not only on his bacon sandwich but also at the bit, desperate to pass on the gossip and ferret out some more details. He called me Nosey, but he was probably worse than I was; in fact he was a Shirley Parker level gossip, although she called it 'taking a keen interest in the local community'. Being nosey, in other words.

Kai was my next stop and he only lived a few streets away, but before I could get there my phone rang.

'Mum, where are you?' asked Daisy. I told her. 'Okay, it's just that Jade and I are getting a lift to Exeter, and I'm going to meet up with Joe once he's finished recording something. I'm going to be out all day so I can't take the dog.'

'Who's giving you a lift?' None of Daisy's friends could drive, as far as I was aware, and I'd seen too many boy racers wrapping their cars (and their passengers) around lamp posts to feel comfortable about her getting a lift with someone I didn't know.

'One of the girls from the samba band. She's very careful.'

'Okay… What about Nana? Can't she take Germaine?'

'Nana's going round to Bob's. She says he likes dogs but he's not a fan of dog hair, and you know what Germaine's like…' Pomeranians might be cute and fluffy, but unfortunately that fluff's got to go somewhere, and our clothes and sofa all looked like they'd been present at an explosion in a cotton wool factory. I could hardly blame Bob for wanting to protect his soft furnishings from Germaine's fallout.

So that's how Germaine ended up accompanying me to interview Kai, who I could only hope wasn't allergic to dogs.

I needn't have worried though, because as soon as I rang the doorbell of his house barking started. I sincerely hoped Kai wasn't genuinely ill and asleep in bed, because if he had been he was definitely awake now.

I was just about to ring the doorbell again when the door opened. Kai peered out, eyes squinting. He took a moment to recognise me.

'Oh, it's you,' he said, surprised but not hostile. 'Is this about Connor?'

'You heard?'

'Yeah, Ken told me when I rang in sick. Hang on—' He turned round to address the source of the barking. 'Lola, stop it! It's not burglars. Sorry,' he said, turning back to me, 'do you want to come in?' He looked down at Germaine, who for once hadn't joined in with the barking and was instead sitting on the doorstep with a slightly superior air, as if she would never stoop so low as to yap maniacally at someone coming to our door. 'Does your dog like other dogs?'

'Usually,' I said, because although she was normally very friendly to all other living creatures, she did have a thing about the Labrador who lived a few doors down, despite the poor thing being about eighty (in dog years) and too sedate to raise a hackle. Kai reached down behind him before opening the door. His hand was on the collar of a beautiful little Bichon Frisé, who easily rivalled Germaine in the cute, white and fluffy stakes. Germaine immediately stood up and yapped, but it was her excited, pleased-to-meet-you yap, rather than her hey-you-this-is-MY-territory one.

Kai led us inside, down a narrow hallway. As we paused near the open door into the front room my nostrils twitched at the potent and very recognisable smell of marijuana. I wasn't sure if Kai noticed, but he hastily shepherded me onwards into the kitchen, where he flicked the kettle on. The two dogs had followed us and were currently engaged in sniffing each other's bottoms. Not for the first time I was relieved that humans had other ways of introducing themselves.

'I was just making myself a hot honey and lemon,' he said. 'My throat's really sore this morning.' He did sound a bit croaky, and he looked tired.

'Is that why you're off today?' I asked, and he nodded.

'I was fine yesterday, but I was coughing all night and I

hardly slept,' he said. 'I figured they could manage without me for a day. I'm planning to lie on the sofa and binge-watch something on Netflix all day.'

'Is it just you living here?' I asked, hoping that I sounded more concerned that he was on his own with no one to look after him while he was ill, rather than checking for an alibi for the time of the murder.

'It is at the moment,' he said. 'My mum and my sister are away for a few days.'

'Gone somewhere nice?' That probably wasn't relevant, so I was just being nosey, although I could justify it by saying I was testing out his alibi or lack of one.

'They've gone to stay with my uncle and aunty in East Grinstead, and then they're going to a wedding fair near there at the weekend. My sister's getting married next year and Mum's determined she's going to have a big wedding with all the frills.' He grinned. 'My sister's already told me they're eloping, but there's no sense in upsetting Mum until she has to.'

'Oh dear,' I laughed. 'I hope I won't be the same when my daughter gets married, if she ever does.'

'My dad keeps telling her to leave Hannah to plan it herself, but she won't listen.' He anticipated my next question. 'My mum and dad aren't together anymore but everyone's still friends. He lives in Truro.'

No alibi, then. But Kai seemed like a good-natured sort of person; surely he wouldn't push someone down the stairs, no matter how much of a sexist dick they were?

The kettle clicked off. 'Would you like a cup of tea, or a

coffee?' he asked, pouring hot water into a cup of lemon juice and honey.

'Tea would be nice,' I said. 'I'm not a big coffee drinker.'

'Me neither,' he said, getting out another mug. 'I have to be in the mood for it.' I wondered if the right mood for coffee would also be the right mood for pushing someone down the stairs. Didn't ask him that, though. It doesn't do to upset the person making you a cup of tea, in case they maliciously put too much milk in it.

We walked through to a small but comfortable living room, full of plants and books and a couple of big squashy armchairs, but no TV.

'You're not watching Netflix in here, then,' I said. Kai grinned.

'No. Mum calls this the snug. No telly allowed. That's in the front room, but it's full of dirty mugs at the moment so I'm not taking you in there.' Dirty mugs and weed, I thought.

'You've been on your own a few days, then.'

'Ha, yeah. I'm normally quite tidy – well, not if you ask my mum – but I've just been really knackered the last few days. Probably leading up to me being ill now.'

'Yeah, probably.' We sat in silence for a moment, sipping our drinks.

'So go on then,' said Kai. 'Ask me whatever you came here to ask.'

'Okay,' I said. 'Ken said you told him that Connor was a misogynist, or something like that. You didn't agree with the way he went on, anyway.'

'No, I didn't,' said Kai. 'He was a dick. He was always getting at me and Shaggy, saying we were soy boys and simps—'

'What exactly does that mean?' I asked. 'I've heard about "alpha males" and all that rubbish, but I don't understand all of it.'

'Basically, we treat women like human beings. My girlfriend – my ex-girlfriend – she's really intelligent, she got like a first in Psychology and now she's doing a PhD, really smart, you know?' He sighed. 'We split up a few weeks ago.'

'Oh, I'm sorry.'

'Thanks, but it's fine. It was on the cards for a while, really. She was never going to stay round here, was she? I don't blame her for wanting different things out of life than I do.'

'What do you want out of life?' I asked. Again, not relevant at all, but I couldn't help being interested.

He shrugged. 'Now that's a question. I don't know, I'm still working it out. She knew she wanted to be a shrink or something when she was twelve. I mean, that's mad, innit? To know that early. I just wanted to leave school when I was twelve.'

'Yeah, I know what you mean,' I said, although I didn't really; I'd always wanted to follow in my dad's footsteps and be a copper, but in London, where crime never slept, not Penstowan, where nothing ever happened.

'Anyway, after we split up, I was upset about it even though I knew it was coming, and Connor heard about it and just said I was a soy boy for wanting a woman like that in the first place, and that if I didn't know my own worth these hoes would always treat me like dirt. Which, one, didn't exactly make me feel better, and, two, it just wasn't true. There's nothing wrong with a woman wanting an education and a career.'

'And if she didn't have a career and make her own money, then she'd be a gold-digger,' I said, and he nodded.

'Exactly! Although good luck digging for gold from a casual labourer like me.' He laughed, but it turned into a cough. He took a sip of honey and lemon and cleared his throat. 'That's the other thing Connor always bangs on about – money. He reckoned he was going to be bringing in big bucks from this investment platform he'd heard about, but when he showed it to a couple of the other lads they all told him it was a scam. He wouldn't have it, though. Reckoned he'd have the deposit for a Lambo in a couple of months. The stupid thing is he'll have been making good money anyway as a bricklayer, but it sounds like he's been putting loads of it into this investment thing. I hope for his sake it isn't a scam—' He stopped, looking suddenly sombre. 'Not that it'll make any difference to him now, will it? God, I can't actually believe he's dead.'

'It's a shock,' I said gently. 'Did he have a girlfriend?'

'Connor, shackle himself to just one woman?' He snorted. 'I don't think so. He'd have told you it was through choice, like no stupid ho was going to trap him, but I think his personality took care of that. Or maybe I'm wrong and he really was beating them off with a stick. Maybe the women I know just have better taste.' He shook his head. 'Nah, I think if he was seeing someone he'd have gone on and on about how hot but stupid she was and how much sex he was making her have with him.'

'A real charmer, then,' I said. 'How long had you known Connor?'

'About a year?' Kai mused. 'I met him on another job for Tommy Devlin.'

'You weren't at school together?'

'Nah, he's – he was older than me, so he'd have been a few years above me. But I don't even know if he grew up round here. We never talked about anything normal like that, it was all this alpha male crap.'

We were quiet for a moment, watching the two dogs. They'd finished sniffing round each other and Lola was now showing Germaine round the house, or so it seemed; they were in and out of the room, Germaine happily trotting behind her new friend and snuffling around the furniture.

'They've hit it off,' I said, and Kai smiled.

'They're both so cute.' He sighed. 'That's another thing that apparently makes me a beta rather than an alpha, the fact that I love animals and I'm not embarrassed to be seen walking a fluffy white dog. Connor said I look gay walking Lola. I told him I was taking that as a compliment, because all the gay men I know are really good-looking.' He grinned. 'And they all dress better than him.'

I laughed. 'That wouldn't be hard. All he had to do was get a suit two sizes bigger and he would've looked okay.' We both laughed, a little guiltily, and Germaine and Lola both yapped, as if in agreement. 'So when was the last time you saw him?'

'Yesterday morning at work. He came in and started giving it all the usual rubbish—'

'Like what?'

'Asked me if my balls had dropped yet.' He rolled his eyes. 'I know you're not supposed to speak ill of the dead, or their dress sense for that matter, but he really was a dick.'

'Sounds like it. What time was that, can you remember?'

'Would've been around ten? We'd stopped for a tea break.'

'And did you see him again after that?'

'No,' said Kai. 'Simon said he left early, not long after lunch.'

'Simon's one of the other labourers, yeah?' I asked, trying to remember. I thought he was one of the names Ken had given me, but I hadn't had a chance to talk to him.

'Yeah, he was helping Connor in one of the rooms upstairs. He was taking the piss out of him, saying he'd gone to meet his investment adviser.' He sniggered.

'Is that what Connor told him?' Because that wasn't what he'd told Ken.

'Yeah. Simon said he was his normal irritating self until he looked at something on his phone, and then he got the right hump.'

'Maybe you were right about his investment scheme being a scam,' I suggested. Hadn't he said something about getting a message from his bank when Devlin and I had come across him in the caravan, the day before the murder?

'Yeah, maybe.'

I stood up. 'Well, thank you for your time. I hope you feel better soon.'

Kai stood too. 'Thanks. I don't know if anything I've told you will be any help, but at least you know what he was like now.'

'Yeah…' I almost wished I didn't, because hearing about the way he'd gone on made me feel soiled. Soiled and a bit depressed. How many men felt the same way about women as Connor had? We'd fought so hard for equality and we'd come so far, but there seemed to be so many men online now who just hated women; how many were there in 'real' life who felt the same way? And why? As well as being a danger to women, many of them were a danger to themselves. Depression and loneliness were rife among younger men, and male suicides had gone up in recent years. As Daisy would no doubt have commented, toxic masculinity and the patriarchy hurt men almost as much as it hurt women. I smiled to myself; if Daisy and Joe ever broke up, I'd introduce her to Kai – they'd get on like a house on fire, although I might have to have words with him about his weed habit…

I called to Germaine, who actually came running (wonders will never cease), clipped on her lead, and turned back. 'Oh, one more thing,' I said, attempting to sound nonchalant, like it had just occurred to me. I've always been a fan of Columbo. 'Where were you between ten o'clock last night and midnight?'

Kai narrowed his eyes, but he looked more amused than annoyed. 'Are you asking me for an alibi?'

'Yeah, I suppose I am. The police will be asking everyone who worked on site with him—' I didn't think they would actually ask everyone, but he didn't need to know that '—so this just gives you the opportunity to get your story straight before they ask you.'

'I was here. Like I said, I wasn't well and I was awake for most of the night, coughing.' He gave me a rueful smile. 'And I was on my own, so there's no one to back me up. Almost like I didn't do anything wrong so I didn't bother inventing an alibi…'

I bade him farewell and left him to spend his sick day watching the boxset of *Narcos* on telly, then walked down to the beach to give Germaine a run. In the summer we weren't allowed to let her off the lead on the beach, in case she pooped on a holidaymaker (or something like that), but between October and April she was allowed to run free. I found a stick that had probably been abandoned by another dog and threw it for her, but she just looked at me in disgust and trotted off to nose into a rock pool.

I strolled along the sand, one eye on the dog, and thought through what I'd just learned, but I kept getting distracted by other dogs and their owners, by screeching seagulls, and by the fact that it might be cold and a bit eerie with the mist drifting in off the sea, but it was still beautiful here. I love living near the sea. I love the smell of salt and seaweed and ozone, I love the way the cold breeze brushes away the cobwebs and makes you feel alive, and I love the low murmur of the waves as they creep up the beach. Being near the sea can fill you full of joy, or sometimes melancholy, but it always makes you feel something.

I was interrupted by the buzz of my phone in my pocket.

Hey babe, I'm back at the station. Pop in for a brainstorm? xxx

---

Germaine put her head on one side and looked as cute as she possibly could. Taking her to the police station was always a bit of an issue, but it did depend on who was on the desk. The main desk sergeant, Sally, loved dogs and always had a couple of treats tucked away in her desk – although they were there more to placate any snarling bulldogs or Rottweilers officers might have to deal with in the execution of their duties, because a lot of the small-time criminals around here seemed to have big, angry dogs – but she drew the line at letting me take Germaine upstairs to Nathan's office. Equally, she'd taken a dim view that time I'd asked her to dog-sit for me while I went up there. But today I was in luck, because lack of staffing meant the constabulary had recently called in a part-time civilian desk jockey, who was none other than my dad's old colleague, ex-desk sergeant Harry Adams. As we entered the station Harry's face broke out into a big smile, and he came out into the foyer to make a fuss of both Germaine and me.

'I was wondering when you'd turn up,' he said, squatting down to ruffle Germaine's hair.

'You talking to me or the dog?'

'Both of you. You want a treat, do you?' This last was, I assumed, addressed to the dog.

'Of course she wants a treat. When has she ever turned one down?' I said. 'Come to think of it, when have I?'

He laughed. 'Oh yeah, I remember you as a little un. Always wanted one of me jelly babies, didn't you?' He patted his tummy, which was looking very flat. 'Had to give them up for me 'ealth. If you want something sweet you'll have to make do with a satsuma.'

'Ugh no, that's far too healthy,' I said. 'You're looking well, though. Being back at work suits you.'

'Yeah, it does. Particular as it's only two mornings a week, and no weekends. Want me to look after this good girl while you go upstairs? Or is Nathan okay with her being up there?'

'Well, you look like you're bored, so…'

He laughed. 'It would be my pleasure to look after Miss Germaine. I'll buzz you in.'

I left Sergeant Adams – he'd told me to call him Harry but I'd grown up with him being Sergeant Adams, and it was a hard habit to break – teaching Germaine how to sit and shake paws with him. She already knew how to do it, so she was just humouring him. As I passed the door to the room that had once been my dad's office I felt a pang; they'd kept it empty for ages, in his memory, then as a storeroom, but now they used it for occasional meetings.

That was fine. It would've felt really weird to have Nathan or anyone else sitting behind my dad's desk.

'Hey.' Nathan saw me enter and came across the room to meet me, giving me a very chaste and discreet peck on the cheek. 'Glad you could join us. Does that mean you've got something to share?' He lowered his voice. 'Because so far we've got bugger all.'

'Maybe,' I said. Matt and Sunil were at their desks, next to the big whiteboard that got wheeled out for murders and complex cases, and also to work out the seating plan for Sunil's wedding reception, which had been massive and, like many weddings, an object lesson in familial diplomacy.

'So what have we got?' I asked, as Nathan and I stood in front of the board. Matt laughed.

'Listen to her, acting like she's in charge.'

'She's my wife,' said Nathan. 'Of course she's in charge.'

'Happy wife, happy life,' said Sunil, who did indeed have a happy wife, two small happy children, and a happy life.

'Yeah, yeah,' I said, waving away the good-natured banter. 'I just wanted to get in and say it before Nathan did.'

'Okay,' said Nathan, becoming businesslike. 'We spoke to the victim's parents. Both of them absolutely shocked, he was a model son, who would do such a thing, etc., etc.'

'Hmm,' I said. 'That's not what I've heard.'

'No,' said Nathan, 'nor us. According to them he was very popular, had lots of friends, so many that they didn't see him very often even though he only lived around the corner from them. Always out.'

'Did they mention any names? Or a girlfriend?' I asked. Matt nodded.

'Girlfriend, yeah. They said he'd told them he was seeing someone, but they hadn't met her. They'd been on at him to bring her round for Sunday lunch but he said she was a bit shy, so he kept putting them off.'

'That's interesting,' I said. 'Because Kai – one of the labourers I just spoke to – said he didn't have a girlfriend, and that he was the type of person who would definitely have boasted about it if he had.'

'So he was either lying to his mates or to his mum,' said Nathan. 'Which one's more likely?'

Without even a second's pause the rest of us said, 'His mum.' Followed by laughter, some of it no doubt coming from a place of bitter experience.

'My mum used to constantly go on about when was I going to settle down and give her some grandchildren,' said Matt. He was going out with PC Chrissie now, so hopefully he was getting less parental hassle.

'Yeah, so did mine,' said Nathan, and I felt that old familiar guilt about not giving him a baby because I'd been there, done that with Daisy's father, and it was too late for me to have another one now anyway. 'I don't think she was expecting me to present her with a fully grown teenage granddaughter,' he continued, 'but it's all worked out fine.'

'So no girlfriend,' said Sunil. 'That's one less suspect, at least.'

'Yeah,' said Nathan, 'but let's not completely discount it. Keep her on the board for now.'

'Maybe he had a boyfriend,' I said. 'That might be why he was keeping it quiet amongst his workmates, and why he didn't bring them home to meet Mum and Dad.'

'Have you seen what he looked like?' asked Matt, doubtfully. 'Your typical red pill macho man.'

'Yeah, but I reckon a lot of them are in the closet,' I said. 'Look at their online content, it's all to impress other men.' I sniffed, sounding just like my mother when she was unimpressed by something. 'It don't work on most women, anyway.'

'I don't know about that,' said Sunil. 'Him being a closet homosexual, I mean. I had a look at some of his social media, and some of the content he's shared is horribly homophobic.'

'Deep in denial,' I said. Nathan shook his head.

'Not every homophobe is in the closet. Some of them are just horrible people.'

'True,' I admitted. 'So let's just say he probably wasn't in a relationship, but if he was he was keeping it secret for some reason.'

'That covers all the bases, yes.' Nathan rubbed out the word *girlfriend?* where it was written on the board and wrote *relationship?* instead. 'Okay, so let's look at motive instead.'

'He was a dick,' said Sunil, and we all looked at him, slightly shocked. That was the closest Sunil ever came to swearing, unless he was drunk, which had only ever happened once to my knowledge. He blushed. 'Well, he was, wasn't he?'

'He absolutely was,' I agreed.

'People tend not to get murdered solely because they're dicks, though,' said Nathan, which was basically what I'd said earlier to Devlin and Ken. But then that was before I'd seen the sort of thing he'd posted online. 'Otherwise there'd not be many people left.'

'I mean, you're not wrong,' I said, 'but there's being a dick and there's being a dangerous bigot. If he was saying that sort of thing in public, what was he saying in private, amongst friends? Or more to the point, amongst people he thought agreed with him, but who might not have done?'

'You think he said something horrible to the wrong person, and they killed him?' asked Matt.

'Maybe. I don't mean to sound like I'm victim-blaming here, because no one deserves to be murdered over words, but… Maybe it had gone a step further than that? Maybe he'd done something to back up all the controversial stuff he posted?' I thought. 'We know he was influenced by the people he followed. He was using some investment platform one of them had recommended. Maybe that wasn't thc only call to action he followed?'

'Hmm.' Nathan tapped the board marker on his lip, deep in thought. Thankfully he'd put the cap back on and we weren't going to have a repeat of the time he'd ended up with a streak of blue ink running across his chin. 'I don't know about that. We're still digging into his private life, of course, but outside of work he seems to have spent most of his time at the gym, at home, or in the pub.'

'What pubs did he go to?' I asked.

'The Market Arms, mostly.' Nathan grinned. 'Not the Admiral Benbow.' That was Penstowan's only gay pub.

'Some of the people who drink in the Market are a bit rough,' I said. 'Like Tony and his Chamber of Commerce lot…' Nathan laughed.

'Yeah, it's not exactly a hotbed of crime,' he said. 'Not the sort that could get you pushed down the stairs, anyway.'

'That's the other thing, Guv,' said Matt. 'What was he doing in the convent after dark? How did he even get in?'

'You could climb over the fence,' said Nathan, thinking. 'If you really wanted to get in, that is. You're right, the real question is why was he there?'

'To plant more of those dolls Jodie's been looking into?' suggested Sunil.

'It's possible,' I said, 'but I don't know why, I just can't see him doing something like that. They're a witch thing, aren't they? The idea behind them, I mean, not that there's a witch who's been planting them.' I shivered. 'Whoever planted them must know a bit about witches, and I can't see how or why Connor would've had any interest in them. Witchcraft was about empowering women, about female intelligence, and those are two things he really didn't agree with. The noose, now – I could see him doing something like that.'

'But again – why?' asked Nathan. 'Devlin said he'd worked for him for nearly twelve years, since he was an apprentice. Why would he be trying to get the site shut down? Because I can't see any other reason for any of this stuff being planted.'

'No, nor can I.' I sighed. 'Okay, so if he didn't plant them, were they planted to target him? It would be a massive coincidence if the two things weren't connected, and although coincidences do happen all the time and I can't see how they're connected, it doesn't mean they aren't.'

'How's a doll threatening to him, though?' asked Matt, and I had to admit I had no idea.

'Okay, let's move on,' said Nathan. 'Connor left work early yesterday. He told his boss that he was taking his mum to a doctor's appointment, but when I asked her about it she said it wasn't true and that she hadn't seen him for over a week. So where was he going?'

'I might have something there,' I said, remembering what Kai had told me. 'You remember I said he was using this investment platform one of the influencers had recommended? Well one of the other labourers, Simon, who was working with him at the time, told the others that Connor had had some notification on his phone that had put him in a really bad mood, and Simon joked that he'd left early to talk to his investment adviser. The other lads he'd shown it to had all told him it was a scam. Maybe it was? Maybe he'd had some bad news about the money he'd invested and he was going to sort it out? And you remember I said when we looked at his ID that I thought I'd seen him the day before? I'm pretty certain it was him. He told Devlin he'd just had a phone call from the bank and he wanted to follow it up, but Devlin turfed him out of the caravan so we could talk.'

'That's a line of enquiry we need to pursue,' said Nathan. 'Sunil, find out what you can about Connor's financial status. Was he being conned out of money? Was there someone he could've confronted about it?'

'At the convent?' I asked.

'I know it's unlikely, but it's a lead,' said Nathan.

'Maybe one of his co-workers who didn't like him—' started Sunil.

'There were a few of them,' I said.

'—maybe one of them had set up the investment platform as a joke, and he'd fallen for it and started giving them money?'

'That's good,' said Nathan, nodding. He wrote it on the whiteboard:

Investment scam lost him money? Who benefited? Who would want to stop him telling everyone what they'd done?

'That would also explain why they'd meet up at the convent after everyone else had gone.' He turned to me suddenly. 'You thought you saw lights there last night, didn't you?'

'Yeah, I did. And the other night, when we came out of the Market,' I said, remembering that brief flash of light in an upstairs window. 'But the one last night was too early for the murder window.'

'Doesn't mean they weren't still there,' said Nathan, writing it on the board.

'Uniform went and checked, though.'

'But they didn't go in, did they? They checked that the site was locked up, and they waited to see if the light came back on or anyone left the building, but they didn't.'

'True…' Maybe the light I'd seen had been the murderer, getting into position and then lying in wait for Connor. Maybe they'd taken a thermos of coffee with them to keep warm…

Chapter Twelve

I rescued Germaine from Harry (she was an old dog and she was starting to get tired of pretending he was teaching her new tricks) and turned towards home. Nathan had given his team their instructions: Sunil was to take a look at Connor's finances and at the investment platform he'd been using, while Matt was going to trawl CCTV and traffic cams to see if he could track where Connor had gone after he'd left work early. There was no CCTV around the convent, or the wider building site, so unfortunately there was no way of seeing how Connor would've got back in after the gates had been locked, or who might've followed him, but if we – the police, I mean – could find out where he'd gone earlier in the day that might shed some light on a motive. Nathan was going to talk to Connor's parents again and get the names of some of his friends, both on and off the building site.

And me? I was going to work out who'd planted those

flipping dolls and if they'd had anything to do with Connor if it killed me. But where to start?

I'd barely started walking when my phone rang again. I pulled it out and peered at the number, but I didn't recognise it. I almost let it go to voicemail, which is how I normally deal with numbers I don't know, but then I wouldn't normally be in the midst of a murder investigation (although I had been, more times than was probably usual for someone no longer in the force). I answered it.

'Hello?'

'Is that Daisy's mum?' It was a young man's voice, again not one I recognised. My blood ran cold.

'Yes, what's happened? Is she okay?' Please don't let it be one of those phone calls. "I'm sorry to tell you that your child is—" I knew I should've checked who was giving her that lift to Exeter.

'Yeah, I saw her earlier. You might not remember me but I was at school with her? Luke Trevally?'

'Luke? Yeah, I remember you…' He'd entered the town's fancy dress contest during Mermaid Week a few years back, dressed in full drag with a couple of scallop shells stuck on his chest. His mum had told me (well, she'd told another mum, who had told Debbie, who had told me) it had taken two days of frantic washing to get them unstuck. 'Everything okay?'

'Yeah. No. Er – can I come and see you?'

I stood outside the community centre wondering what on earth I was getting myself into now. Luke had insisted that whatever he had to tell me, he had to do it in person.

The community centre and library had succumbed to the All Hallows Eve madness, but it had an excuse: tomorrow's parade would end up there, and the revellers would go inside for a party. The caretaker, Ged, was up a ladder hanging fairy lights around the entrance, wobbling dangerously as he tried to tuck them behind a hanging skeleton that was guarding the door. Rookie mistake. When decorating, the lights always go up first. Ged swore and grabbed a madly swaying bat for support, narrowly avoiding coming a cropper. I should've volunteered to hold the ladder, but it was more entertaining to watch him wobble, and the ladder wasn't that high.

Germaine settled down onto the tarmac by my feet with a weary sigh.

'I know how you feel,' I said. 'I want to go home and have a cup of tea.'

'Mrs Parker? Er – sorry – Mrs Withers?' Luke pulled up on his bike in front of me and dismounted.

'Jodie's fine,' I said. I love Nathan but his surname, not so much. 'What's all this about?'

Luke padlocked his bike to a railing and turned back to me. 'It might be better to show you.'

He led me around the back of the community centre and towards the housing estate that backed onto the convent, the one I could see from the shady convent garden.

'Daisy said there was something going on at the

building site,' he said. 'I went and had a look and there's police everywhere.'

'Yes,' I said, although I didn't go into details. He swallowed hard.

'I think they might be looking for me.'

I stopped dead. 'What? What are you saying? Why would they be looking for you?'

'I was in the convent last night.' He looked at me, hugely anxious – not the cocky young lad I remembered from the Mermaid Festival.

'Okay. What were you doing?' I tried to sound firm, but not harsh. 'You need to tell me, Luke. If you did something, you need to come clean. It'll be better for you in the long run.'

'I know,' he said, miserably. 'I'm sorry.'

I reached out and put a hand on his arm. 'Come on, Luke. You can tell me.'

He sighed. 'Okay. I went to the convent last night at about half six. I wanted to scope it out for a prank.'

'Go on.' That was about the time I'd thought I'd seen a light.

'You know the parade tomorrow night? It'll go past it on the way to the community centre, and I thought it would be funny to set up some fireworks or something there to give everyone a jump scare as they went by. So we went in—'

'"We"?' I seized on the word. He looked mortified. 'Who was with you?'

'I meant "I". I was on my own…' No you weren't, I

thought. I didn't say anything, just stared at him. He dropped his eyes and mumbled, 'Dylan Reed was with me.'

'Okay. So what happened?'

'What happened?' He looked surprised. 'Nothing happened. We broke in, we had a look around, and we realised it would be more hassle than it was worth. So we left.'

'You didn't see anyone else?' I asked.

'No, nobody.'

'Did you damage anything?'

'No, of course not. Well...'

'Go on, Luke.'

'We had the torches on our phones, but Dylan's ran out of juice so we only had mine, and it was well dark. Then we found some camping lanterns there and we turned them on, but they were so bright we got worried someone would be able to see them out in the street.'

'They did,' I said. 'I did.'

'Oh. Well anyway, we turned them off but of course then it was really dark, and I tripped over one of them and it broke. So we left in a hurry.'

'And you didn't see anyone else in the convent, or hanging about outside?' I persisted.

'No, no one. We wouldn't have gone inside if there was anyone else about,' he said. 'Is that why the police are around? Did something else happen?'

'It did,' I said. 'Something much worse than a couple of daft teenagers breaking in and smashing a lantern. You were very lucky that something bad didn't happen to you.'

'Sorry,' he said, hanging his head. I felt a twinge of sympathy for him. Penstowan could be a bit of a boring place out of season if you were a teenager.

'Don't worry about it,' I said. 'But tell me, how did you get in?'

'That's what I was going to show you,' he said, and we started walking again, down an alleyway that ran between the houses and along the back wall of the convent. At one end, out of sight of the nearby houses, was a gap in the brickwork where the thick trunk of an ancient oak tree had disturbed it. There was a wire fence bridging that gap, but it had clearly been there a few years as it too had been disturbed by the tree, stretched and distorted. And in one corner, it had been pulled out of the post holding it up. Luke reached down and pulled the fence back, then slipped in through the gap. It was narrow and I wasn't as slim as he was, but I managed to struggle through it after him.

We were in the corner of the garden, with the side entrance of the convent only about fifteen metres away.

'So that's how you got in without climbing over the big fence round the front, or breaking the padlock,' I said, and he nodded. 'How did you know about the gap in the fence back there?'

'Dylan lives in one of the houses over there.' He waved an arm in the direction of the estate. 'He was taking his dog for a walk a while back, and it chased a squirrel through the gap.'

'Who else knows about the gap?' I asked. 'Is it common knowledge?'

'I don't know. A few of us do. Before the builders came in we used to sneak over here and sit in the garden and have a—' He stopped abruptly. I grinned.

'A few beers? A smoke?' I supplied.

'A laugh,' he said, although I knew my suggestions were closer to the truth. 'Never saw anyone else over here, but that don't mean no one else knows about it.'

'No, it doesn't.' Someone walking their dog had found it, I thought. Maybe other dog walkers had found it too. Who else did I know, connected to the case, who had a dog? One small enough to nose their way through that gap? Who had already admitted they had no alibi, and who had disliked Connor?

I didn't know why, but I really didn't want it to be Kai.

I told Luke not to worry and that I would pass on what he'd told me to the police. I warned him that they would probably need to speak to him at some point, just to confirm what I'd passed on. He nodded.

'And,' I said, 'do not go into the convent or its grounds again! Tell your friends. Otherwise you could potentially get into a whole heap of trouble. What are you not going to do?'

'Go into the convent or its grounds again,' he repeated dutifully. 'I really am sorry. Tell them I'll replace the lantern if they want me to.'

I let him go, and he climbed back onto his bike and rode off in a hurry. So much for going home for a cup of tea. I pulled out my phone.

'Where are you, babe? Are you still at the station?'

'I was just on my way to see Connor's parents again,' said Nathan. 'You found something?'

'Yep. Meet me at the community centre.'

I walked Nathan through exactly what Luke had told me, and showed him the gap in the fence. He climbed through and studied it carefully, maybe hoping for a scrap of material left behind on a sharp bit of wire or something, but there was nothing.

'Well, at least we know who was up there with the lights, and that it had nothing to do with the murder,' he said. 'And we know how Connor got in after dark, although it must've been a bit of a squeeze for him. He was pretty well built.'

'Maybe he was very bendy,' I said, contorting myself into a weird shape to fit through the hole again. Nathan watched me for a moment and then laughed.

'More bendy than you? I doubt it. These gym bros tend to concentrate on building muscle, not flexibility. Whereas you and me, our favourite exercise routine makes us very flexible…' He glanced around and then pulled me into a hug. 'Ever done it in a churchyard?'

I swatted him. 'DCI Withers! Where's your sense of propriety?' I cried, in mock horror. 'In full view of the ghost nuns and everything! And you a Catholic, too.'

He laughed. 'A lapsed Catholic. Very lapsed. I'm more worried about Brett coming round the corner and catching us than the ghostly sisterhood spying on us.' I shivered; I didn't like the thought of spectral sisters watching us from the windows of the convent, but I could imagine it only too clearly.

I pulled away and we both composed ourselves. 'Anyway,' I said, 'this also throws up another question, although hopefully it's one we can get answered soon enough.'

'Which is…?'

'Whose lanterns did they find? Devlin's got those big work lights set up in all the rooms they've been working in, so why would there be camping lanterns?'

'Maybe they were in rooms they haven't started on yet but that they were looking at?' Nathan shook his head. 'I don't know. Did you work out which room the boys found them in?'

'Yeah, one of the attic rooms. I don't know if it was the one the noose was in – Luke didn't mention it, but Devlin had probably already taken it down – but if it was that room then I don't remember seeing any lanterns when we went to look at the noose.'

'No, but were you looking for some? Because I wasn't.'

'No, fair point. Maybe we should go and have a look now?'

Nathan nodded, and we made our way over to the side entrance of the building. We could hear the forensics team in the main hallway, so we walked round to them. It looked like they were close to packing up.

'Don't mind us,' said Nathan. 'We're going upstairs, but

we'll go up the other staircase so we don't disturb you. In case you hear strange noises from above.' The three forensics officers looked at each other.

'Oh man, we've already heard plenty of them,' said Gary.

'Like what? Is someone else in here?' asked Nathan.

'I don't think so,' said Lisa. 'And anyway, they weren't that sort of noise.'

'What did you hear?' I asked, a cold feeling seeping into my stomach.

'I didn't hear anything,' snorted Robbo, 'but these two thought they heard a baby crying.'

'We did hear a baby crying,' insisted Lisa. 'And a woman wailing.' She shuddered. 'I don't mind telling you I'll be glad when we're done with this one.'

'I thought you'd been quick,' said Nathan. He smiled at her. 'Finish up and then go and get a cup of tea. Great work on the stain on the staircase, by the way.' She smiled back and then carried on bagging up evidence.

We walked out of the hallway and back to the side staircase. This would probably have been used by staff – remembering that it had originally been built as a kind of novelty convent for a rich man's problematic spinster sister, who would've been used to having people to cook and clean for her – so it was less grand than the one in the main hallway, but still very impressive by the standards of someone who lived in a three-bedroom semi-detached house (me). We headed up the stairs, both of us tensed, waiting to hear the sounds of wailing and sobbing, but there was nothing. I relaxed, ever so slightly, then thought, in horror movies this is when the big jump scare happens – the moment the characters stop expecting it. I clenched my fists to stop my hands shaking, although I couldn't have told you why they were. It was just an old building, after all. We took the second, narrower staircase up to the attic rooms and went first into the one that had had the noose. Nothing. No noose, no camping lanterns. We came out and crossed the narrow hallway to the second attic room.

'Thinking about it,' I said, 'it must've been this room, because it's to the front of the building. I wouldn't have seen the lights if they'd been in the other room.' I took a deep breath and braced myself before we entered.

'True,' said Nathan, 'and look.' He pointed to the corner of the room, where there were two battery-powered camping lanterns. One stood upright, but the other had fallen over – or been kicked over – and the glass surrounding it had broken. I crouched down to look at it; not glass, but clear plastic, and shards of it had been scattered by Luke and Dylan's retreating, trainer-clad feet.

'Okay, so the next step is to find out who they belong to,' I said. Nathan raised his eyebrows.

'You think that's important? They're probably Devlin's,' he said, but I shook my head.

'They could also belong to whoever's been planting stuff around the site,' I said. 'And that person could be our murderer.' I corrected myself. 'Or murderers.'

'Murderers? Plural? How d'you work that out?' asked Nathan, but then he answered himself. 'Oh – two lanterns…'

'The other thing we should do is have a look at the rooms on the next floor down,' I said, 'to see if any more dolls or nooses or whatever have been planted. Because maybe the killer was here leaving stuff and Connor found them?'

'Although that doesn't explain why he was here in the first place,' said Nathan. 'Unless maybe he suspected someone, and came back to catch them? I don't know. Anyway, Matt and a couple of uniforms did have a look round earlier, but it couldn't hurt for us to as well, while we're here.'

'Are we bagging these up as evidence?'

'No… Not yet.' Nathan took a photo of them on his phone.

We headed down to the next floor. Work had started on all of the rooms on this floor; some of them were still completely open, where the old partitions had been taken down, while some were still in the process of being stripped down. Only two had new stud walls in place, including the one Devlin had shown me the other day.

'Tools and materials, but nothing else,' said Nathan.

'No,' I said, disappointed. I wasn't sure what I'd been hoping for, but it was still disappointing not to find it. I walked over to the window of the room we were in, the room where Devlin had found the first doll in the fireplace, and looked out. It was late afternoon and it was starting to get dark already. Give it a month or two and by this time of day it would feel like night time.

I turned back to Nathan and was about to say we should go when I spotted a dark shadow from the corner of my eye, flitting past us. I made a weird sound – somewhere between a strangled gasp and a high pitched eek! and turned back to look for it, but there was nothing.

'Babe, what is it?' Nathan was understandably concerned. I sounded like I was having a stroke.

'There was a shadow – I thought I saw—' I stuttered incoherently. He crossed the room and put an arm around me.

'There's nothing there,' he said gently. 'It's this place – it's playing with us.'

I shuddered. 'You make it sound like it's alive. It's making my imagination go haywire.' I took out my phone and turned the torch on, shining it into the dark corner where I thought I'd seen whatever it was.

'See? Nothing,' said Nathan. 'Let's go.'

'Hang on,' I said, pulling away from him. 'What's that, on the floor?' I walked over and squatted down, shining the torch on the bare floorboards. Nathan followed and peered at the wooden floor in the circle of torchlight. 'That white stuff, what is it? Ectoplasm?'

Nathan pulled a pair of gloves from his pocket and put them on, then gingerly reached out to touch one of the spots of white. It was firm and slightly raised, so it wasn't a paint splatter, and it looked too white to be plaster or something like that.

'It's wax,' he said, surprised. 'Candle wax.' He looked around. 'No candles, though. I can't think why the builders would need to be burning candles anyway. Certainly not with all this wood and other flammable stuff around.'

'The nuns would probably have used candles, when this place was originally built,' I said. 'But on a bedside table, not on the floor. Even if they'd had particularly drippy candles, would they have dripped on the floor?'

'If these spots of wax had been here that long they'd have been walked over, not just by whoever was living here but recently, by the builders working in this room,' said Nathan. 'The wax would be all scuffed up, I'd have thought, but these are perfect little white blobs.'

'So someone has been burning candles here very recently, on the floor,' I said. 'You know who puts candles on the floor and burns them?'

'People without electric lights and tables,' he said, trying to make a joke, but it would take more than that to placate the hairs on the back of my neck, which were standing to attention.

'Witches,' I said. 'People casting spells or trying to summon demons. I've seen it on the telly. They draw a pentagram, or a pentacle – I don't remember which one it is, but one's just a five-pointed star and the other's got a circle round it for protection—'

'A pentacle. That's what they use in witchcraft,' said

Nathan. I stared at him. 'What can I say? Teenage me had a massive crush on Fairuza Balk in *The Craft*.'

'Ooh, good film, Teenage Nathan,' I said. 'But anyway – you know what this means? Someone was here trying to summon something.'

'Possibly.' Nathan turned his own torch on and slowly crossed the room, swinging the beam slowly side to side so he could examine the floor. I stood up and did the same. 'Can you see any more wax?'

'No…' I kept looking.

'Or chalk marks? That's what they use to draw the pentacle.'

'I know! Get you with your Wiccan stuff. Do I need to dress up as a witch tomorrow? Or just a load of eyeliner and dark lipstick so I look like your teenage crush?'

Nathan laughed, which finally lightened the mood. 'I don't think "teenage Goth" is your style.' He reached the other side of the room and turned back to me. 'I've got nothing. You?'

'Nope. No more wax, and no chalk outline apart from the one downstairs in the hall.' I straightened up. 'Of course, they could've cleaned it all up really well and just missed that bit over there – it's right in the corner of the room. You wouldn't draw a pentacle over there, would you? I wouldn't, anyway, and nor would Fairuza. We'd draw it right in the middle of the room.'

'Yeah, so would I,' agreed Nathan. 'Which is probably why they missed that bit.' He looked at me, a sudden huge grin on his face. 'I love this case. I mean, not forgetting that someone's died, but come on – haunted convent, weird lights at night, the sound of a baby crying, and now satanic rituals? It beats my hit-and-run case, doesn't it?'

I laughed. 'DCI Withers, that's the second time today you've said something inappropriate. I think you've been possessed…'

Chapter Thirteen

PC Brett did a double-take as we left the convent and walked out to the front of the building site, which felt unnaturally quiet for what was normally a hive of industry; no builders, of course, but also no protestors. The Penstowan grapevine had clearly been all aquiver, and news of the murder must be all around town by now. No need to stand out in the cold and rapidly encroaching dark to protest if the police had already shut the site down.

'DCI Withers, I thought you'd left—' Brett started. Nathan gave a brief smile.

'We did,' he said, but he didn't explain further. I got the feeling he didn't like Brett any more than I did. 'Have Mr Devlin and Mr Campbell both left?'

'Mr Devlin's in his office,' said Brett, nodding over to the caravan, which must double as an office as well the break room. We left Brett to stand guard and headed over there.

Nathan knocked on the door and then poked his head in

without waiting for an answer. Devlin was sitting on the lumpy sofa, laptop open on the coffee table in front of him.

'Oh, you're back,' he said. 'Any leads?'

'Too soon for that,' said Nathan, stepping inside. I followed him. 'I'm surprised to see you still here, seeing as there's no work going on.'

Devlin gestured to his laptop. 'No work out there, no, but it means I can catch up on the admin. Quieter here than at home with the wife and daughter about.'

'Kids, huh?' I said, attempting to be sympathetic but at the same time feeling disloyal to my own kid, because I always loved spending time with her. I always loved the school holidays, especially when Daisy was little. I'd take time off and we'd go out, or do craft stuff at home. Maybe Devlin wasn't into finger painting or days out at the zoo.

'There's always some mess to clear up,' he said. He definitely didn't like finger painting, then.

'Just needed to ask you a couple of quick questions,' said Nathan. 'We came across a couple of camping lanterns in one of the attic rooms. Do they belong to you?'

'Camping lanterns?' Devlin looked alarmed. 'You mean like the gas-powered ones?'

'No, batteries,' I said. 'About this big.' I demonstrated with my hands. Now he looked mystified.

'No. Why would we need them? We've got work lights.'

'That's what we thought,' said Nathan. 'Would any of your lads have brought them in, maybe?'

'Well – maybe. But I don't know why they would.'

'Okay. Also, we found candle wax on the floor—'

'Candle wax?' Devlin looked even more mystified. 'What do you mean, you found it on the floor?'

'Like someone's lit a candle and it's dripped,' I explained. Devlin shook his head.

'We certainly wouldn't be using candles or any naked flames. Have you seen all the flammable material up there? Wood and plasterboard and all that? I'd have the Health and Safety people all over me.'

'That's also what we thought,' said Nathan. 'Okay, thank you for your time. We'll be in touch.' He turned and left the caravan, and I followed, now feeling mystified myself.

'Is that it?' I asked as we got outside.

'What?'

'You didn't tell him about the secret back way into the site. Surely you should let him know so he can block it up?' Nathan just looked at me, smiling, with his head to one side. 'Ah… I get it. You want it left open?'

'Yep.'

'You think whoever's been leaving the dolls, who may or may not be the murderer, is going to come back and finish what they started?' I asked. 'Presuming shoving Connor Milburn down the stairs wasn't them finishing the job.'

'I think they might.' Nathan nodded to Brett as we left the site and headed back round to the community centre, where I'd left Germaine with Maggie Tiddy. She was there doing some last-minute preparation for the parade the next night, and as a frustrated dog lover (she couldn't have one at the B&B she ran) she loved any excuse to dog-sit. 'That's why I left the lanterns there, as well. I don't want them to know we're onto them.'

'Not tonight though, surely?' I asked. 'Not with Cornwall's finest on guard.'

Nathan gave a snort before he could stop himself. 'Brett? Yeah… No, probably not tonight, but who knows? They might not turn up at all. I just have this feeling like it's not over yet.'

'No,' I admitted, 'I know what you mean.' We went through the double glass doors into the community centre and found Maggie, tickling Germaine's tummy.

'You look busy,' said Nathan, with a grin. Maggie laughed.

'Yeah, Germaine's been helping me…' Hearing her own name the dog rolled over, looking mortified at having been caught in such an undignified position, and trotted over to Nathan, completely ignoring me.

'You know who's the boss, don't you?' said Nathan, making a fuss of her.

'Yeah,' said Maggie. 'She is. Are you both still on to act as stewards tomorrow night?' I looked at Nathan, because being in the middle of a murder investigation often meant cancelling plans or just having to be on call, but he nodded.

'Of course. Looking forward to it. Joining in with another one of your weird Cornish customs…'

'It's just an excuse to crack open the scrumpy,' I said. We left Maggie to her preparations and walked over to the police station, where Nathan had left his car. He unlocked it and opened the passenger door for me, and the back door for Germaine. 'Oh, are you done for the day?' I asked.

'Yeah. I was going to go and see Connor's parents again, but I sent Sunil instead.'

'You're letting him go out on his own?' I sighed. 'They grow up so fast, don't they?'

We climbed into the car and headed home. Halfway there my phone rang.

'Carmen, hi,' I said, answering it and putting it on speakerphone. 'Everything okay?'

'I was going to ask you that,' she said. 'I heard about what happened at St Ann's. Poor young man.'

'Tony passed on the gossip, did he?' I asked. 'Hang on, I didn't tell him who the victim was. How did he know to tell you?' Nathan rolled his eyes.

'Come on, this is Tony we're talking about,' he said. 'The Penhaligons know everyone in this town, alive or, it would appear, dead.'

'True.'

'Anyway, I spoke to the bishop,' said Carmen. 'He's coming along tomorrow so I thought I should fill him in on the town gossip before he got here. And he said if there's anything in the St Ann's files that you need, you can have it.'

'Really? We don't have a warrant,' I said, and Nathan rolled his eyes again, this time at me. I bit my tongue; sometimes I needed to learn to be quiet and not remind people of their legal rights.

'Yeah, I know, but he said as St Ann's closed such a long

time ago and most of the people in the files are probably dead by now, it couldn't hurt.'

'That's really helpful,' said Nathan. 'Thanks, Carmen.'

'I looked at all the ones in your office,' I said. 'I don't think there was anything there. But maybe the ones in the crypt…' I gulped. Nathan looked at me.

'They're in the church crypt?' he said.

'Yes,' said Carmen. 'It's a long story. Do you want to pop over now, or in the morning?'

'In the morning,' I said, shivering at the thought of going down to the crypt in the dark. But then it was always dark in a crypt, wasn't it, no matter what time of day or night it was.

'We'll swing by on our way home now, if that's okay,' said Nathan, and I thought, Nighttime in the crypt it is, then…

It wasn't really night by the time we reached the church – it was only about five thirty – but it felt dark enough to be. Yesterday's fog, which had cleared by this morning, was now drifting back with a vengeance, and the headlights of Nathan's car picked out the shapes of gravestones in the mist as we pulled into the car park. Germaine gave a little whimper, but she soon perked up when she realised where we were.

We knocked on the vicarage door and were greeted by Carmen, today clad in a bright blue sweatshirt with purple and yellow leopard print spots on it. 'Nice top,' I said. 'I loved the pink one you had on yesterday, too.'

'I'm dopamine dressing,' she said, which I nodded at

and Nathan looked bemused by. 'Being a vicar naturally means a lot of black and white clothing, but I need some colour this time of year.' She grabbed a set of keys from a hall table, not the ones she'd used to unlock the church office, but a brass ring with some big old iron keys rattling from it. 'Let's go!'

She led the way over to the church, unlocking the heavy wooden doors. 'I hate locking the church,' she said. 'It goes against everything we stand for. But you always get some idiots – I mean, "misguided souls"—' I could almost hear the air quotes '—around Halloween, thinking it's a jolly jape to come into the church and spray graffiti, or leave dead animals on the altar.'

'No!' I cried, horrified. 'That's terrible. They don't really do that, do they?'

She nodded. 'Yes, unfortunately. I had a spate of dead crows on the altar last year, three nights in a row. The rest of the year it's fine.' She stood back to let us into the church, although I almost didn't want to enter it now. I'd always found St Botolph's peaceful, but now I expected to see a big black crow perched on the altar, its beady eyes staring at me.

I didn't see one though, of course, and then Carmen led us across the building to a low stone archway, surrounding a small wooden door, which she unlocked with another one of the huge keys. She pushed the door open – I was expecting it to creak, and I was simultaneously glad and disappointed when it didn't – and stood back to let us go first again. Germaine howled and refused to budge another inch, so I picked her up as Nathan and I exchanged nervous glances, and then stepped into the darkness beyond…

Which was then flooded with light as Carmen reached out and flicked on a switch. There was a short flight of stone steps downwards, and then the room opened out into a vaulted space. The ceiling was low and it felt cold, but not unpleasantly so; it wasn't the sort of chill that settles into your bones, more the sort that wakes you up, refreshes you, and makes you more alert.

The room, which I'd expected to be full of, I don't know, bones or coffins, or to look something like the catacombs in Paris, which I'd visited a few years back, was instead full of filing cabinets and shelving, all illuminated by fluorescent strip lighting. Nathan was obviously as surprised as I was.

'This is not what I was expecting when you said "crypt",' he admitted. She smiled.

'It was intended as a crypt, but never really used as one,' she said. 'The church was built with money raised by two of the wealthiest families in the area, and of course every church had a crypt where you'd expect to find the remains of those people, but they decided they wanted to be buried outside instead, with magnificent headstones so everyone could see just how much money they had. You know that massive angel statue, the one right on the edge of the graveyard with the best view of the sea in the distance? That's for the Trevanion family, who were the biggest donors to the church.'

'So this crypt's never seen a dead body?' I asked,

anxious to clarify it. I don't know why, because goodness knows I've seen quite a lot of dead bodies myself.

'Never. It was left empty for a while, but if the old stories are to be believed it quite quickly got used as a place to store contraband, mostly alcohol and occasionally stuff the locals stole from shipwrecks.'

'Wow,' said Nathan. 'I didn't know the church had form for fencing stolen goods.'

We all laughed. 'Apparently that went on for years, until a new bishop came along and put a stop to it,' said Carmen. 'He had the vicar flogged and excommunicated from the church.'

'Bit harsh,' I said.

'Yes,' said Carmen. 'I don't think our current bishop would do that, but I'm not about to find out…'

She left us to go through the filing cabinets at our leisure, taking Germaine with her (to the dog's obvious relief), but there were so many we didn't know where to start. We stared at them, and then at each other, as overhead the fluorescent lights hummed and flickered.

'If we have to go through all this lot we'll be here all night,' said Nathan.

'We will not be here all night,' I said firmly, because even a crypt that doesn't have dead people interred in it feels kind of eerie. At that the lights flickered again and they all went out. Except for one, which shone on a single filing cabinet in the middle of the row. 'Well that's not weird or anything, is it?' I said, trying to sound light-hearted but feeling somewhat freaked out.

'I guess we'll start with that one, then,' said Nathan, and I nodded. He walked over to the cabinet and I scuttled after him, wanting to stay as close as possible to him as I could without literally jumping into his arms. He pulled open the top drawer and started to rifle through the files. I peered over his shoulder.

'Stop!' I said, and he stopped. I reached and pulled out the file he'd paused on.

'What is it?'

'I don't know yet, I'm just trying something out…' I scanned the file. 'It's an old personnel file. There's a list of secular staff who worked at the hospital, and another of the nuns who lived and worked there at the same time.'

'What period of time does it cover?'

'Late Sixties to early Eighties, when the convent and the hospital both finally closed down,' I said. 'So some of these people could actually still be alive, despite what the bishop said. They'd be quite old by now, though, probably older than Mum.'

'Do you think any of that's relevant, though?' asked Nathan. 'It's a bit random, even for you.' The one remaining light flickered, threatening to go out. I gulped.

'Yes. Yes, I do. Don't ask me why…' And then all the lights came back on again, shining strong and bright and not even humming. Nathan and I exchanged looks and then made for the exit at top speed.

We didn't hang around after collecting Germaine, thanking Carmen and saying goodbye – who wants to loiter in a dark, foggy graveyard, the night before Halloween, particularly after what had just happened? Although I wasn't exactly sure what had just happened. Nathan floored the accelerator, as keen to get away from that place as Germaine and I were, and we didn't speak until we were almost home.

'Well, that was…' Nathan started, but his voice trailed off.

'Wasn't it?' I agreed. 'Although whether or not anything in that file is really relevant, I don't know. I just feel like it might be.'

'Yeah, I know what you mean,' said Nathan. He shook his head. 'Did I say I love this case? I'm not sure if I do anymore. I'm feeling a bit freaked out. Like the time my mum went to see a clairvoyant when we were on a day out to Blackpool one year, and I went in with her.'

'I can't imagine your mum seeing a fortune teller,' I said, incredulous. 'She's far too down to earth.'

'Yeah, well this was not long after my sister died,' he said. Nathan's sister, Laura, had passed away from leukaemia when she was just seventeen years old. Nathan had been fourteen at the time, and it had (understandably) hit the whole family hard. 'I think Mum was desperate to know that she was all right – I mean, she wasn't all right was she, she was dead – but… I don't know.' He slowed the car down as we went round a tight bend.

'What happened?' I asked softly.

'The medium didn't ask us any questions. She just immediately said, "I'm so sorry for your loss," which was probably a safe assumption to make – most of her clients were probably there hoping to speak to someone they'd lost – but then she said, "She was so young," and my mum just lost it.'

'Poor Liz,' I said. I was fond of both of my in-laws, and I could only imagine how tough it must be to lose a child.

'But then the medium looked at me and said, "She says she knows you tried to keep it alive, but it doesn't matter because she'll always be with you."' He smiled. 'Do you remember those Tamagotchi toys, the virtual pet things? She had this pink one she'd bought to play with on the bus – she had a long ride to sixth-form college – and just before the end I told her I'd keep it alive for her. It was like, as long as I kept that daft thing alive it meant she was still with me. But a kid at school took it off me because it was pink and, obviously, that meant I must be gay, and by the time I got it back it had died.'

'Oh, Nath!' I said, sniffing furiously and wiping my eyes. He laughed gently.

'Don't you start crying, woman, you'll set me off,' he said. 'It freaked me out a bit, but it was reassuring too. I don't think I believe in God or Heaven or whatever, but it's nice to know that death isn't necessarily the end.' Germaine, who was sitting on my lap, reached out and put her nose on Nathan's leg to let him know that she was with him, too. I sniffled even harder – my hormones were out of control again – and then pulled myself together.

'So that means you'll never be rid of me, in that case,' I said.

'Good.'

We made it home without me bursting into tears again. Daisy and Mum were both in the kitchen, staring into the cupboards as if waiting for inspiration to strike.

'What's for dinner?' asked Mum.

'Yes, thank you, I did have a good day!' I said brightly. 'How about you?'

'It was fine up until about twenty minutes ago, when my stomach started to think my throat had been cut…'

'You do have a kitchen of your own,' I pointed out.

'Yeah, but that don't mean there's any food in the cupboards,' she said, and I had to concede that that was true. Luckily there was plenty of food in my cupboards, or at least enough to make a meal out of, so I set everyone to work. Nathan scrubbed some salad potatoes and put them on to boil, while Daisy laid the table and Mum – well, Mum just sort of swanned around, looking busy without actually doing anything.

I made a quick sauce vierge good quality extra virgin olive oil, mixed with a couple of de-seeded and finely diced tomatoes, olives, and some finely minced garlic and anchovy fillets, finished with a squeeze of fresh lemon juice and a handful of chopped parsley, then seasoned with salt and pepper. I pan-fried some fillets of sea bass while Nathan tossed the cooked potatoes in some butter, and then dished up the fish, spuds and some green beans before giving them a generous drizzle of the sauce. Daisy and I both hate uncooked tomatoes and we're not that keen on olives, either, but in this dish they're delicious. With the weather being miserable we'd eaten a lot of typically English stodgy winter food, which is what your body craves in the cold, but after a few days of that I needed something lighter like this simple, French-inspired dish, just to mix things up a bit.

It didn't take long to cook, and it took even less time for everyone to polish it off. Nathan and I sat back in our chairs and let Mum and Daisy clear up.

'We should have a look at this file, then,' said Nathan.

'Yeah,' I said. 'It would be good to know what we're actually looking for, though…'

Nathan brought the file in from where he'd left it on the hall table, and we started to go through the contents. As I'd already deduced from my split-second glance at it earlier, the file was a record of everyone who'd lived and worked at the convent and the cottage hospital. I sorted the papers out into two piles: Nuns and Hospital Staff.

'No patients,' I said.

'No. Maybe they got rid of them when the hospital closed, or passed them onto the NHS or something,' suggested Nathan. 'They'd be confidential, wouldn't they? Particularly in those days. No one would want it to come out that they'd had an illegitimate child.'

'No, I suppose not,' I said. I scanned the names of the nuns, but nothing leapt out at me, and as I watched Nathan do the same with the (much smaller) list of hospital staff it looked to me like he was having the same problem. With nothing much to go on, what were we looking for? And how could anyone who'd been at the convent that long ago have anything to do with a murder in 2026? I sighed and pushed the papers away from me. 'This feels a bit pointless. I don't even know why we got these.'

'Nor do I,' admitted Nathan. 'There was just something that, I don't know, compelled me to go and get them.' He ran his eye down a list of names. 'There's noth—' He stopped abruptly.

'What is it?'

'One of the names rings a bell. This one.' I followed his finger and frowned. The name was spelt Caoimhe but I had no idea how to say it.

'Ca-o-im-he? Who's that?'

'It's pronounced Keeva,' said Nathan.

'No it isn't!' I cried. 'Get outta here. How on earth do you get Keeva from that?'

'It's Irish,' he said. 'The matron of the hospital from 1978 until it closed in 1982 was Caoimhe Doyle.'

'So?'

'So the little old lady who got knocked down in that hit-and-run was called Caoimhe Mackintosh.'

I stared at him, wide-eyed. 'You think it's the same person?'

'Could be. How many Caoimhes are there in Cornwall?'

'But if she worked at the hospital in 1978 she'd be ancient now. She'd be—'

'Seventy-eight,' said Nathan. 'At least, that's how old Caoimhe Mackintosh was. That would've made her...'

He did some quick sums in his head. 'That would've made her thirty-four when the hospital closed down.'

'Does the file give her address?' I asked, craning my head to look.

'Yeah. It says here she lived at number 3, Trebah Cottages, Pencarrow Street. Where's that? I know the street but I can't think where those cottages are.'

'They got pulled down years ago,' I said. 'You know where they built the big Tesco's? They demolished a whole row of houses there to make room.'

'Did your mum protest against that?' teased Nathan. I laughed.

'No. One, she didn't know Jocasta then, and two, she wanted a big Tesco's.' I looked down at the rest of the woman's details. 'Date of birth for Matron Doyle was 23rd of July 1948. So that makes her…' I tried to do the sums in my head, but I'm terrible at maths.

'Seventy-eight. Just like my hit-and-run victim.' Nathan sat back, deep in thought. 'It must be the same woman.'

'Okay, so the matron of this hospital dies years later in a hit-and-run,' I said. 'Is there anything to suggest it wasn't an accident?'

'No,' admitted Nathan. 'Although it was very handy for the driver that it happened on a stretch of road with no CCTV cameras.'

'There are loads of roads round here with no CCTV cameras, especially out in the sticks,' I said. 'In fact it's harder to find places that have got them, which we've discovered to our cost in previous investigations.'

'Yes, that's true… And what motive would someone have?'

'Well,' I said, surprised that he couldn't guess, 'it might have something to do with her being in charge of a maternity hospital that forced young women to give up their babies for adoption.'

'You what?' asked Nathan in shock.

'Of course, you weren't here when Mum was telling the rest of us about the place, were you?' I said. 'It was run by the church and aimed at unmarried young women, yeah?' He nodded. 'Well, in some cases the girl's mother would stay locally as well, and then they'd both go home with the baby and pretend the mother had given birth, not the girl. So the baby would grow up thinking their grandma was their mum, and their actual mum was their sister.'

'Like that storyline in Eastenders,' said Nathan, and I nodded.

'Yeah. I think that happened a lot back then. But some of the girls weren't so lucky – they didn't have parents who were willing to take the baby. And they couldn't bring it up on their own. I mean, they could, but even in the Eighties everyone looked down on single mothers, particularly young ones, and I don't know how much financial help they would've got. So the idea was the girls would give birth here, hand the baby over for adoption, and then go back to their old lives like nothing had happened.'

'That's a tough thing to do, though,' said Nathan. 'Walking away from your baby.'

'Yeah, although for some of the girls it probably was the

best thing for them and for the child. But some of the girls no doubt wanted to keep their babies.'

'And they weren't allowed to?' Nathan looked horrified. I shook my head.

'No, not if what my mum told us is right. She even helped one girl run away from the convent one night with her baby.'

'But some were forced to give them up?' Nathan whistled through his teeth. 'That's a motive, then.'

'Yeah, it could be. If the Matron was seventy-eight when she died, then the killer – assuming it was one of her ex-patients – would be, what, late fifties? Early sixties?'

'Something like that, yeah.' Nathan rifled through the papers again in frustration. 'But even knowing that doesn't really help, does it? Because we don't know the names of any of her patients.'

'No. And it could still have been an accident, although it feels less likely now.' I tapped my fingers on the table, trying to get my thoughts in order. 'So, do you think the person who ran her over is the same person who's been planting the dolls?'

'Could be,' said Nathan.

'And the same person who killed Connor?'

'Could be,' said Nathan again, but with a note of doubt in his voice. 'Although what motive would they have for his murder? How does it tie in with what went on forty-odd years ago?'

'No idea,' I admitted. 'It's a big coincidence if none of

these things are linked, but coincidences do happen all the time, don't they?'

'Yeah…' Nathan shook himself and gathered the papers together, putting them back inside the cardboard folder. 'Let's stop for the night, shall we? We're just going round in circles. And I think Daisy was after a lift somewhere.'

'Yes please,' said Daisy, placing a cup of tea in front of me and then another in front of Nathan. 'I could walk, but it's dark and cold…'

'Where you going?'

'The community centre,' she said. 'We've got last-minute band practice.'

'You must all know what you're doing by now?' I said. 'You've been practising every other day.'

'Yeah, but a few people have missed rehearsals and Maggie wants to make sure we're perfect.'

I laughed. 'You're walking along banging drums and blowing whistles. How perfect do you need to be?'

Daisy looked most affronted. 'Don't let Maggie or Jocasta hear you say that! We do all have to be beating the same rhythm, you know.'

'I know. Sorry, sweetheart. Of course I'll take you. Will you need picking up?'

'Hopefully not. Teri said she'd give us a lift back.'

'Terry who? Do I know him?'

'Teri's a she. Teri Devlin. Her dad's the one running the building site.' Daisy grimaced. 'She was a bit pissed off when she heard I went to the protest.'

'Hang on, how old is she?' I asked, surprised. 'I thought

she was still a little girl, the way Tommy Devlin talks about her.'

She laughed. 'Ha, yeah, that's what she says – that he still treats her like a child. She was in the year above me at school. She's the one who gave me a lift to Exeter.'

'Ah, right…' So Tommy Devlin still saw his daughter as a little girl. I couldn't blame him; most of us want to hang onto our kids for as long as we possibly can, and sometimes that means we don't recognise it – or want to recognise it – when they stop being children. They grow up so fast. At least Devlin (and I) had been around to watch our kids grow up, unlike the poor girls who'd been sent to the convent, all those years ago…

Chapter Fourteen

I dropped Daisy off at the community centre and drove home, to find Sunil sitting at the kitchen table with Nathan.

'Hi, Jodie,' he said, as I dropped my car keys on the table and shrugged off my coat. 'Just updating the boss on what Connor Milburn's parents told me this afternoon.'

'Well I'm here now, so go ahead,' I said, pulling up a chair and sitting down. Nathan looked highly amused.

'Yes, Sunil, please do fill in "the boss"...'

Sunil took out his notebook and consulted it. 'I asked them about Connor's online presence and all the things he was sharing and posting,' he said. 'Mrs Milburn refused to believe that her son had been posting misogynist content and she became quite upset, but Mr Milburn admitted that he'd known about it and had had words with Connor to get him to see sense. This was after he sent Mrs Milburn out to the kitchen to make some tea, though. He said she knew deep down that Connor had picked up some dodgy ideas but it upset her to admit it.'

'Did he know how long Connor had been engaging with misogynistic content?' asked Nathan. 'Or have any idea why he started?'

'Mr Milburn said that he put it down to Connor breaking up with his long-term girlfriend a couple of years ago,' said Sunil. 'Name of Emma Blake. Connor was devastated, although Mrs Milburn reckoned he'd had a lucky escape.'

'Oh yeah?' Nathan raised his eyebrows. 'How's that, then?'

Sunil smiled. 'I think it's more of a case of "no one's good enough for my boy", rather than anything the ex-girlfriend did. That's the impression I got from his dad, who seems sensible.'

'So Connor's heartbroken, and that leads to him hating all women?' I asked.

'Pretty much,' said Sunil, 'although I think Mrs Milburn probably added fuel to that particular fire. Lots of talk about "girls today" and how "modern" women don't care about stuff like families or babies.'

'Daisy'd call that "internalised misogyny",' said Nathan. I nodded.

'And then he found the online bros with their nasty ideas about women, and that was that,' I said. 'It probably made him feel better about the break-up if he could blame it all on women in general. Do we know why they split up?'

'No. Mr Milburn said they seemed happy, and then all of

a sudden they weren't together anymore,' said Sunil. 'He did say that his son could have a temper, though.'

'Maybe she'd had enough of that,' Nathan said. 'Or maybe they just split up. People do. We'll need to speak to her, though.'

'She lives in Bude,' said Sunil. 'Do you want me to go this evening?'

'No, Sunil, you get home to those daughters of yours, give Eesha a break,' said Nathan. 'You need to get back for bath time.'

Sunil smiled. 'Yes, I do. If that's all right with you, Guv?'

'Of course. Leave me Emma Blake's address and Jodie and I will go and see her in the morning.'

It had been a long, tiring, and quite puzzling day. After Sunil left, Nathan changed out of his work clothes and put the file we'd taken from the church into his work bag, which he then put in the hall cupboard next to his coat. It was his way of drawing a line under the day, which didn't always work because sometimes the day wasn't quite ready to draw a line under him. That night, however, we were left to watch the telly in peace, consciously not talking or even thinking too much about the case, because as Nathan had said earlier we were in danger of going round and round in circles. Sometimes when that happens, you end up convincing yourself of a particular theory, twisting the facts, or even inadvertently making stuff up to fit it. The human mind – a detective's mind, anyway – enjoys a mystery, but only if it feels like it's getting somewhere with it. When you keep going over and over the same thing and still coming up with nothing, that's when you find yourself slipping down rabbit holes and running headfirst into dead ends.

We watched a very confusing film about time travel, which was absolutely the right choice as it confused us so much it drove all thoughts of the case from our minds, until about ten o'clock when Germaine leapt up and ran to the front door, barking.

'What's up with her?' asked Nathan. I stood up and peered through the curtains, out into the street. A car – a small white Toyota with black bumpers and a black rear end – had pulled up outside our house and was sitting there, engine idling.

'It's just Daisy getting dropped off,' I said. 'Germaine knew before she'd even got out of the car. She must've used her doggy sixth sense.' I headed for the door.

'Where you going?'

'Germaine just wants to say hello to this new friend, that's all…'

'Yeah right, you just want to have a nose at her yourself. Don't embarrass Daisy!'

But it was too late for that, as I'd already opened the door and let the dog out, who went bounding down the path to where Daisy was now standing, dancing around her and barking in sheer, unadulterated joy.

'Sorry!' I called, following her. 'She got out. She just wanted to say hello.' Daisy narrowed her eyes at me, knowing that there was no way the dog could open the front door on her own, but then the driver got out of the car.

Teri was tall and slim and looked older than her nineteen years, clad in black jeans and a hoodie with a band logo on it in red. Her hair was long, dyed black, and she wore heavy eyeliner. But as she came round to the side of the car and squatted down to ruffle Germaine's fur, a broad smile on her face, she looked like a schoolgirl.

'Oh my God, Daze, she's sooo cute! You weren't lying,' said Teri. She was nothing like her father, I thought.

'Good practice?' I asked. Teri nodded, smiling almost shyly at me before focusing on the dog again.

'Yeah, it was great,' said Daisy. 'I'm starving, we got any Jaffa Cakes? You want to come in and have a cup of tea?' This to Teri, who reluctantly gave Germaine a last pat and stood up.

'Nah, better get back or the olds will be on at me,' she said. 'Nice to meet you, Mrs Withers.'

We watched her drive away and then went into the house. Daisy flopped on the sofa.

'Teri seems nice,' I said. Although to be fair I'd say that about anyone who treated my dog like that.

'Yeah,' said Daisy. 'I never really knew her at school, I just knew of her. Everyone did.'

'Why's that?' asked Nathan.

'Well, she's a bit of a weirdo. She's into all this witchy Goth stuff—'

'Oh, Nathan would've loved her when he was a teenager,' I said, grinning at him. Daisy grimaced.

'Eww, no. She's practically my age, and you're well old. No offence.'

'None taken,' said Nathan. 'I go for the more mature woman these days, anyway.' He grinned at me. 'No offence.'

'Ha! I'm not going to get offended by that. Debbie once described me as "old but really immature for my age", so...'

'Best way to be,' said Nathan.

'See?' said Daisy. 'I don't care that she's a weirdo, because I'm surrounded by them at home.' But there was more to it than that. My kind, beautiful daughter had always had a thing for waifs, strays and outcasts, and had always befriended the kid sitting on their own at lunch. And they'd always repaid her by being amazing, loyal friends.

'I like her car,' I said. 'It looks like a panda.'

'That's what Teri says,' said Daisy. 'She calls it Ling-Ling. Cute, innit? In case you were wondering what to get me for Christmas...'

Nathan and I took Germaine out for a last walk before bed – she was more reluctant to leave the house than we were, but we knew from bitter experience that it was necessary – and then headed upstairs, where we both collapsed into a deep, dreamless sleep.

I was awake bright and early the next day. I rolled over to wake Nathan with a kiss, but he already had his eyes open, staring up at the ceiling.

'Morning, babe,' I said. 'It's far too early in the day for you to look that deep in thought.'

'Lots to think about,' he said, stretching and putting his arm out so I could snuggle in. 'I half expected a phone call in the night from Brett telling me our mysterious doll-planter had turned up, but it looks like it was all quiet on the western front.'

'You really think they'll go back? After there's been a murder, and there's police crawling all over the site?'

'I do, yeah. They left the lanterns there for a reason, didn't they? They hadn't finished.'

'Yeah,' I said, doubtfully, 'or maybe they had. Maybe Connor was the endgame.'

'So why leave the lanterns behind? Why leave any trace?' asked Nathan. He sighed. 'I don't know if or how they're connected to the case, but we'll leave them there for now.'

'So if the bad guys come back for them, they won't know we're onto them, they'll do whatever it was they came to do, and then you'll swoop in and arrest them.'

'Yes,' said Nathan. 'Of course, you might be right. The dolls and the noose, the whole spooky charade might just have been paving the way for Connor's murder and throwing the scent off the real motive for it. In which case they probably won't come back. And then we'll bag the lanterns up and fingerprint them.'

'They might not need to, if their plan was to stop the development going ahead,' I said. 'Will Devlin want to carry on with it, after someone's died there?'

'I would've thought so,' said Nathan. 'How much will those two buildings and the land around it have cost him? He might shut down the site for a while, out of respect, but he probably can't afford to stop work on it for ever. Who'd buy it off him now?'

'Yeah, you're probably right. So what's the plan today?' I grinned at him. 'Assuming I'm part of that plan.'

'I need to talk to Connor's ex-girlfriend,' said Nathan, sitting up. 'You can come along as it's just a chat. The only thing I can't have you sit in on is formal interviews.' He sighed dramatically. 'Oh to have a suspect to formally interview…'

I patted him on the back. 'There, there, DCI Withers, you'll have one soon. Maybe even more than one, if you're lucky.'

'Oh no, just having one sole obvious suspect is lucky. Having loads is a pain in the bum.' He smiled ruefully. 'Although having none is worse.'

Daisy was having a lazy day today, in preparation for her big night on the parade, so we left Germaine with her and headed out.

'Is nine o'clock on a Saturday morning too early to call on someone?' I asked. Nathan shook his head.

'It's late enough. At least I'll knock on her door, I won't be battering it down like something out of The Sweeney.'

'Get yer trousers on, luv, you're nicked,' I growled, in

my best impression of the terribly sexist Seventies cop show. Nathan laughed.

'Oh my God, you're so sexy when you do your Jack Regan impression,' he said.

'Really? You need help, babe…'

We drove to Emma Blake's house in Bude. Sea fog still clung to the houses along the coast road, but the sky held the faintest tinge of orange; the sun was struggling to burn its way through the clouds. By lunchtime it would either have won and we'd have a lovely day, or it would've given up and the fog would be even thicker. That's what it's like living here, particularly in the autumn: it can be beautiful weather one day, and then the next, fog can roll in off the sea and suffocate everything for a whole week.

Emma's house was a tiny two-up two-down stone cottage in a row of others just like it. Although it was small it was neat and pretty, with sage green paintwork on the door and window frames. The front garden was just big enough for a wrought-iron bench under the bay window, with a couple of pots either side containing topiary trees teased into spirals. Nathan cleared the garden path in two strides and knocked on the door, grasping the black iron knocker in the shape of a mermaid. I wondered if I could take a photo of it before someone answered so I could look for one just like it for our front door, but the door opened so quickly I didn't even get a chance to take my phone out.

'Ms Blake?' Nathan held out his warrant card. 'DCI Nathan Withers. Do you have a moment?'

The woman who'd answered the door nodded. She

didn't look surprised. She was tall and slim, in her late twenties by the looks of it, and dressed in yoga pants and an oversized sweatshirt.

'I thought I'd get a call from you. Come in.' She stood back to let us through the door, which led straight into the front room. 'Please, take a seat. Can I get you a cup of tea or anything?'

'Not for me, thank you,' said Nathan, and I made agreeing noises. Emma went over to a gold-coloured velvet armchair (she had very good taste, and I wondered if it would be unprofessional of me to ask where she'd bought it from) and picked up a fluffy white cat who was staring at us with deep suspicion. She sat down with the cat on her lap and stroked it, and then laughed.

'I've been expecting you, Mr Bond,' she said, and then looked shocked at herself. 'Sorry, that's probably a bit inappropriate in the circumstances. I take it you're here to ask me about Connor?'

'Yes,' said Nathan, sitting on the sofa. I sat next to him. 'You used to be an item?'

'We were engaged,' she said. 'I ended it, must be two and half years ago by now. So although I'm sad he's dead, I've done my crying over him already.' But as she spoke her eyes welled up with tears. She sniffed them back.

'Can we ask why you split up?' I asked gently.

'Why do you need to know?' She looked at me, and then at Nathan. 'Oh, right. You want to know if I still bore enough of a grudge to kill him.'

'Did you?' Nathan stared steadily at her. She didn't look away.

'No, I didn't. I came to the conclusion I was much better off without him.' She stroked the cat again, and picked a piece of garden debris from its fluffy coat before speaking again. 'We were engaged, but we should never have been. We wanted different things from life.'

'Like what?'

'I wanted children, for one thing, and he didn't. He really didn't…' She sighed. 'Have you met his mum?'

'I have,' said Nathan. 'Not the best circumstances for meeting someone for the first time, though.'

'No, I suppose not. Anyway, she has it in her head that her precious son was the injured party and I was a heartless Jezebel – I mean, God knows what he told her. But Gerry – his stepdad – he knew what Con was like.'

'So what happened?' I pushed.

'I got pregnant,' she said. 'It was an accident, but I was happy about it and I thought he would be too, once he got used to it.'

'But he wasn't,' said Nathan, and she nodded.

'He pretended to be, at first, but I knew he wasn't really.'

'How did you know?' I asked.

'Because I was dying to tell everyone, and he didn't even want to tell his parents until I started showing and it became obvious. But it never became obvious, because I had a miscarriage at eight weeks.'

'Oh no, I'm so sorry,' I said. She gave me a wan smile.

'Thank you. I actually think now that it was for the best

after the way he reacted. I was gutted, but he didn't even attempt to look sad about it.'

'I'm sorry, that sounds really tough,' said Nathan.

'It was. We limped on for another couple of months, until I couldn't even stand to look at him because he was so unbothered by the whole thing. I gave him his ring back and told him to leave.'

'You were living here together?'

'Yes, but it's my house, I bought it before we got together.'

'How did he take the break-up?' I asked.

'He was completely ridiculous about it. He told me that I was being unreasonable because I expected him to mourn a baby I'd never even had. He said I was neurotic because I was grieving for something that had never been alive. But she had been alive, she'd been alive inside me.'

'She?' asked Nathan. She smiled.

'Of course I don't know what sex my baby would've been, but I felt like she was a girl. Perhaps I just hoped she was, so she wouldn't be a boy and take after her father. I already knew deep down, you see, that he wasn't the right one for me.'

'But you managed to get him to leave your house?' said Nathan.

'Yes. He wasn't happy about it, but it's my name on the deeds, not his. He went back to his parents. He's still living there, as far as I know. I mean, he was still…' Her voice trailed off, faltering slightly. She cleared her throat. 'So no, I didn't bear him a grudge and I didn't want him dead. I still can't believe that he is.'

'When was the last time you saw him?' I asked. 'You're in Bude and he was in Holsworthy, it would probably be quite difficult to avoid bumping into each other now and again.'

'It must've been about a month ago. I was getting petrol at Morrisons and he was filling up at the next pump along. We said hello and he started telling me how amazing everything was going for him, he was just about to move into his own place, he had this sexy young girlfriend, all the usual bullshit.' She rolled her eyes. 'Every time I saw him, which thankfully wasn't very often, he'd tell me the same old thing. How much money he was earning, how popular he was, how he had this new girlfriend, younger and sexier than me. I never believed any of it, but I honestly wouldn't have cared if it was true. I moved on a long time ago.'

We thanked her for her time and left her cuddling the cat.

'She's more upset about it than she lets on,' said Nathan, and I nodded.

'Yeah, you can't once have been engaged to someone and not feel something when they die,' I said. 'At least, I assume you can't, although if something happened to Richard—' my useless ex and Daisy's dad '—my reaction would be, "Oh dear, what a pity. So anyway… ".'

Nathan laughed. 'Yeah, but he's a piece of work so that's fair enough. Do you think she did actually have anything against Connor?'

'Do I think she wanted him dead? No, I don't. She seems to have her life very much together,' I said. 'I loved her armchair.'

'Ha! I knew it, the way you were staring at it. I'm surprised you didn't ask where she got it. But if you think someone's incapable of murder just because they've got good taste in furniture, I hate to tell you you're probably wrong.'

'Yeah, but her whole house is very calm, organised, peaceful… And her cat too, what a cutie.' Nathan rolled his eyes. 'Don't you roll your eyes at me, mister! You know what I'm getting at. She seems to be living her best life, and if you're doing that you're not going to risk it for the sake of getting your own back on a low-life ex who probably did you a favour by showing their true colours and making you dump them.'

'I'm not entirely sure I agree with your reasoning,' said Nathan, 'but I do agree with where it got you. I don't think she fits. Happy people don't tend to commit murder.'

'No, they don't. But I think you're missing the real question here.'

Nathan looked at me with his eyebrows raised. 'I am? And what question is that?'

'Would that colour armchair go in our front room?'

Nathan dropped me back home and went off to the station, although he wasn't entirely sure what his next move would be. I knew what mine was: making a cake to take to the event that was taking place in the community centre that night.

I'd decided against pumpkin spice cupcakes, after all. I prefer my pumpkin to be in a savoury dish, like the roasted pumpkin, carrot and coriander soup I was planning to make for lunch with the leftover pumpkin. Instead, I'd settled on something that felt really autumnal to me; not just seasonal, but it also made me think of Halloween parties and bonfires and fireworks round at the Penhaligons' when Tony and I were kids. Tony's mum, Brenda, always made toffee apples for us kids, arguing that yes, they might be covered in a ton of sugar and golden syrup, but they were still fruit, so they weren't as unhealthy as other sweet treats. She was delusional, obviously, but they were delicious. And I was taking that childhood memory and turning it into a cake.

I whipped up a basic sponge with some diced apples folded into it. While that was cooling, I made a rich toffee sauce with cream, brown sugar and butter, and caramelised some slices of apple and a handful of pecans. Daisy and Mum both wandered into the kitchen and reached for a slice of apple, which I allowed as long as they peeled and sliced me another one. I piled the apple and nuts on top of the cake and drizzled it with the toffee sauce, which had started to thicken up as it cooled down. By the time I took it to the community centre it would be thick and gooey enough to hold the toppings in place, but not hard enough to break anyone's teeth. Hopefully…

Nathan was still out and Daisy needed something in town, so I drove the two of us down there and left her to it while I popped into Penhaligon's. There were a couple of things I needed for the evening, and I didn't want anyone to see them just yet. I found what I was looking for, took a picture, and texted it to Nathan. ***Are you sure this is what you want?*** I asked. He obviously wasn't very busy, because almost immediately I got a thumbs-up back, followed by a ***Thanks, babe xxx***

'What have you got in there?' asked Daisy, peering at my bag when I met her at the car.

'Never you mind,' I said. 'All will be revealed later…'

Chapter Fifteen

One thing you need to understand about the Cornish is that we love a good street party. Whether that's a carnival, a village fete, a festival or a parade, give us an excuse and we'll all be out there dancing, drinking (possibly a little too much), and basically enjoying all sorts of shenanigans. The other thing you need to know about us (but which I think applies equally to the rest of the UK) is that we love to take 'important' people, or anyone who thinks they're better than the rest of us, down a peg or two. We invented satire (well, technically the ancient Greeks probably did, but we perfected it). We also really enjoy burning things. The two are often connected.

Depending on where in the world you're from, you might have heard of Guy Fawkes and the infamous Gunpowder Plot. In 1604 England was not a good place to be a Catholic (this is a huge understatement: anyone found conducting Catholic Mass or hiding a priest would be subjected to some extremely imaginative and horrific forms of torture and execution). Catholics, of course, took a rather dim view of this, and a group of plotters including the aforementioned Mr Fawkes came up with a plan to assassinate the Protestant king of England, King James, by sticking a busload (or whatever the seventeenth- century equivalent was) of gunpowder underneath the Houses of Parliament and making it go BOOM while Parliament was in session. The plot failed, which was great for the king but not so much for the unfortunate Guy and his co-conspirators.

Someone, somewhere, decided that this plot would be a great thing to celebrate every 5th November, with fireworks and a bonfire taking the place of gunpowder (which is why it's known as either Guy Fawkes or Bonfire or Firework Night). Presumably at first it was a celebration of the failure of the plot; one of the centrepieces of any 5th November party was (and still is) a bonfire, with a mannequin or figure ('the guy') representing Guy Fawkes burnt on top of it. However, nowadays the guy is more likely to resemble or represent exactly the sort of person the Gunpowder Plotters were keen to blow up. Politicians or other divisive personalities can now find themselves represented on many a bonfire. Some places are famous for their effigies, which they parade through the streets before setting them alight and waving sparklers at them. One year, while I was living up country, I went to a bonfire celebration in Lewes, a smallish town in East Sussex which has become famous for its satirical effigies. That particular year there had been a scandal about the then Prime Minister engaging in, shall we say 'lewd behaviour' with an 'unusual' partner during his time at an elite and very expensive public school (note for non-UK readers – 'public school' actually means a private, fee-paying one. Confusing, I know). Cue effigies of both the PM and, um, a large pig's head being marched through the streets of Lewes. There are always a lot of visitors to their bonfire celebrations, but that year it got on the news and everything. Anyway…

Until quite recently here in the UK Halloween wasn't really a 'thing'; you might've got a few Earth mother types (like Jocasta) dancing around in the moonlight without their bras on and chanting 'Death to the Patriarchy' or what have you, but no one really went trick-or-treating. Our parents had spent 364 days of the year telling us not to take sweets from strangers, so they weren't about to suddenly let us go knocking on people's doors demanding fun-size Mars bars with menaces. And although the creeping Americanisation of the western world means that our shops are now full of plastic skeletons, pumpkin lanterns, and multi bags of Maltesers in the run-up to Halloween (and our cafés add pumpkin spice lattes to the menu), Bonfire Night is still the big pre-Christmas party, so much so that in rural and seaside areas lots of towns have their own bonfire committees and their own parade. The parade normally involves the usual suspects (there's always someone who loves getting frocked up, and in Penstowan that's Tony and the rest of the Penstowan Players Amateur Dramatics society) dressing up as devils or, if you're by the sea, pirates, or, if you can't decide between the two, pirate devils. Basically, if your costume involves a striped top, a bandana, horns, make-up, and/or tights, then you're good to go. These piratical devils march through the streets, banging drums (for some reason there's always a samba band made up of drums and whistles, which is where Daisy and her fellow band members came in) and dragging flaming braziers on wheels behind them, filling the air with smoke and chucking the odd firecracker into the crowd to make everyone jump. It's more fun and even more chaotic than that might sound.

Locally, all the towns around Penstowan stagger their bonfire celebrations so we can go to each other's (some of the samba bands are quite incestuous, sharing drummers and instruments), with the parades happening over several weekends usually stretching from two weeks before the official Bonfire Night and two weeks after. And this year Penstowan had hit the jackpot by drawing the night of the 31st October, which meant we could combine Bonfire Night with Halloween and really go all out on the spooky theme.

The parade was due to start at 7:30, with everyone meeting up outside the council buildings. From there we – I say 'we', as Nathan and I had somehow allowed ourselves to be coerced into acting as stewards – would march round the one-way system, along Fore Street, up to the library and then into the big car park by the community centre, which had various food stalls and a stage set up inside for the end-of-march party. I'd agreed to contribute a cake to one of the food stalls, but at that time of night, at that time of year, all anyone really wanted was something to warm them up, which meant hot food or alcohol. The hot food was being provided by the local Sikh community, who were there as part of a multi-faith event organised by Carmen, while the alcohol was being sold by a local cider and craft beer brewer. After everyone had warmed themselves up, it would be back outside and onto the beach, where the bonfire was waiting and where (by that point) tonight's 'guy' would've been lifted into place, ready for burning.

Nathan and I popped into the community centre beforehand to say hello and drop off my toffee apple cake. We found Carmen at one of the food counters, talking to a very smiley Indian man who was feeding her something from a large spoon.

'Oh my,' said Carmen, swallowing. 'That is absolutely delicious, Mr Sandhu. I've never had pumpkin dhal before.'

'Mandeep, please. Mr Sandhu is my father.' He smiled even more broadly. 'I'm so glad you like it.'

'I love it. Would it be rude to ask for the recipe?'

'Not at all! I would be very happy to give you it, next time I see you.' He smiled at Nathan and me and then went back to his cooking.

'Oh my God, that was amazing,' said Carmen, licking her lips. 'I'm definitely in the right place this evening.'

'You weren't tempted to dress up as a witch and come and join us?' asked Nathan, eyeing her outfit, which once again gave a nod to the concept of 'dopamine dressing' by combining her sensible black shirt and white dog collar with a pair of purple trousers covered in colourful bats, cats and witches' hats.

'Tony tried to get me to, but I thought best not, what with me being the vicar,' she said with a grin. 'This whole event is meant to reassure my parishioners and the other local religions that Halloween doesn't have to be about worshipping the devil. We're reframing it as a celebration of Good overcoming Evil. This is the one night of the year where Satanic forces are allowed out to roam the streets before we banish them back to where they came from.'

'Nice reframing,' I said.

'Thank you. The bishop took a little bit of persuading, but I told him the locals would all be out in force, drinking and dancing and being terrible pagans, so we really had to do something to protect their immortal souls, and he fell for it.' She snorted. 'I mean, he agreed that it was our duty, and that it sounded like a lot of fun. He's probably here somewhere, dressed up as a masked pirate so no one will recognise him. He does enjoy a pint of cider.'

'The church has changed a lot since I used to get dragged along as a kid,' noted Nathan. I laughed.

'We're all heathens in my family, but I have to admit if there'd been more drunken dancing and dressing up as Long John Silver I probably would've gone.'

'Jesus did turn water into wine, so I reckon he enjoyed a party,' said Carmen. 'Within moderation.'

It was just past seven o'clock, so Nathan and I bade her farewell for the moment – I was definitely coming back for some of that dhal later – and headed off to the meeting point. Daisy and Jocasta were already there, dressed in woolly jumpers, tutus, striped tights and big boots, ready to set off with the band. I waved to Teri, who was handing out drumsticks nearby, and who gave me a little smile in return, probably thinking, *Oh God, Daisy's weird mum's here.* My own weird mum was going to be cheering everyone on out on Fore Street with Bob, while Germaine was spending the evening away from all the noise at a kennel down the road in Bude. I hated putting her in the kennel but we'd met the ladies who ran it, Lottie and Andrea, while out on walks, and Germaine really liked and trusted them (and their own dog, a Corgi called Madge). It would be just like going on a sleepover. It would be much quieter there than back at our house, and she'd be spoilt rotten tomorrow when we picked her up.

'Where's your costume?' asked Debbie, bustling up to us. She was dressed as a slutty witch, deviating slightly from the usual Bonfire Parade costume in deference to it being Halloween. At least she hadn't come as a slutty nurse, which I'd seen a few younger women dressed as going into the pub on our way there. I'm not sure quite how 'slutty nurse' became part of the Halloween lexicon, but it definitely has. I blame the Americans.

'We're stewards,' said Nathan. 'We're supposed to look sensible and reliable.'

'Boring!'

'Yeah, that's why we're wearing these…' I said, flinging off my coat to reveal one of the costumes I'd bought earlier that day in Penhaligon's. Mine was a long red cloak and a head band with a couple of horns on it. I put it on, studying my reflection in a nearby window; no one wants wonky horns, do they? Next to me Nathan struggled out of his own jacket, revealing a hessian tunic and a hump on his back. He reached into his pocket and took out a Quasimodo mask, pulling it over his face. 'We couldn't turn up in these, we had to pop in and see Carmen first…'

'Oh, that's much better!' cried Debbie. 'Nathan, I've never seen you looking so handsome.'

'Yeah yeah, just try and control yourself,' said Nathan, sliding his mask up onto the top of his head. 'You're a married woman.' He looked around. 'We need somewhere to leave our coats.' I hadn't thought of that, but Maggie Tiddy, who was busy organising/fussing over the samba band, overheard him.

'You can leave them at ours,' she said, strapping a drum to her own chest. 'Brian's still at home, he won't leave until the last moment because he says it's too cold to be standing around.' Brian had a point, to be fair. Nathan took our coats while I stamped my feet to stay warm. He had to keep shrugging to stop his hump sliding down as he headed over to the Tiddys' B&B. But I had asked him if he was sure that was the costume he wanted.

'What on earth does Nathan look like?' snorted Daisy, attempting to snuggle up next to me, which was almost impossible as she had a large drum strapped to her. 'No wonder you didn't want to show me earlier. I can't believe you bought yourself a sexy devil costume and made him wear that.'

'It was his choice,' I said. 'He wanted to look like an Igor.'

'A what?'

'An Igor. You know, mad scientists always have an Igor to mix their potions, hook up the lightning conductor, source young virgins from the village, that sort of thing.' I thought for a moment. 'I should probably have dressed up as the mad scientist.'

'Your hair's already right for it,' she said. 'I'm freezing. It's not tutu weather.'

'It's tutu cold for that outfit,' I agreed, earning a roll of her eyes. 'You'll be all right once you start dancing. Try and get yourself near a fire pit.'

Nathan got back to us just as a whistle blew, marshalling the drummers and marchers (and us stewards) into line.

'Where's Tony?' I asked Debbie. She turned and pointed behind us, where a motorised float was just drawing up. 'Oh my God, I might've known.'

The float carried tonight's guy – a monstrously bloated, orange-faced figure with a mop of white blonde hair, clad in a star-spangled adult diaper. It was HUGE. And standing in front of it (making sure it didn't fall off and roll into the crowd, causing mass casualties) was Tony, supported by a couple more people I recognised as members of the Penstowan Players. Tony was clad in a figure-hugging red cat suit – very figure-hugging – and was wearing a massive pair of horns on his head. In his hand he held a long red trident, which he was waving about and jabbing at the effigy. He saw us and waved before returning to his very camp devilish cavorting.

'He's overcompensating for something,' said Nathan. Debbie snorted.

'In that cat suit? I don't think he's got anything to compensate for.' She saw me and Nathan staring at her and got a bit defensive. 'What? You've got eyes in your head, you can see it from here! It's big enough to scare the horses!'

'Padding,' I said, and Nathan laughed.

'One, two, three…' Maggie counted the band in and the music started, sending us on our way.

Daisy and Jocasta strode ahead of us, keeping time with their drums. Nathan and I hung back a little from the band so we could hear ourselves think, and fell into step with Debbie and a couple of demon pirates.

'So,' I said, trying not to shout but having to a bit, 'I didn't get to talk to you properly when you got home from work. How did the rest of your day go? Did you find anything else out?'

Nathan started to speak from behind his rubber mask, then stopped and pulled it off again, stuffing it into his pocket. I'd suspected he wouldn't last long in it. He started again. 'Sunil did his usual magic trick and got us Connor's financial records in super-quick time. Honestly, that man can sweet-talk banks and phone companies and all sorts of financial institutions into releasing people's records before the ink's even dry on the warrant. It's a good job he's on our side.'

'What did you find?'

'As suspected, Connor's investment platform is a scam. It's basically a pyramid scheme. That's why he was telling all his mates at work about it, because the only way to really make any money from it is to get other people to sign up.' He shook his head. 'Even then, he would never have got all his money back, let alone make a profit from it.'

'Did you track down who runs it?' I asked. 'Could he have realised he was being conned and confronted them?'

'As far as Sunil was able to track them down, the developers seem to be based in the Middle East,' said Nathan. 'There's a physical address in Dubai, which is probably a front or maybe even not a real place, but the IP address is in UAE somewhere. And even that could have been routed there from somewhere else. That's where he went, on Thursday afternoon – to the bank, to see if he could get his money back. I'm assuming he lied to everyone at work because he was embarrassed about it.'

'So he couldn't have confronted the scammers and then been pushed down the stairs to shut him up,' I said, trying to simultaneously make myself heard by Nathan but also keep my voice down to stop the demon pirates hearing me. Luckily they were too busy throwing firecrackers into the crowd to be interested in me. It struck me that as stewards we should probably stop them doing that, as it was quite dangerous. 'There goes one line of enquiry. What about his phone? Any joy there?'

'We haven't been able to get into it yet,' he said. 'Damn these people who actually have impossible-to-guess passcodes rather than just using their birthday.' He looked at me pointedly but I didn't say anything, although he probably knew I was thinking, *I really should change my passcode…* 'But Sunil sweet-talked the phone company as well, and we should have his phone records by Monday.' He shrugged and bent over, trying to keep his hunch, which had started slipping down again, in place.

'You're going to regret that costume,' I said, laughing.

'What makes you say that?'

'Because Quasimodo didn't strut along like a cocky Scouser, did he? He scuttled along, all bent over.'

'I'm Igor, not Quasimodo,' insisted Nathan. 'But you might have a point.'

'So what's our next move?' I asked. He raised an eyebrow, which, combined with him being hunched over, looked authentically Igor-ish. 'I mean, what's your next move?'

He gave up and stood up straight. 'Well, tonight we're going to enjoy the parade whilst also keeping an eye on the convent. Just in case.'

'Do you still think the killer's going to return to the scene of the crime? And tonight? With at least half the town out on the street?'

'At least half the town making a lot of noise and causing distractions?' said Nathan. 'Yes, I do.' He pointed over his shoulder. 'Call it a hunch.' I groaned and reached out to straighten his hump, which had slipped so far down now that it was starting to look like one of those old-fashioned bustles women used to wear that made their bottoms stick out like a shelf. 'I think they'll want to go back and at the very least retrieve those lanterns before anyone finds them, because they don't know we already have. If it was me, I'd be planting another couple of dolls or nooses or something, to make it look like supernatural forces were behind Connor's death.'

'Like he was killed because nobody heeded the warning from the dolls?' I asked.

'Yes. We can't rule out the possibility that the plan all along was to murder Connor, for reasons we don't yet know, and the dolls were there as a distraction.'

'To make it look like it's about the convent, rather than Connor?'

'Yep.'

'Clever,' I said. 'If you're right. Which you might be,' I said quickly. 'I'm not dissing your theory, even though you have form for dissing mine.'

'Okay, what's your theory, then?'

'I haven't got one,' I admitted. 'I'm just not convinced that the sort of person who'd have a grudge against Connor would also know about witch dolls.'

'Anyone who's been to the Witchcraft Museum would know about them, though,' insisted Nathan. 'And that would cover at least half the local population, surely?'

'True,' I said. 'Anyway, I take it you've got someone stationed at the convent?'

'Brett has been secreted in a hedge in the garden round the side of the building,' said Nathan. We both looked at each other and smirked.

'Oh, he'll love that,' I said. 'He's on his own?'

'Yes. We couldn't have an obvious police presence there, could we? We've left the crime scene tape up, and the front gate is locked, of course, so it looks like we've left it secure but unguarded.'

'But of course it's not secure, because of the gap in the fence round the back,' I said. He nodded.

'Matt and Chrissie are waiting outside the community centre,' he continued. 'They're dressed up, so it looks like they're there for the party, but they'll also be able to keep an eye on anyone heading around the back to the secret entrance. And Sunil and a couple of uniforms are stationed along the route, exactly as they normally would be. Not that I expect anything to kick off on the parade itself.'

'We're more likely to need medical assistance,' I said, jumping as a firecracker exploded next to me, 'if one of this lot set fire to themselves. Either that or Tony has someone's eye out with that thing he's waving about.'

'You mean his trident, or…' Nathan looked at me for a moment, and then we both burst out laughing.

'Padding,' I said.

We followed the parade along Fore Street. The fog which had blanketed Penstowan all day was driven back by the flaming torches and braziers of the marchers. As I watched them dancing ahead of us I suddenly realised why Nathan had insisted on being an Igor: it really did look like a mob of angry villagers, descending on Frankenstein's castle (or in this case, department store – Penhaligon's was the biggest building on the street) waving pitchforks and baying for blood. Although to be fair this mob were more likely to be baying for alcohol. A pagan festival where everyone dressed up and even wore masks felt like the perfect place to indulge in a little bit of bad behaviour; the perfect opportunity to go wild in anonymity. The street was lined with people cheering and dancing to the samba band; far too good-natured for a Frankenstein re-enactment, although there was the occasional cry or shriek from a small child, scared of the firecrackers. They were very loud.

'This is mad,' said Nathan, grinning at me. 'The whole town must be here.' Before I could reply he frowned, reached into his pocket for his phone, and peered at it.

'How did you hear that?'

'I didn't, I felt it vibrating.' He opened it and looked at the screen, then held it up to me. 'It's happening. Come on!'

We turned towards the pavement, but there was no way we were getting through that crowd.

'This way!' I said, running further into the parade. We dodged and weaved in and out of the assembled pirates, demons, witches, and (weirdly) a pair of unicorns, then danced around the band and past Tony's motorised float. It had to be the most surreal chase I'd ever been involved in. Nathan waved at uniformed police officers on the route and they joined us, heading for the community centre.

Matt and Chrissie, dressed as Morticia and Gomez Addams, were there, looking out for us.

'Ready?' asked Nathan. Chrissie nodded.

'We thought we should wait for you, Guv,' said Matt.

Nathan sent Sunil, who had the key to the site gate, around to the front with a couple of uniforms. Then he turned to Matt, Chrissie, and me and spoke quietly. 'Round the back. Let's get in without them noticing until we're right on top of them.'

We ran around to the back of the convent then slipped quietly through the gap in the fence. Or at least Nathan tried to but his hump got caught. The rest of us immediately got a fit of the giggles, until he glared at us to stop. I quickly helped him discard his hump and then we all squeezed through.

We tiptoed quietly around to the side of the convent and then stopped in shock. The sight that met us was not at all what we'd expected.

In the corner of the garden, by a large yew tree, two figures were lit by camping lanterns – no doubt the ones we'd found the day before in the attic room. One of the figures was tall and lean, hooded, and dressed in a long, dark robe. A scythe was propped up against a nearby crumbling stone statue. The other figure was smaller and rounder, dressed in a nun's habit, their head covered by a white wimple that glowed slightly in the gloom. The figures' dress was disturbing enough, but what they were doing upped the eerie factor by about a hundred per cent.

They were digging.

I looked at Nathan. 'What do we do now?'

'DCI Withers!' A voice hissed at us, making all of us jump.

'Jesus Christ!' breathed Nathan, turning round. 'Oh, Brett. Good call on texting me.'

'What do we do?'

Nathan held a hand up, silencing Brett, and turned back to watch the diggers. 'On my word... Go!'

I hung back – I'm not a police officer, after all, and I can't actually arrest anyone – but I followed close enough behind to see what was going on. There was no way I was going to miss this.

'Police! Hold it right there!' shouted Nathan, holding out his warrant card. The two figures jumped and turned around. The shorter one dropped their shovel and bent down to pick something up from the hole they'd dug. 'You! Leave it!' shouted Nathan, but they ignored him.

'Holy shit,' I whispered, because the figure now held a small bundle in their arms. I knew exactly what it was without even looking.

The taller figure threw back their hood. 'Don't hurt my nana,' they said. I gasped in surprise.

'Shaggy?'

Nathan turned to look at me. 'You've got to be kidding me. Shaggy? This already feels a bit Scooby Doo.'

'Real name Lewis,' I explained. 'One of Devlin's labourers. And his nana, apparently.' The nun tore off her wimple, revealing a gentle-faced lady in her late fifties, early sixties.

'What's going on here?' asked Nathan, as Chrissie stepped forward to take the bundle from the woman's hands. She gasped in shock as she saw what it was, pulling her hands away as if she'd been burnt.

'Oh my God!' she cried, struggling to compose herself again.

'The poor little mite won't hurt you,' said the woman, softly. I stepped forward too then, reaching out but changing my mind as the woman hugged the bundle more tightly.

'A baby,' I said, and she nodded. 'A baby that was born here, in the maternity unit?'

'Yes. One that deserved so much better than she got.' She hugged it close, although from what I could see there wasn't much left to cuddle; the only way I could really tell that it had once been a baby was from the remains of the blanket it had been swaddled in. It – she – had obviously been buried for a long time, and there could be little more than skeletal remains. As we stood there a cold breeze blew through the garden, a cold breeze that seemed to have the sound of a baby's cries floating on it. I looked up at the convent, feeling unseen eyes watching us. I shivered. The others seemed to feel it too.

'I think we need to continue this down at the station,' said Nathan.

Chapter Sixteen

Nathan put Lewis and his nana, Susan, into separate interview rooms and let them stew for a few minutes, although not without a cup of tea each to warm them up. He'd discarded his hump and hessian tunic, changing into the spare shirt he kept in the office.

'So what do you think, Guv?' asked Sunil, who had arrived on the scene from the front of the building just in time to catch up on the action and help escort the two of them to the station. It had been impossible to get a car through the crowds in the surrounding streets without turning on the lights and sirens, and Nathan hadn't wanted to create panic or even start anyone speculating over events, so we'd marched them through the throng as if we were all mates, dressed up and having a great time. 'Do you think we've caught Connor's killers?'

'No,' I said without thinking, before Nathan could

answer. He looked at me. 'Sorry, I shouldn't have said anything.'

'As it goes, I don't think they're killers either,' he said. 'Can you imagine Susan pushing someone down the stairs? Because I can't.'

'Nor can I,' said Matt. 'She reminds me of my auntie Carol.' He paused. 'Now, my auntie Barbara, I could see her shoving someone down a flight of stairs…' Nathan and I exchanged looks and then decided not to question him on that.

'Let's leave Lewis to think things over for a while longer,' said Nathan. 'Let him think about what trouble he's in while we interview his nan. Matt, I want you to take the lead on this with Sunil. I want to watch her reaction. Keep your phone on, Sunil.'

I wasn't allowed into the interview room, but the station had recently been renovated with new cameras and a control room, so Nathan and I sat ourselves down in front of the monitors and the two-way mirror and watched as Matt and Sunil entered the room.

They did the usual preamble – stated their own names and ranks, then got Susan to state hers for the benefit of the tape machine which was recording the interview – and then Matt opened his mouth to speak. Susan, however, got there first.

'Everything that's happened here, it was all my fault,' she said. 'Lewis only helped me because I asked him to. He's a good boy.'

'Lewis is your grandson, yes?' asked Matt, although we already knew he was.

'Yes. Well, he's not legally, but yes.' Susan looked at the two confused officers in front of her. 'I fostered his mother when she was a teenager, and after she aged out of the care system we stayed in contact. She moved back in with me when she was twenty, when she got pregnant with him, and we've basically been family ever since.'

'Oh, right,' said Matt, making notes. 'So do you want to tell us exactly what's been going on?'

'Yes,' said Susan without hesitation. 'But it's a long story.'

'Take your time,' said Sunil kindly. 'We're not in a rush. Get it off your chest.'

'Thank you, I will.' Susan took a sip of tea, pulled herself together, and then began. 'In 1979 I took my vows and joined the sisterhood of St Ann's. I was twenty years old and I didn't really know anything of the world, but I knew I wanted to help people, and I'd heard that St Ann's was very progressive.'

'She was a nun!' I said to Nathan. He looked amused.

'Yes, I know, she literally just said that.'

'I was surprised, that's all.'

'There were various jobs around the convent, but because of my age, I think, I was put to work as an assistant in the maternity unit. I was probably the closest in age to the girls in our care, you see, and they thought that I would be able to relate and communicate with them best.'

'How old were most of these girls?' asked Matt.

'Most of them were in their teens, anything from fifteen to eighteen, although we did have a couple of poor girls who were younger. My job was to keep them compliant, I suppose, stop them causing trouble.'

'Why would they cause trouble?' asked Sunil innocently. She gave him a soft smile.

'Ah, you're too young, I think, to understand what it was like back then. Underage mothers were seen as troublemakers, even those who'd ended up pregnant through sexual abuse. It was seen as their own fault, somehow. God help me, even I judged some of them when I first started working there. I thought they were loose women, that they'd been willing partners in sin and that they needed saving. To be fair some of them had been willing partners, but that didn't give me the right to judge them. It certainly didn't give society the right to condemn them and not the men who had got them pregnant. But anyway, I wanted to help and in some cases what we did was best for everyone involved.'

'What did you do?' asked Matt. 'Not just you specifically, but the convent in general?'

'We gave them a place to shelter from the outside world. In practice that meant they could stay with us, far away from their friends and family back home, all throughout their pregnancy, so no one need ever know that they'd had a child out of wedlock. When the time came, some of the babies were claimed by the girls' parents and brought up as theirs, but most of them were adopted.' Susan paused for a moment, looking intently at Matt and Sunil. 'The adoptions weren't always voluntary.'

Sunil gave a little gasp, and I knew he was thinking of his own daughters. If someone had tried to take them away from him… Matt just nodded.

'So far, this just confirms what Mum told us about the convent,' I said, and Nathan nodded.

'Yeah. But good to hear about it from someone who was actually part of it.' He stared through the two-way glass into the room. 'Come on, Matt, ask her about the body she just dug up. Ask her about the hospital staff.' He typed a quick text into his phone.

'So where does the baby from this evening come into it?' asked Matt. I grinned at Nathan; he'd trained his lads so well it was like they had some kind of psychic link.

Susan sighed heavily. 'The poor little mite. By the time her mother came to us I was starting to realise that not everyone at the hospital always had the girls' best interests at heart. There was a doctor from the hospital in Bideford who would occasionally come along and do inspections, but the rest of the time it was run by Matron.'

'Caoimhe Doyle,' said Matt, reading the text Nathan had just sent him. Susan nodded.

'Yes. She was a heartless cow.' She blushed. 'Pardon my language, but she was. She didn't seem to realise the young mums had feelings. Some of the girls wanted to be there, they wanted to give up their babies and go back to their old lives, but even then some of them changed their minds when the time came. She just ignored their wishes completely. I don't know for certain, but I think she had a deal with this man who ran an adoption agency. Mr Keller. I never knew his first name. She didn't want me having anything to do with him. I think money changed hands.'

'That's awful,' murmured Nathan.

'Even the girls who felt it was best for their babies if they were given to a new family, they were still heartbroken when it was time to hand them over. One of the things they worried about was that their baby would think they weren't wanted, and often that wasn't the case at all. So I started making dolls, little rag dolls with a dress made out of something the mother had worn, so they knew that a part of them would go with their baby when they went to their new family.'

'The doll in the fireplace!' I said. 'She must've made it for one of the girls. But how did it end up there?'

'This girl turned up one day. She was fifteen years old, and she was tough. Really tough, and she had a real mouth on her. The other nuns were scandalised, but I talked to her and she told me about her family. They were very poor, but some of the other girls came from poor backgrounds, it wasn't unusual. But this girl – Jessica Delaney, her name was – her family were so uncaring, and just plain cruel. She told me she wasn't planning to go back to them after she'd had her baby, she was going to go away and make a new life for them both.' She shook her head. 'I should've told her straightaway to leave, that they'd never let her take the baby with her, but I didn't. I didn't think she'd be able to cope.'

'What happened to her?' asked Sunil.

'Some of the nuns – the ones who worked in the hospital with me – and Matron, they all said she was a troublemaker. She was, to be honest. She never did as she was told. The girls all had jobs to do, in the laundry, or in the kitchen, and she could be a hard worker when she wanted to be, but she didn't like being ordered about. And the sisters who had taken against her, they did treat her very badly, which just made her all the more difficult and rude. The girls slept in dormitories until they were close to giving birth, which were cramped but warm, at least. But they punished her for talking back by making her sleep in the attic. She pretended she didn't mind, because she had a room all to herself, but it wasn't a fit place for anyone to sleep, let alone a pregnant young woman. It was freezing cold, and there was mould on the walls and ceiling, and there wasn't even a proper bed. I told them it was dangerous to let her sleep there, but Matron stepped in and said she'd be fine, Jessica was as strong as an ox, and it would do her good to be taken down a peg or two.'

'I'm guessing she wasn't fine, though,' said Matt.

'She wasn't. They kept her up there for weeks. No one was allowed to go up there, and she was only allowed down for meals. If she was late, she didn't get any food. She went into labour four weeks early. I don't know if it was brought on by the conditions, but they can't have helped.'

I looked over at Nathan, and saw my own horror reflected straight back at me.

'Oh my God,' I said.

'She died in childbirth and so did her little girl,' said Susan. It must've been years ago, but she still looked traumatised by the memory. 'And because no one was allowed up there, she wasn't found until two days later.'

'Oh no,' said Sunil.

'I found her. She'd wrapped her baby up to try and keep her warm, but I think she was probably still-born. Jessica herself died from massive blood loss, still holding her baby.' She wiped her eyes, and I subconsciously did the same. 'All hell broke loose. Mr Keller came, and he and Matron shut themselves away in her office, working out what to do. The only people who knew about it were me, the two of them, and one of the other girls, who'd liked Jessica and had alerted me to the fact she'd missed a couple of meals. Matron came to my room and told me that they would take care of Jessica, and send her back to her family so they could bury her, but I had to take care of the baby. When I asked her what she meant, she told me to put her in the incinerator.'

Nathan reached out and put an arm around me. I always blame my hormones when I get weepy, but who could listen to this and not be moved to tears? I gratefully buried my face in his shoulder for a moment, and then pulled myself together.

'But you didn't do that,' stated Matt. 'Instead, you buried her in the garden.'

'Yes,' said Susan. 'That poor child had never done anything wrong. She deserved a proper burial, but I couldn't give her one. So I did the best I could. I'd made a doll for her, with one of Jessica's skirts, and I wanted to bury it with her, but I didn't have time. I had to just get her into the garden and find her a peaceful resting place before someone saw what I was doing.'

'Get Matt to ask her about the doll,' I said. Nathan typed in a text, and in the interview room Matt read it.

'The doll you made. If you didn't bury it with the baby, what happened to it?'

'I hid it inside the fireplace in my room,' said Susan. 'I didn't know what else to do with it. I still hoped that one day I'd be able to bury it with the child, but I never got the chance to. A couple of months later the Mother Superior came and told me that I was being transferred to another convent, but by then I'd decided that life as a nun wasn't for me, and I left the order completely.'

Nathan knocked on the window and Matt and Sunil looked up, then stopped the tape and left the room. A minute later they were in the control room with us. They both looked shaken.

'What a terrible story,' said Matt. 'I feel sorry for her, even though she should've reported it at the time.'

'She was young, though,' I said. 'And she would've been quite naive, too. She hadn't seen much of adult life outside of holy orders, had she?'

'No,' said Nathan. He turned to look at her through the window, and we all watched her for a moment. She looked to be on the verge of tears, but she was holding it back. 'Make her another cup of tea, and let her have a rest. We'll have a crack at Lewis next.'

Nathan and I got home just after midnight. I was surprised to see that Mum, Daisy, and Joe (who was staying over that night) were waiting up for us. Daisy greeted us at the door and looked a bit surprised when I reached out and grabbed her for a big hug.

'Mother!' she complained, but she must've realised how much I needed a hug from my baby as she relaxed and wrapped her arms around me. I sniffled and pulled away after a couple of minutes, plastering a smile on my face which fooled nobody.

'It's been a bit of a night,' said Nathan, with great understatement.

'I'll get the kettle on,' said Mum, leaping up and making for the kitchen, but not before she'd stopped and given me a kiss on the cheek and a reassuring rub on the back.

'Don't I get one of those?' asked Nathan, and she laughed and did the same to him.

'There you go, love. You don't need it, though. You're not as soft as us Parkers.'

'I know you probably can't talk about it—' said Daisy, with a hopeful lilt in her voice.

'Not just yet,' said Nathan, 'but I'm sure your mum will tell you all about it when she can.'

'Okay. In that case, we're off to bed.' Daisy shot Nathan a quick glance first though, and I saw him nod slightly and murmur, 'She'll be fine.'

'Night, sweetheart,' I said. 'Night, Joe.' We watched

them leave the room before we both collapsed on the sofa. Mum brought through two mugs of tea and a bag of mini Twix bars.

'I half-inched these from a couple of young scallywags what were about to post a firecracker through next door's letterbox,' she said. 'They'll think twice about doing that again. Now, if they'd been about to post it through her at number nine's door…' She grinned and then left us with uncharacteristic diplomacy.

'I think Shirley might be sickening for something,' said Nathan, and I laughed, grateful that he was trying to lighten the mood.

'I know, right? She didn't even try and pump us for any gossip. I'll call the doctor tomorrow.'

Nathan and I drank our tea and slowly worked our way through the chocolate. Finally we'd both recovered enough to talk.

'So Susan wanted work to stop on the convent until she'd had time to move the baby,' I said. 'The plans for the site included building a couple of houses on the garden, meaning the builders might well have dug up the body when they started on the foundations.'

'I don't think she did it just to stop it being discovered, though,' said Nathan. 'I think she genuinely wanted to make sure the baby was laid to rest somewhere.'

'Yeah, I think so too. She's spent the last thirty years living so close to the convent, she was like the guardian of the poor thing's grave.' Susan had told us how she'd gone back to her parents in Dorking, but had eventually ended up marrying a Cornish man and moving back to Penstowan of all places where, after discovering she couldn't have children – punishment, she thought, for her part in the mistreatment of the mothers in the maternity hospital – she and her late husband had fostered a variety of kids from disadvantaged backgrounds, giving them happy childhoods despite the bad starts they'd had. Including Lewis's mum, who had become a permanent (if unofficial) part of her family, along later on with Lewis and his brother and sister. That, I thought, would have more than made up for any supposed sin against the girls of St Ann's hospital.

Lewis, aware that she'd been upset about the convent being redeveloped, had told his 'nana' about the creepy doll that had been found, saying that maybe the site would turn out to be haunted and Devlin would be forced to close it down. After wrestling with her conscience, Susan had told him all about her past and her reasons for wanting the work to stop. It was a testament to the closeness of their relationship that Lewis had immediately volunteered to help close it down, even though it would put him out of a job. His nana's happiness was more important than money. It had been his idea, in fact, to make some more dolls, seeing how much the original one had freaked everyone out. He'd even gone to a local charity shop and bought some old curtains to use. The two of them had hurriedly made a batch of dolls – they were quite simple, and she was retired with lots of spare time, so it didn't take long to make them – and had only stopped when they'd run out of usable material.

'So then you made the noose,' Nathan had said to him, and he'd nodded. 'And you drew a chalk circle on the floor.' We didn't know for certain that anyone had done that, of course – we were just guessing, going by the candle wax we'd found on the floor. But Lewis had looked mystified by that.

'No, we never did that.' He shook his head. 'We didn't even think about that. God, that would've been a lot easier to do than plant all those dolls...'

'But they didn't kill Connor,' I said. 'They both have alibis, which I know we have to check in the morning, but honestly, where's their motive? Lewis thought Connor was an idiot, but the same could be said for most of the blokes working with him.'

'Yeah,' said Nathan. 'We've solved one mystery, but not the most important one.' He yawned. 'I think we should get a good night's sleep and start fresh in the morning.'

'I think you're right,' I said, stifling a massive yawn of my own and standing up.

'Although, if you still have those sexy devil horns...'

Chapter Seventeen

Sunday was usually the day we allowed ourselves a lie-in. But that rule didn't apply when we – I mean, Nathan – was in the middle of a murder case. We were both up and dressed by eight-thirty, eating breakfast in the kitchen and discussing our plans for the day.

'I'm not sure what we can do about the murder now until we get Connor's phone records,' said Nathan.

'But you do have plans for something else, don't you?' I said, swallowing a piece of toast. 'You have that look in your eye.'

He grinned. 'Remind me to never play poker with you. Unless it's strip poker, in which case I don't mind losing. Yes, I do have plans. Something that came up yesterday while we were talking to Susan.'

'You're going to find Jessica Delaney,' I said. 'Well, her parents, at least.' He looked surprised for a moment and then shook his head in wonder.

'I don't know, you really can see into my head, can't you?'

'Not really,' I said, 'I just think we're on the same wavelength. Because I'd be interested to know what this mysterious Mr Keller and Caoimhe Doyle told them about their daughter's death.'

'Exactly. I—' But he didn't get any further before his phone beeped with a text message. 'Sunil's up early,' he said, picking it up and calling his DC. 'Sunil – no, I was up… Ha, yes of course she is. I'll put you on speakerphone.'

Nathan lay his phone on the table between us and hit speakerphone.

'Morning, Jodie,' said Sunil. He sounded very sleepy.

'Bloody hell, Sunil, you sound like you've been up all night,' I said.

'I have. I couldn't sleep, and then the twins started – they're teething and they wouldn't settle – so I took them for a drive and we ended up back at the station.'

Nathan looked at me, shaking his head. 'Sunil, the minute we hang up you go back to bed, okay?'

'Yes, Guv, I will.' The sound of an enormous yawn being unsuccessfully smothered came down the phone to us. 'Anyway, I thought I'd put my time to good use, so I decided to track down Jessica Delaney's death certificate.'

'Great minds think alike,' said Nathan. 'That was exactly what I planned to do today. Did you find it?'

'No. There isn't one.'

Nathan and I exchanged looks. 'Are you sure?' I asked.

'I mean, I know you are, you're so thorough at this kind of thing, but – are you sure sure?'

'Yes, I am sure sure. Her death wasn't registered. The first thing that's supposed to happen when someone dies is that a medical certificate is issued confirming the cause of death. The matron may not have been able to do that, but Susan said there was a doctor who came and did inspections, didn't she? So I would've thought he'd be called in to confirm the death. But there would be a record of that medical certificate, and I can't find one.'

'And anyway, a doctor would've seen that she'd died from childbirth complications,' I said. 'The first thing they'd want to know is, where's the baby?'

'Okay…' said Nathan, thinking. 'What about Jessica's family? It would've been down to them to register the death before they buried her. Have you managed to track any of them down?'

'Yes,' said Sunil. 'I found Jessica's birth certificate, and from that I was able to see her parents' details and her place of birth. I looked on their local register, in case her parents had filed it but it hadn't ended up on the national register for some reason, but nothing. I did find their death certificates. Her mum died in 1993 of lung cancer, her dad in 2001 of pneumonia.'

'Right,' said Nathan, sitting back and looking at me.

'They didn't know,' I said. 'No one told them their daughter was dead. They certainly didn't return her to them. They died not knowing where she was.' In the background of the call came the sudden wail of a baby crying, joined almost immediately by a second. 'Oh my God, Sunil, don't tell me you've still got the girls with you?'

'Er…'

'You'd better get them home before Eesha files *your* death certificate,' said Nathan.

'Okay, Guv.' The call abruptly finished.

'What is he like?' Nathan shook his head. 'Anyway, what do we think happened to Jessica's body?'

'There's a lot of cliffs around here,' I said casually.

'You think they threw her off one?' Nathan looked thoughtful. 'That would work. Plenty of people are swept out to sea and aren't found until they wash up months or even years later. It'd be difficult at that point to tell the cause of death was post-labour haemorrhaging, or to ID her. Nothing to tie her to the hospital that way.'

'And also nothing to stop them doing the same as Susan did, burying the body,' I said. 'Although they probably had the advantage of being able to take Jessica off-site and bury her somewhere else.'

'Probably,' said Nathan, seizing on the word. He gave me a grim smile. 'Your mate Tommy Devlin is not going to be happy about this.'

Devlin wasn't happy, as predicted. No one wants a dead body discovered on land they own, and the fact we thought there could be two dead bodies was not the news anyone would want to receive first thing on a Sunday morning. But he swallowed whatever swear words he'd been about to unleash and agreed to meet us at the building site in an hour.

The fog had finally cleared, and it was a bright and sunny morning, the temperature a pleasant enough fifteen degrees – warm for the time of year. We stood and watched as Ken unlocked the gate and stood aside to let a digger rumble in. We followed.

They started around the side of the convent, the metal teeth of the machine biting into the hard soil.

'We probably won't have to dig too deep,' said Nathan. 'They would've been digging the hole by hand, in a hurry, so they can't have gone too far down.'

We watched for a while, but there wasn't a lot we could do except wait and see if they found anything, so we left Matt and Chrissie there (both now dressed more soberly than the night before, in a suit and uniform respectively) to keep an eye on things and keep us updated. As we left we passed Devlin, about to get into his car. Except it wasn't the slightly battered van I'd seen him use before, it was that little black and white Toyota. He looked faintly ridiculous trying to squeeze himself into it.

'I'd have thought Ling-Ling was too small for you,' I said, smiling. He looked confused for a moment and then his face cleared.

'Oh yeah, that's what my daughter calls it,' he said.

'Your girl's in the band with her, isn't she? They seem to get on well.'

'They do. Only now Daisy's got car envy. She wants one of these for Christmas.'

Devlin laughed. 'Teri been saying it's hers again, I bet. It's mine for when I'm not working, although I did buy it with her borrowing it occasionally in mind. I can't see her driving my van, it's not trendy enough.' He looked serious again, and gestured back towards the convent. 'Do you really think you're going to find another body in there?'

'We really don't know,' said Nathan. 'But if there is one, better for us to find it than one of your lads dig it up while they're working.'

'Yeah, I can't disagree with you there.'

We left Devlin to his contortions and headed to Rowe's for a cup of tea, the lady behind the counter thankfully having given up trying to upsell the pumpkin spice lattes.

'Do you think Jessica's buried there?' I asked. Nathan shook his head.

'I don't know. I actually think probably not, but we have to look,' he said. 'There are parts of the garden where she definitely can't be, where there are trees which would have been there at the time and the ground would've been too hard and too full of roots to dig deep enough. If she's not there, she could be anywhere.'

'Yeah,' I said. I sighed. 'It will just feel wrong if we don't find her. Susan did what she could for the baby, and I'd like to do right by Jessica too. They deserve to be together, finally.'

'Yeah.' Nathan reached for my hand and gave it a squeeze. 'I feel the same. We'll do everything we can to find her.' His phone rang.

'Have they found her?' I asked.

'I don't know, it's Sunil.' He answered. 'Sunil, I thought you were supposed to be in bed? You're no use to me if you're hallucinating from exhaustion.'

I leant in close so I could hear Sunil – we couldn't put him on speakerphone here, not in public where anyone could hear.

'I know Guv, I'm at home and in my pyjamas, I promise. But I heard they were digging up the convent grounds and I thought, what if she's not there?'

'We've thought the same,' said Nathan.

'And I thought we've not really looked into this Mr Keller character, so I did a tiny bit of digging of the online variety and I found him. I think it's him, anyway. Harry Keller, lived in Penstowan until April 1981.'

'Okay…'

'Well, according to Susan's official statement, this all happened in November 1980, didn't it? He'd been living in the same house for pretty much his whole life – it was his family home – and then he abruptly decided to sell up and move overseas.'

'Could be a coincidence,' said Nathan. 'Where did he live?'

'Garrick Road. His house backed on to a campsite. A campsite with a lot of land around it, and it would've been closed at that time of year.'

I looked at Nathan. 'They're digging in the wrong place.'

If Tommy Devlin had been unhappy at being made to dig up his building site, it was nothing compared to the reaction of the current occupants of 143 Garrick Road or the owners of the Blue View campsite it backed onto. But after their initial shock, horror and anger, they all agreed to let the police search the land.

Before we called off the digger at the convent – although they were close to finishing there anyway, as the gardens weren't that big – Sunil contacted a friend of his who worked at Exeter University.

'She's a professor of Forensic Archaeology and Anthropology,' he told us. 'This sort of thing's right up her street.'

And it clearly was. Dr Myra Syed was endearingly bouncy and enthusiastic about her work, which normally consisted of teaching, and I thought she was very excited to have an opportunity to be literally back in the field. She asked us a few questions about what had been the Keller house. There was a gate in the back garden fence into the grounds of the campsite, and there'd been one there for ever as far as the current owners knew. They used it when they took their dog for a walk, and their son had used it as a shortcut when he had a summer job at the campsite years ago. We all agreed it made sense that, if Keller and the matron had taken Jessica's body to his house, they'd have taken her through that gate and out into the fields beyond. We walked through what might've happened, stepping through the gate.

'The burial site is probably not too far from here,' said Dr Syed, and we all nodded in agreement. 'They would have wanted to bury her under cover of darkness, and they would've been carrying her. From what you've told me, at most there would've been two people handling the body, but possibly only one – this Mr Keller – so that would make the burial site even closer to the gate.' She stood and surveyed the land. 'There's a bank of trees over there, which would shelter them from onlookers while they were digging, and they would probably want to be able to identify where they left her just in case they had to move her.'

'That makes sense,' I said, impressed. 'That wouldn't have occurred to me.' Dr Syed smiled.

'That's because you've never had to illegally bury someone,' she said, and I nodded and then thought, Hang on – does that mean you have?!

She strode towards the trees and the rest of us followed: me, Nathan, and Sunil, who despite having apparently been in his pyjamas earlier was now fully dressed and seemingly wide awake, although I suspected he would crash mid-afternoon.

'In the cases I've studied, these things usually follow a pattern,' she said, still walking. 'After the Spanish Civil War, where lots of people mysteriously "disappeared", bodies were usually found at least a kilometre, but no more than ten kilometres, away from the site where they'd been held and tortured, and always within a hundred metres of a main road. So I'm guessing they wanted to bury her away from the convent, to try and hide any connection with what happened there – especially if other girls were being mistreated, or had even died there in the past. So they could've driven her to the house, which is, what, three or four kilometres away? Then, of course, the final leg of moving her would be on foot, so it wouldn't be too far away…' She stopped, just short of the trees where it would've been difficult to dig, and studied the landscape.

'What are we looking for?' asked Nathan.

'Burial sites can change the topography of the landscape,' she said. 'With mass graves, of course, it's much more obvious. But even one grave can alter it. If they dig down too far, once the earth settles it can leave a depression. If they don't dig down far enough, it can leave a mound – usually faint, but noticeable if you look closely enough.'

I scanned the ground around the trees but I couldn't see anything. 'What do you think?' I asked her. She frowned.

'It's difficult to tell for certain… But I think that patch over there—' She pointed to a patch of land that looked exactly the same as all the other patches of land around it to me. 'I think there's a slight mound there, don't you?'

'Er…' I said, because I didn't see it, until all of sudden it kind of popped out at me, like one of those Magic Eye pictures that were popular years ago, when a picture of a candlestick turns out to be the silhouettes of two people looking at each other or something.

'Yes,' she said more firmly. 'I can't say for definite there's something under there, but that's where I'd concentrate my search.'

'Well,' I said, sitting back in my chair. 'This puts a new spin on your hit-and-run "accident", doesn't it? Now we know Matron was a wrong un.'

'Yes, it does,' said Nathan. 'Unfortunately it hasn't given us any more clues to the identity of the driver. It could've been someone she forced into giving up their baby, but as we don't have a list of the girls who were at the hospital I'm not sure we'll ever know. We asked Susan about it, but she was shocked to hear that Matron was living relatively nearby, and she didn't remember the names of any of the other girls.' He gave a small smile. 'I'm not totally convinced she'd tell us even she did suspect someone, and I can't say I entirely blame her.'

We were back at the station. The owners of the campsite had allowed us to tape off the area to be dug while they waited for a team of searchers to arrive. In the interests of police/public relations we'd agreed to use manpower, rather than Devlin's digger. Now we could turn our thoughts to other matters.

Nathan leaned back in his own chair, mirroring me. 'Yesterday I had two deaths to investigate. Now we've got four.'

'Although at least we know what happened to the latest two,' I pointed out.

'True. I can't nick anyone for them, though…'

'Oi, Sunil, wake up!' We turned to see Matt shaking Sunil by the shoulder. He was slumped in front of his computer, looking like he was about to doze off. Nathan and I went over to them.

'Sunil, go home,' said Nathan, kindly but insistently.

'Are you sure, Guv?'

Nathan laughed. 'I've been telling you to go back to bed all morning. Get uniform to give you a lift, you shouldn't be driving in this state.'

'Okay,' said Sunil, managing to look guilty and relieved all at the same time. 'Before I go, I was just—'

'Looking at Connor's social media, we know,' said Matt. I reached out and took the detective constable's coat from the back of his chair and handed it to him.

'We've got this. Go!' Nathan pointed to the door, and Sunil fled through it.

'Your lads are so loyal,' I said, smiling at my husband. 'Just like my dad's were. Old Davey would've done anything for him, and Sunil and Matt would do the same for you.'

'Dunno about that,' said Matt, overhearing, but I knew I was right.

'So, had Sunil come up with anything on the social media front?' asked Nathan, sitting in the recently vacated chair. We hadn't even given Sunil time to log out of his computer, and we could see what he'd been looking at.

I perched on the desk and looked down at Sunil's notes. 'He posted mostly on Instagram and TikTok, although he was on Facebook too. Followed a lot of "manosphere" accounts, reposted misogynistic content and the odd racist meme too – nice combination, that – but the only original stuff he posted were selfies of himself posing in front of fancy cars, which I assume weren't his—'

'He had a 2012 Nissan Navarra,' supplied Matt. 'It's parked in the Beachside car park. Parking warden spotted it yesterday morning. The parking ticket had expired. Connor must've left it there on Thursday night when he went to meet his killer.'

'Why would he park there?' I wondered. 'There're much closer places to park.'

'Maybe he went somewhere else first,' suggested Matt. 'There's at least two pubs between that car park and the convent.'

'We need to get onto them, then,' said Nathan. 'See if he did go in either of them first. They should have cameras as well, so we can see if he was with anyone. Maybe he was meeting someone he knew online?' He scrolled down the list of accounts Connor had followed. 'Hmm. Most of these look like they live overseas. Not in Cornwall, anyway. So they're not people he really knew.'

'What about his own followers?' I asked. Nathan switched lists.

'Half of them have AI avatars for profile photos, and nicknames or just random letters and numbers… BadBoy92, BBBro74732, 4ReelBro, TD462007, Ivana_JerkUov69—'

'Ooh, Ivana sounds nice,' I said, sniggering. 'A real classy young lady and absolutely not a pornbot or anything.'

Nathan laughed. 'Oh no, you think she's not a real person? Shit…' He took out his phone and pretended to delete her from his contacts. I rolled my eyes.

'As if! You'd be terrified if someone like that contacted you.'

'And that's why I'm not on social media.'

'What, not at all?' Matt looked stupefied.

'Nope.'

'Not even Facebook?'

'No,' I said. 'He's a complete weirdo. He only knows people in real life.'

'That is weird,' agreed Matt seriously.

'Anyway, back to the victim and away from me,' said Nathan. 'We need to get access to his messages.'

'Sunil's already on it,' said Matt. 'Social media companies always drag their feet over access, though.'

'Yeah, they do…' Nathan was still scrolling the list of followers, clicking on some here and there. 'He did have a few real-life friends, going by this.' He clicked on a profile. 'Kai Stevens, lives here in Penstowan. Didn't you talk to a Kai?'

'Yeah, I did.' I frowned and bent down to look at the computer screen. 'Kai didn't like him, though. I'm surprised they were friends online.'

'It doesn't look like they actually interacted with each other,' said Matt, also leaning in. 'You know what it's like, someone you vaguely know sends you a friend request and you accept it, but you're not really friends.'

'Yeah,' I said. 'But still… Kai said Connor regularly took the piss out of him, and Shaggy and probably some of the others, too. Kai told me he broke up with his girlfriend a few weeks ago and he was quite upset about it, and Connor was pretty horrible about that, too.'

'Isn't Kai the one who didn't come in to work on Friday?' asked Nathan, spinning in his chair to look at me properly.

'Yeah.'

The three of us exchanged looks.

'In itself that doesn't mean anything,' said Nathan. 'But avoiding work on the day one of your colleagues is found dead, a colleague you didn't get on with… It doesn't look good, does it?'

'If I'd killed someone I'd want to be there when they were found, so I could register my shock and look as horrified as possible,' I said. I'd liked Kai and I really didn't want it to be him, but I had to admit he might have a motive.

'But you've been around murder cases,' Matt pointed out. 'You know what looks suspicious. This Kai bloke wouldn't. And a lot of murderers aren't that clever.'

'He also might've been worried about looking guilty,' said Nathan gently. He could tell I didn't want to suspect Kai. 'If deep down he's a nice person, like you thought, he might not have been able to hide his guilt and thought it was safer to stay away.'

'He doesn't have an alibi, either,' I admitted. 'He lives with his mum and sister, but they're away. He had the house to himself.'

'I think we need to have another word with Kai, don't you?' said Nathan.

'Bloody hell,' said Matt. He'd stepped back to his own desk and had been shuffling through some papers. 'I knew I'd heard that name before. When I interviewed Lewis about planting the dolls, I asked him how he'd known about the back way into the convent. He said one of his workmates had told him.'

'Who?' asked Nathan, but it was obvious.

'Kai Stevens...'

'Bugger,' I said, with feeling. 'But is this enough to bring him in for questioning?'

'It is,' said Nathan, 'but I'd feel better if we had a bit more. Where does he live? If he went to the convent that night, would we be able to pick him up on camera anywhere en route?'

'He'd have to go past the community centre,' I said. 'They've got a camera, I think?'

'Yeah, they do,' said Matt. 'We didn't initially look at the footage from there because we didn't know about the hole in the fence, and we were thinking the murderer must've climbed over the fence at the front, so it wouldn't have caught them. But if they went in round the back they might've passed the community centre, and the library. They've both got cameras.'

'The community centre will be open today,' I said. 'They'll be clearing up after last night.'

Nathan stood up. 'Let's get down there before they finish up, then. Babe, you'd better come with us, because you're the only one who's spoken to Kai and will be able to recognise him if he's on camera.'

We walked down to the centre. It was so close to the station it would've taken longer to drive round to it than to go on foot. It was a hive of rather tired activity, with the food stall holders from last night clearing up rubbish alongside Ged the caretaker, who I'd seen nearly come a cropper with the Halloween decorations a couple of days previously, and the manager of the centre, who I recognised despite no longer being dressed as a sexy vampire, as she had been about twelve hours ago. No Carmen, though; being a vicar meant Sunday was her busiest time of the week.

Nathan showed the manager his warrant card and after a few brief words, she ushered us into her office and pulled up the CCTV footage before leaving to get back to haranguing Ged.

Matt wound the footage back to Thursday night. There were various people coming and going, as the centre had been open for Conversational Italian and Zumba (presumably two different classes, because quite frankly learning another language was hard enough without having to conjugate a verb in Italian whilst shaking your booty). But as the last Lycra-clad Zumba attendee left, the street outside grew quieter and quieter.

'No one about,' I said, not sure if I was relieved or frustrated. But then there was movement; a figure in a black puffer jacket with the hood pulled up briefly came into view, striding past.

'We can't see his face,' said Matt, but that didn't matter because the figure was accompanied by a tiny ball of white fluff.

'Lola,' I said.

Chapter Eighteen

So there I was, back in the control room watching Nathan and Matt interview Kai. His mum and sister were back from their trip, thankfully; I'd been worried that Lola would be left on her own if Nathan had enough to charge him with and kept him in, and she was too cute for that.

'So, Kai, tell us again where you were on Thursday night between ten pm and midnight,' said Nathan.

'I told you, I was at home. On my own, so before you ask no, no one can corroborate that.' Kai sounded fed up, and still a bit croaky from his cold. 'I didn't kill anyone, so I didn't bother to invent an alibi.'

'You were at home all night?' pressed Nathan. 'You didn't leave home at all?'

'No, I didn't,' said Kai, but now he looked wary. 'Oh – hang on, I did leave. I took the dog for a walk.'

'At eleven thirty at night?' said Matt.

'I don't know what the time was, but yeah, it must've been around then…'

'That's weird, because when you spoke to my colleague the other day you didn't mention it, even though she asked you and you'd been talking about dogs,' said Nathan. 'And if I remember rightly, you claimed to have been feeling quite ill. Seems irresponsible to go out so late on such a cold night if you've got a bad cough.'

'Asking for trouble,' agreed Matt.

'I told you, the dog needed walking.'

'The dog's tiny. That time of night, if she'd needed to go outside you could've let her into the garden. The houses down your street all have gardens, don't they?' said Matt. 'Not like some of them round here.'

'I know what you're suggesting, but you're wrong. I didn't go to the convent, and I didn't kill Connor.' Kai sat back and folded his arms across his chest.

'The CCTV footage from outside the community centre looks a lot like you were heading that way,' said Nathan mildly.

'Yeah, well, I often walk the dog round there—'

'In the middle of the night?'

What else could Kai have been up to? I wondered. I didn't buy that he was taking the dog for a walk that late at night – I mean, I know some people do do that, but for starters he'd been ill (genuinely, I thought – he'd been very croaky and looked run down when I'd spoken to him on Friday), and on top of that he'd have been getting up early the next day for work; Ken had said that most of the builders were usually at work by half seven. I suddenly remembered the smell I'd noticed as we'd passed his front room. He'd hastily moved me on to the kitchen and then into the snug, probably because he'd noticed my nostrils twitching. I picked up my phone and texted Nathan.

Ask him about weed. Was he buying or selling? I'd guess selling.

In the interview room, Nathan glanced at the phone and read my text. He gave a brief smile.

'Maybe you were there to meet somebody?' he said. Kai groaned.

'I told you, I wasn't there to meet Connor.'

'Then who were you there to meet?'

'What? I wasn't. I—'

'Kai, if you weren't there to lure Connor to his death then I don't care what you were up to. My only interest is in how it might eliminate you from our enquiries. If you met someone, for whatever reason, you need to tell us. Because at the moment we are this close—' Nathan held his thumb and forefinger up, with a space of about one millimetre between them '—to charging you with murder.'

No you're not, I thought, *you still haven't got anywhere near enough evidence*. But Kai wouldn't know that, of course.

Kai groaned. 'If I tell you, you won't take it any further?'

'Kai, whatever you were actually doing, a murder charge trumps it. Tell us.' Nathan looked at him steadily. Kai hesitated for a moment, and then slumped in his chair.

'Shit. I was meeting a bloke who wanted to buy some weed off me.'

Yes! I allowed myself a fist pump, safe in the knowledge no one would see me do it. I was glad to get Kai off the hook, but I was also very pleased with myself for working it out.

'Why did you meet there?' asked Matt.

'He lives on the estate, the one behind the convent,' said Kai. 'I wouldn't normally go out and deliver so late, but he kept on and on, being a right pain in the arse, and in the end I agreed to. I didn't want him coming to my place. My mum might've been away at the time, but it's still her house.'

'What's his name?' asked Nathan. Kai hesitated again. 'You do understand that unless he backs you up you're still potentially facing a murder charge?'

Kai sighed and reached into his pocket, taking out his phone. 'Here. This is the last text message he sent me, agreeing where to meet. I deleted all the others, there were about ten of them. You can check phone records, yeah? If you check mine you'll see them. His name's Jack, I don't know his surname or his address.'

'So how did he know to contact you?'

'Word of mouth.'

Nathan let Kai go, with a veiled warning about being on the police radar now. He scuttled away, looking mildly terrified.

'Bless him,' I said, 'he ain't exactly Pablo Escobar, is he?'

'More like Pablo Milky Bar,' agreed Nathan. 'You know

how I feel about weed, but for the moment it's still illegal. We're hardly going to bother setting up a sting on him, but it won't be a bad thing if he thinks twice about selling it in future.'

'True. So what next?' I asked. 'It feels like we're back to square one again.'

'No, we're not,' said Nathan.

'No?'

'Nope. We didn't see anyone else on the CCTV footage from the community centre, did we? Apart from a lot of exhausted-looking Zumba participants, and I don't know why any of them would want to kill Connor.'

'It's a bugger getting blood out of Lycra as well,' I said. 'I wouldn't want to risk it.'

Nathan laughed. 'Exactly! So we've narrowed things down a bit, haven't we?'

'The Zumba people were suspects?'

'What? No, of course n— Oh, you're pulling my leg. What I mean is, we've narrowed down the direction the killer could've approached from. Anyone coming from town would've had to walk past the community centre, or park nearby, and there weren't any cars left as far as we could see once the last people had left the centre. There could have been a car or two parked nearby, but that camera covers quite a wide angle, and once we get hold of the footage from the library camera I reckon we'll be able to see more or less the whole street.'

'So if someone got in through the hole in the fence, the only direction they could've come from would be the housing estate?' I said, working it out. 'And they'd have to come on foot, because there's no parking on the roads around there, only on people's driveways.'

'Yes. But there's still the possibility they got in over the fence round the front.'

I wrinkled my nose in disagreement. 'Really? That fence is pretty high, and I don't know how strong it is – surely it would be noticeable if people kept climbing all over it.'

'Maybe, but as Lewis was going in the back way to plant the dolls, that means it only had to stand up to two people climbing over it – Connor once, and his killer twice, once going in and once coming out. Of course there is another possibility that we haven't really considered yet.'

'What's that?' I asked.

'That the killer had a key.'

'But the only people who have a key are Tommy Devlin and Ken whatshisface,' I protested. 'Why would they kill Connor? They're already under enough pressure to down tools, what with the protest and then the dolls and that. They'll have to stop work on the site now, for a while, at least.'

'I know,' admitted Nathan. 'It doesn't make sense for it to be either of them. But maybe there's more than two keys. Maybe there's a spare and someone got hold of it. Or maybe the killer knows how to pick a lock. It's not that hard.'

'You know how to pick a lock?' I looked at him in amazement. He grinned.

'Yes. Well, a Yale lock, anyway. I've never tried to do a

padlock. And I know how to hot wire a car too, although it's harder with new cars.'

'I keep forgetting you're a Scouse scally,' I teased him. 'I bet you used to nick car stereos and hubcaps and Volkswagen badges when you were fifteen.'

'Crosby's not inner-city Liverpool—'

'"Liverpool on Sea". That's what you called it when we first met.'

'Only because no one south of Birmingham knows where Crosby is.' He laughed. 'How do we always end up talking about something completely irrelevant?'

'It's a skill,' I said. 'But yes, I suppose someone could either have found the spare key, if there is one, or sprung the padlock somehow.'

'So to sum up: they either approached the convent from the front, in which case they could've come from any direction, and there aren't any cameras close enough to be helpful in picking them up. Not until we have some idea who we're looking for, anyway. Or they could've walked to the convent and gone in round the back, only if that was the case we probably would've seen them on the community centre camera, and we didn't. We didn't even see Connor, so he at least must've gone in the front way. Or the killer could've come from the direction of the housing estate, which means they either live there and walked, or they drove there and parked on someone's drive, as there's no on-road parking. So they've got a friend or family member who lives on the estate. Oh, and there's only one way into the estate, which is via the road that goes behind the community centre.' Nathan sighed. 'Has that covered all the possibilities?'

'I think so,' I said. 'In other words, it's all a bit bloody complicated, innit?'

'Just a bit,' said Nathan. 'We need to find someone with a proper motive.'

The only way to find a motive for Connor's murder was to dig deeper into his background. But it was a Sunday, we'd had a late night and, despite the fact I sometimes conveniently forget or ignore it, I'm not an official copper. So I was able to make my excuses (which in this case were simply 'I'm off, babe, I'm knackered') and leave Nathan and Matt to it.

I walked slowly home. It was cold but even with HRT I still tended to be several degrees hotter than non-menopausal people, so I was soon warm enough to unzip my coat and enjoy the cool breeze. As I walked I went over what we knew about Connor, which seemed to consist of very little and most of that was contradictory. He was keen to project this image of being successful, financially and with women; but his 'investments' were all just part of a scam and he was even further away from putting down a deposit on a Lamborghini than he would've been if he'd just saved up. He either had a girlfriend who he was reluctant to introduce to his parents (citing her apparent shyness), or he was single and busy enjoying as much casual sex as he wanted and not letting 'hoes' tell him what to do. I could understand him lying to his parents, especially from what I'd heard of his mum, who no doubt was very keen for him to settle down and give her some grandchildren – although from what Emma Blake had told us, that last bit was unlikely to ever happen. And Kai had dismissed the casual sex angle; he'd said (and from what I could glean from Connor's social media presence, I thought he was probably right) that if Connor had had a girlfriend, or a string of one-night stands for that matter, he would've been boasting about them at work. But he wasn't. So was he in a relationship that he wanted to keep quiet? He could have been gay, I supposed – one thing that all men in the 'manosphere' seem to have in common is the desire to impress other men, which could be because they are in denial about their own sexuality, but I thought it was more likely that deep down they were just terrified of women…

'Penny for your thoughts,' said Debbie. I jumped; she was standing right in front of me, holding a pasty which smelt really good. I'd grabbed a quick sandwich for my lunch, but it hadn't been particularly filling and it was three o'clock now, which in my book was afternoon tea time.

'What you up to?' I asked. She gestured behind her with the pasty in the vague direction of the community centre.

'I had to pop in and fill in an accident report for last night,' she said.

'You had an accident?' I asked, concerned. 'Are you all right?'

'No, not me – of course, you'd gone by then, hadn't

you?' She chuckled. 'You're not the only one who had a bit of drama last night.'

'No? What happened?' I motioned to a nearby bench and we sat down. 'Spill it.'

'It wasn't that dramatic. I'm surprised Daisy didn't tell you,' she said. 'It was her mate, Teri. She came over all funny during the parade. She managed to keep it together long enough to get back to the community centre for the party, but she passed out and hit her head on a table as she fell.'

'Poor girl, is she okay?' I asked.

'Yeah. Probably just low blood sugar. You know what these young girls are like, they never eat enough.' She took a big bite of the pasty and my tummy rumbled. She swallowed. 'Sorry, I'm always so hungry these days.'

'Hormones,' I said. 'I mean, I've always eaten like a pig, but perimenopause genuinely does mess with the hormone that tells you you've had enough to eat, so you can blame it on that.'

'It's always good to have an excuse, isn't it?' She grinned. 'I told that Teri to get herself down to the surgery tomorrow for a blood test, just to make sure everything's okay, but she didn't seem keen.'

'Maybe she doesn't like needles,' I said. We sat and chatted for a few more minutes. I got the impression there was something she wanted to say to me, but she wasn't sure how to start, which was very unlike her. 'Okay, out with it.'

'With what?'

'Whatever it is you want to tell me. I can feel it itching to come out.'

Debbie did a dramatic glance from side to side to make sure no one else was about, then turned back to me.

'Okay. That poor bloke that died? He was one of my patients. I shouldn't really be telling you any of this, but I know you're treating it as murder and, well, I don't know if it really was.'

I looked at her in astonishment. 'What are you saying? Was Connor depressed? Do you think he killed himself?'

'I don't know. I know he was worried about the future, though.' She looked around again, then lowered her voice. 'I had him in for some blood tests, a couple of weeks ago. We were testing him for Huntington's disease.'

'Bloody hell. What made him think he had it?'

'His dad and his grandad both had it, and it can be hereditary. He said he'd been worried for years about having it and passing it on to his kids, so he'd finally plucked up the courage to come and have a test.'

I inhaled sharply. That was why he'd been so adamant about not having children.

'Did he have it?' I asked. 'If you can tell me that.'

Debbie gave a small laugh. 'I've told you too much already, so I might as well tell you that no, he didn't have the gene mutation that would lead to Huntington's. But I got the feeling he'd been worrying about it for so long and had so thoroughly convinced himself that he did have it, that he hadn't really taken in the fact that he was going to be okay. I know it sounds weird, but when you've lived with the fear of something like that, when you find out that you're going to be okay the immediate reaction isn't relief, it's denial.'

'Wow,' I said, my mind somewhat blown.

'Obviously I'm not supposed to talk about patients, but I thought I should tell you and then, if you think it's relevant, you could tell Nathan,' she said. 'Just keep my name out of it.'

'I will,' I promised. We talked a little more, my mind still reeling, before Debbie headed off to the supermarket on her way home (they shut at four on a Sunday) and I continued walking.

I got home to find Daisy in the kitchen, absentmindedly tossing a ball to Germaine, who had been rescued from her doggy sleepover that morning by Mum and Bob, and scrolling on her phone.

'That poor attention-starved animal,' I said. She looked up and frowned.

'I'm multi-tasking, that's all. You want tea?'

'Daft question.'

She laughed and stood up to put the kettle on, dropping her phone onto the kitchen table. I caught sight of the web page she was looking at, and my heart leapt. Early Signs and Symptoms of Pregnancy. Oh God, I thought. Was this why she'd changed her mind about going to university? Was she dropping out to be a teenage mum? Don't get me wrong, I think there's a lot to be said for having kids at a young age; you've got more energy, and you're still young enough when they grow up to go out and have a career.

If you wait until you're older and more established, being a parent is even more exhausting, and if you take time off to raise your baby your career can stall or in some cases, never recover. At least Daisy had a decent partner; I could see Joe changing a nappy far more easily than I could see him running for the hills. But that would mean having a baby in the house again. It might even mean Joe coming to live with us, too – in fact I hoped it would, because it would give him the opportunity to be a proper hands-on father, and not leave Daisy with all the responsibility. But the house would be so crowded. I'd also end up having to look after it, and as much as I did sometimes feel a bit broody and guilty for not giving Nathan a child, did I really want dirty nappies all over the house, and everybody grumpy from lack of sleep? Daisy was so grown up, it was nice to be able to have time to myself now…

Stop it, I told myself. If my daughter was pregnant it was her I should be thinking about, not me. I cleared my throat.

'So…' I said, trying to sound casual, but I obviously didn't because she turned round and gave me a funny look. 'What have you been up to?' *Having sex*, I immediately thought, and chastised myself for it.

Daisy sighed. 'You saw what was on my phone, didn't you?'

'Yes, sweetheart, I did. You know you can—'

'And you jumped to conclusions, didn't you? I bet you were just standing there, working out where to put the nursery and wondering if Joe would move in.'

'Of course I wasn't,' I said hastily, because of course that was exactly what I'd been doing. 'But,' I added, because if she was pregnant I wanted her to know that was okay, 'if I had been…'

She rolled her eyes. 'It's all right, Mum, I'm not pregnant.'

I exhaled heavily. 'Oh thank God. So why are you looking up symptoms?'

'Because…' She paused for a moment. 'Because I think one of my friends might be.'

'Not Jade?' I gasped, and then calmed down. 'No, of course not. Is she still asexual?'

'Yes, she is, and no she's not. I mean, round the other way. No, she's not pregnant, yes, she's still not interested in sex. It's not a phase, Mother.'

'I know it's not,' I said, although I kind of thought it was, because I couldn't imagine not being interested in sex. Horses for courses, though. 'So who is it? You don't have to tell me, but I won't tell anyone. I probably don't even know their parents. What about the father? Do you think he'd stick around?'

'I don't know anything about him, not even his name. She's really secretive about him. Jade reckons it's someone we all know and she's embarrassed of him, but I think it's because he's already got a girlfriend and they're cheating on her.' She sighed. 'I don't even know for sure if she is pregnant, just that she's been acting a bit funny. And she looks really pale, but that might just be because she's a vegan and she doesn't eat enough. That's why I was looking up the signs.'

'Bless you, you're just trying to be a good friend,' I said. 'That's all you can do. Make sure she knows you're there for her, and then if she does need to talk she'll know she's got you. And if she needs an adult to talk to, she's got me too.'

'Thanks, Mum.'

Nathan was late getting home that night. Mum, Daisy and I had finished our dinner by the time he got in, but I'd saved him some and popped it in the microwave to warm up while he changed. He plopped down on the sofa and tucked into dinner (fish pie, one of his favourites) with the plate on his lap. I was dying to ask him what had kept him at the station so late, but I did have the decency to let him finish his food first.

He put his knife and fork on the plate, then placed the plate on the floor, where Germaine immediately started to explore the (minimal) leftovers. I bent down and grabbed it before she could lick it, and held it above my head so she couldn't reach it.

Nathan laughed. 'I know you're itching to ask me what's happened. Are you really going to stand there with your arm up?'

I lowered my arm. 'No, probably not. Come on, then, spill. Have you worked out who killed Connor?'

'No, unfortunately not. Not yet. We'll have his phone

records tomorrow, and the information from his fitness watch, which might be helpful in narrowing down the time of death, although we've already got a pretty good idea of when it happened.' He yawned and stretched. 'No, we had a breakthrough on the hit-and-run.'

'What?' I was so surprised I sat down on the sofa. Germaine took advantage of my attention being elsewhere and shoved her furry nose onto the plate, and I was so distracted I let her. 'You know who killed the matron? But surely that's also a lead on the convent case?'

'Yes we do, and no, it isn't,' said Nathan. 'A bloke walked into a police station in Reading and said he did it.'

'Reading? What? How did he— Why did he—'

'I've been on the phone with the officer who interviewed him there, so I'm getting all this secondhand, but apparently he'd been down here visiting some long-lost relative. He doesn't know the area very well and he got lost driving back to his hotel, so he ended up down this dark country lane. He knew that he'd hit something, so he did stop and get out to see what it was, but he didn't spot her.'

'He didn't spot a woman's body lying in the road?'

'No. To be fair, it was really dark and she was very frail and light – she got tossed in the air, basically, and ended up in a hedge, so it is feasible that he couldn't find her, although I would question how hard he looked,' said Nathan. 'He thought he'd hit a dog, or a small deer or something. He drove back to his hotel, spent the night there, and then drove home. He didn't know anything about a woman being killed until the relative he'd been visiting down here mentioned it, because he was due to come back again in a few weeks.'

'His car must've been damaged,' I said.

'It's one of these big SUVs, so there was some damage but nothing to suggest he'd hit anything other than a deer,' said Nathan. 'Of course, if someone had examined it carefully at the time they might've found pieces of her clothing snagged on it, but he saw the blood – not much of it, according to him – and took it through a car wash before getting the dents looked at.'

'And he's got no connection to the convent, or to Connor?' I asked. Nathan shook his head.

'None whatsoever. Which is disappointing, but actually makes life easier.'

'Hmm. Who was this "long-lost relative" he was visiting?' I asked. There was a little alarm going off in the back of my head. 'Maybe he was adopted as a baby, and he was coming to visit his birth mother…?'

Nathan shook his head. 'You're not giving up on this, are you? You wanted her to be mown down on purpose as payback for her dirty deeds, didn't you?'

'Not wanted, as such… It would feel a bit like poetic justice, though, wouldn't it?'

'I can't deny that,' said Nathan. 'But the Chief Constable at Reading is happy to call it an accident if we are, apparently, so that's that. Although he'll get charged for leaving the scene and probably dangerous driving.'

'You're not going to check if I'm right and it was his birth mother—'

'Nope,' said Nathan firmly. 'I'm happy to leave it at that. Aren't you?' He gave me a look that made me think that even if there was more to it than that, justice had been served. Plus it would be almost impossible to prove it had been deliberate.

Germaine, having licked the plate so clean she'd practically taken the pattern off the china, gave a satisfied little humph and started washing her bits.

'At least the dog's happy,' said Nathan. He peered at me closely. 'And what have you uncovered this afternoon? Because you've found something, haven't you?'

'Not so much found as been told,' I admitted, and I told him what Debbie had told me about Connor's health scare. 'So,' I finished, 'could we actually be looking at one accident and one suicide?'

Nathan frowned and shook his head. 'No, I don't think so,' he said. 'There would be easier ways to do yourself in, wouldn't there? Easier and more guaranteed to work. But it does shed some light on Connor, and why he was so against starting a family with Emma.' He sighed. 'It's such a shame, isn't it? If he'd had the tests done sooner he'd have been able to stop worrying about passing the gene on, and that might've meant he'd stayed with her, and maybe he would've been happy with the life he had rather than focusing on money and materialistic things. What a sad waste.'

Chapter Nineteen

'So,' said Sunil. 'I've got the data from the victim's fitness tracker, and it's quite interesting…'

It was the next day. I'd managed to insinuate myself into today's investigating and was standing next to Sunil's desk with Nathan and Matt, waiting to hear what the DC had come up with. He looked very pleased with himself.

'I'd been wondering not just who he'd gone back to the convent to meet, but why,' continued Sunil. 'Why would you go back to a building site in the middle of the night? He might've left something behind, but he'd have been able to get it the next day when he went back to work.'

'I was wondering that too,' I admitted. 'After we spoke to Kai and he admitted being out on a drug drop-off, I thought it might be something like that. But why would they arrange to do that inside the convent? Much quicker and less likely to be noticed if they just did a quick swap on the street.'

'Yeah, I don't think it was drugs,' said Sunil. He angled his computer screen so we could see the data. 'See here, this is Connor's heart rate. The baseline is here—' he pointed to the screen '—and as you can see, it's pretty much the same all day. But then around eight forty-five it starts to rise, and it's elevated for about thirty minutes before slowing down again. It picks up again at nine forty, peaks at nine fifty-seven, and then slows right down again over the next fifteen minutes before stopping completely.'

'That's when he died?' asked Matt, and Sunil nodded.

'Yes, at thirteen minutes past ten. So what was he doing that got his heart pumping so hard for that thirty or so minutes?' He looked at us expectantly. 'What could've tempted him into the convent?'

'Oh my God, he was having a shag!' I burst out, and Nathan and Matt gawped at me for a second before laughing. 'I mean, he was having sexual intercourse…'

'That's a definite possibility,' agreed Nathan. 'The pathologist won't have done the post-mortem examination yet, but that's one of the things she'll check. She should be able to see if he had sex before he died. Sunil, get on the phone to her and see if she can at least do that today.'

'I will. So do you think that's why he was there?' asked Sunil eagerly. 'He was meeting someone for sex?'

'Well, I can't think of many other things that would induce a young man to meet someone in a spooky old building in the middle of the night,' said Nathan. 'But until we hear from the pathologist we can't rule anything else out. It could still have been a drug deal, though not with

Kai, or he could just have been meeting someone to talk about or do something else where nobody would be able to see or overhear them.'

'But the elevated heart rate—' I said. Sunil deflated slightly.

'If you have a physical fight or even just a fierce argument, that can raise your heart rate,' he admitted. 'And if you take drugs or do something else that's dangerous or illegal, that would do it too.'

'Although your heart rate would stay raised longer than that if you'd just done a line of coke or something, I'd have thought,' I said.

'It could be anything,' said Nathan. 'I know Devlin reckoned he didn't have a problem with people stealing from the site, but maybe that's what Connor was there for. Those work lights must be worth something, and then there's stuff like the period architectural features – if they were being ripped out as part of the renovation, they'd be worth nicking and selling on.' He paused, looking at the data on Sunil's screen again, tapping his fingers on the desk as he thought. 'I don't know, though. I still like the idea he was there for sex.'

'Not a very romantic place to do it,' said Matt. I snapped my fingers.

'The candle wax!' I cried. Matt cringed.

'Wax? That's kinky.'

'What? No, you perv! We found candle wax on the floor in one of the rooms on the first floor. Maybe they were trying to improve the ambience by lighting a few scented candles, give the place a romantic glow or something.'

'Yes…' said Nathan. I could tell he was picturing it in his head. 'Still not somewhere I'd choose to go for a romantic rendezvous, but the candles would've made it a bit better.'

'Okay,' said Matt. 'But why go there in the first place? He had his own flat. Why not go there?'

'Because he was trying to keep their relationship a secret,' I said. I pointed to the murder board. 'Look, we even wrote *relationship?* because his parents said he had a girlfriend, but Kai was adamant he'd have been boasting about his sexual conquests if he'd been seeing someone. So if he was seeing someone, why would he want to keep it secret?'

'Because he was gay?' suggested Sunil. 'Although I still can't see that.'

'Or she's married,' said Matt.

'Yes!' said Nathan. 'That would explain why they couldn't go to her place. And maybe he thought if they met at his place, someone who knew her might see them.'

'Yeah, that makes sense,' I said. 'That would account for why he parked where he did – to make it look like he was going to the pub, not off having secret nookie with someone else's wife.'

'And at that time of night, on a Thursday, that car park wouldn't have been very busy anyway,' said Matt. 'So he might not have been seen at all.'

'Right,' said Nathan, in the tone of voice that meant action.

'Sunil, speak to the pathologist and then get onto the phone company and the social media people, put a rocket up them and tell them the longer they keep us waiting for Connor's records the more likely it is that someone will get away with murder. Guilt them into getting their arses in gear.'

'On it,' said Sunil, immediately picking up his phone.

'Matt, pull up as much CCTV footage as you can of the roads around the convent. I know there's not much coverage near the convent itself, but the roads in and out of that end of town, anything leading to the car park where Connor left his car – anything you think could possibly be relevant.'

'Will do,' said Matt.

'What about us?' I asked.

'We're going to see Tommy Devlin to find out if anyone else had a key to the site, or could possibly have access to one,' said Nathan. 'We also need to have a look at his staff records, see who lives near the site, particularly on the estate, who could've got there on foot or maybe could've gone round the back entrance without being caught by the community centre's camera. He said he had all his contractors' details on file, but he's not sent them to us as yet.'

'Okey dokey.'

We drove to Devlin's house, which was on the way to Launceston. It was a big modern detached house, all big glass windows and sharp lines.

'Not my cup of tea,' I said.

'It's a bit "footballers' wives", isn't it?' said Nathan. 'Glamorous but not a lot of character.'

The house had an enormous driveway, big enough to accommodate Devlin's van, a sporty two-seater Mercedes soft top (which was my cup of tea, but out of my budget), and, of course, Ling Ling, the black and white Toyota. Nathan pulled up behind it and we got out, our footsteps crunching on the gravel.

I was about to ring the doorbell but Nathan grabbed my arm to stop me. The sound of raised voices reached us from inside the house. Nathan looked at me and we both strained to hear what was being said, but we couldn't. We could tell, however, that whoever was in there wasn't happy. Nathan nodded and released my arm, and I rang the bell.

It took a while for someone to answer. A woman in her fifties – I assumed it was Mrs Devlin – opened the door and peered at us from eyes that were red rimmed.

'I'm sorry, this is not a good time—' she started, but she stopped when Nathan held up his warrant card.

'I'm sorry to interrupt you, Mrs Devlin...?' he said politely. She nodded. 'But we do need a word with your husband.'

'Yes, of course, okay.' She hastily pulled herself together and then let us in. She motioned for us to wait in the hall, but of course we ignored that and followed her down to a living room at the back of the house, where the raised voices were coming from.

'How could you be so bloody stupid—'

'Tommy,' she said, then again, louder. 'Tommy! The police are here to talk to you.'

Tommy Devlin never looked very happy to see us, and I supposed I couldn't blame him. He shut up abruptly and glared at his daughter, who was sitting curled up on the sofa in front of him, before rearranging his features into something friendlier for us.

'Sorry, DCI Withers, you've caught us in the middle of something,' he said.

'We won't take up too much of your time,' said Nathan. 'I just wanted to ask you about access to the site.'

'You've already asked me this,' said Devlin, struggling to keep his patience. I looked at Teri, wanting to check that she was okay, but however angry Devlin might be with her, I didn't think he was the type to actually hurt her.

'I know, but we just need to confirm it,' said Nathan. 'The site gate is secured with a padlock, yes? Which you and Ken Cromwell have keys for.'

'Yes, that's right.' Devlin fidgeted, wanting us to go. I knew that would make Nathan take even longer.

'Are there any spare keys to it? Do you or Mr Cromwell have other keys for it?'

'No, we don't. It only came with two. I thought you'd established the killer got in round the back, anyway, like those two on Saturday night?'

'We're still looking into that,' said Nathan, smoothly.

His phone rang. He looked at it, and then back at Devlin. 'Sorry, I really have to take this. Do you mind if I…?' He didn't wait for an answer, but left the room to take the call. *Thanks, Nath,* I thought. This wasn't awkward at all.

'Um,' I said. Great conversationalist, I am. 'Nice house. Did you build it?'

'No.'

'Oh. Right. Still… Nice house.' Shoot me now, I thought. But then Nathan came back into the room. He looked at me and held his phone out. On the screen was a video taken from somewhere in Penstowan; it looked like it was near the car park where Connor's car had been left, and the time stamp was twenty past eight on Thursday night. As I watched, a distinctive black and white car drove through the frame, in the direction (as far as I could make out) of the convent.

'Ling Ling,' I said, and both Tommy and Teri looked up at me. They looked alarmed. And then I remembered the names of some of Connor's Instagram followers: one of them had been TD followed by a string of numbers. Tommy Devlin, or Teri Devlin?

'Care to tell me where you were on Thursday night between the hours of ten and midnight?' asked Nathan. Father and daughter shared a panicked look. I saw Teri open her mouth to speak, but her father spoke first.

'I was in Penstowan,' he said. 'I admit it.'

'And what were you doing in Penstowan?' asked Nathan. Devlin swallowed hard.

'I was meeting Connor at the convent.'

'Dad!' burst out Teri, but he glared at her and shook his head.

'I'm sorry, sweetheart, but it's best you hear it from me,' he said. 'It was me. I killed him.'

'Tommy!' Behind us Mrs Devlin sounded shocked, and she looked like she might swoon, but she reached behind her and found an armchair to fall into.

'I'm sorry, but he was – he wronged my daughter,' said Devlin. 'Nobody hurts my little girl.'

'Dad, no—'

'I did it for you,' he said, turning to look at Teri. 'It's my job to keep you safe. I did it for you.'

We drove Devlin to the police station and put him in an interview room.

'Sunil, any luck with the phone records?' asked Nathan.

'They've promised we'll have them by the end of the day,' said Sunil. 'But we don't need them so much now, do we, if he's confessed?'

'Hmm.'

Nathan and Matt went into the interview room, while Sunil and I sat in the control room, watching.

Tommy Devlin told Nathan that he'd discovered Connor was sleeping with his daughter. As the dead man was thirty-two, and his daughter was only nineteen, he'd understandably been both furious with him and very concerned for Teri. He'd arranged to meet him at the convent in order to threaten him to leave her alone, but things had got out of hand.

'Why did Connor agree to meet you?' asked Nathan. 'He must've known you'd be angry with him, maybe even violent towards him.'

'I sent him a message from my daughter's phone,' said Devlin, after a moment's hesitation. 'She told me they used to meet there so no one would see them.' He grimaced. 'If only she'd told me sooner, I'd have put a stop to it before it went too far.'

'So you pretended to be Teri. You arranged a rendezvous with him, and then pushed him down the stairs,' said Matt.

'Yes.'

'What happened before you pushed him?' asked Nathan.

'What do you mean?'

'Did you argue?'

'Yeah. Yeah, of course we did. And then I lost my temper and pushed him down the stairs.'

No mention of throwing coffee in his face, I thought. If that's what it had been. And that thought was followed by: Daisy's pregnant friend's a vegan. Would she drink black coffee, as she couldn't have dairy?

I was about to tap on the glass when Sunil received a phone call. 'The pathologist,' he said to me, before answering it. 'DC Bakshi.'

I watched the interview, listening to Sunil's half of the conversation, which was brief.

'Thanks, doc,' he said. 'I think you might've just solved

our case.' He disconnected the call and looked at me. 'We need to interrupt this...'

Five minutes later Nathan was back in the interview room. He restarted the tape recording.

'So, Mr Devlin,' he said. 'You've told us that you were with the victim in the convent from eight thirty. We've just had a call from the pathologist who has reason to believe that Connor Milburn had sexual intercourse shortly before his death.' He stared at Devlin, completely straight-faced. 'Tell me, Mr Devlin, were you having a homosexual relationship with Mr Milburn?'

'What? No, of course I bloody wasn't!' Devlin was red in the face, not just from anger but from fear, too. Because his flimsy story was about to come crashing down.

'Mr Devlin, you're a good father. You want to protect your daughter, of course you do. But this isn't helping.'

'I told you, I killed the bastard, not Teri!'

'I think Teri borrowed the car, as she often did, and went to meet Connor at the convent, where they had sexual intercourse.' In the control room I cringed; poor Devlin, he didn't need reminding of that. 'Do you keep all your keys together, Mr Devlin? All of mine go in a little dish on a side table by the front door. I'm sure she would've known where your key for the padlock was, anyway, and she took it when she took the car key. Afterwards, I think she told him that she was pregnant. We know from his previous girlfriend that he didn't want children, so I'm assuming he didn't take it well.' Devlin stared at Nathan in complete shock, but I thought it was shock at Nathan putting two and two together, not at his daughter being pregnant. That, I thought, was what they'd been arguing about when we got to their house.

'It would be so upsetting, wouldn't it, to be young and pregnant and scared, and then your boyfriend tells you he wants nothing to do with a baby and you're on your own. The betrayal, well, it would be enough to make anyone furious.' Nathan spoke softly, but his words were hitting their intended target.

'No…' protested Devlin weakly, but it was obvious that Nathan was right.

'I've sent a couple of officers to pick up your daughter,' said Nathan, 'so I'm sure we'll soon get to the bottom of this.'

'He deserved it!' shouted Devlin. 'Whoever killed him, he deserved it!'

And I thought he might be right, but that didn't make it okay.

'I can't believe it,' said Daisy.

Nathan and I were at home, after a very busy day at the station. The news would get out soon enough, but I wanted Daisy to hear it from us first. She hadn't been friends with Teri for very long, but she'd liked her and had been concerned enough when she'd realised her new friend was pregnant. And now she was being charged in connection with Connor's death.

Teri Devlin had arrived at the station before the uniforms sent to get her had even left. She'd known she couldn't let her father take the blame for what she'd done.

Our assumptions had been more or less spot on. Teri had known where her dad had kept his keys, so when she and Connor had been looking for a place to get together she'd suggested the convent. It had appealed to her because, as Devlin had said himself, she liked 'weird' things. Connor had been the one to take along candles and blankets to make it more inviting, and it sounded like he had actually cared about her – up to a point. Not enough to be open about their relationship and risk the wrath of Tommy Devlin (which I thought was justified, because no one in their thirties should be going out with someone still in their teens), and definitely not enough to want children with her. Maybe the irony of his situation – getting a teenage girl pregnant, knowing now that he could have kids without passing on a genetic time bomb to them – had allowed him to feel some very delayed guilt and maybe even grief over the family he might've had with Emma, making him even crueller in his rejection when she'd told him. While Teri'd enjoyed the sneaking around – it had made it feel more exciting and romantic – the realisation that he'd only ever seen her as someone to have a bit of fun with had been an unwelcome surprise. She'd taken a flask of coffee along with her that night to keep them warm – black, because as a vegan she didn't drink dairy, and he couldn't drink the almond milk that she usually replaced it with because of a nut allergy – but that had meant it had stayed far too hot to drink. Not too hot to throw in his face, though, as they argued their way down the stairs. It had caused him to step back in shock and pain, losing his footing and tumbling all the way to the bottom, where the impact against the stone floor had knocked him out. She'd been terrified of what he would do to her when he came round and had left him there, locking the padlock on the gate behind her to slow him down if he pursued her.

'So she didn't mean to kill him,' said Daisy. 'Will she be charged with murder or will it be manslaughter?'

'I don't know,' said Nathan. 'That's down to the CPS to decide.'

'They can't send her to prison, though, can they? She's pregnant.'

'She'll be sent to a mother and baby unit,' I said gently. 'She'll have the baby there, and then it'll be able to stay with her in prison until it's eighteen months old. Her mum and dad said they'll look after the child after that, until she's released.'

'Poor Teri…' sniffed Daisy, and I had to agree.

Nathan reached out and pulled the two of us into a group hug, which I think Daisy and I both needed, and then released us with a sigh. 'Do you believe in ghosts? Because it feels to me like that whole building was haunted. All the sadness and pain that happened to the girls there, it feels like the walls just absorbed it all like a sponge and now and then it leaks out to infect anyone reckless enough to step inside.' He saw me and Daisy looking at him incredulously and smiled. 'Ignore me, I'm being daft.'

'No you're not,' I said. 'Jocasta would say the convent needs sage-ing, but I don't think that's enough. The whole site needs bulldozing.'

It was a week later. The sun was out and it was surprisingly warm for a November afternoon. Nathan and I parked the car and walked through the graveyard, where a large crowd of mourners had gathered. We joined them. Carmen stood in front of a newly dug grave, where two coffins, one tiny, one adult-sized, waited to be lowered. She said a few words, but I barely heard them because the sight of that baby coffin had numbed everything else for me. Afterwards, I wiped my eyes as Tony and Carmen came over.

'The town did us proud,' said Tony, and Carmen nodded, looking teary-eyed herself.

'They did Jessica and her baby proud,' I corrected him. 'They're finally together.' And on the wind the faint sound of a baby crying could be heard, before softly fading away.

Epilogue

Four months later, another crowd. Not as big as the one at the funeral of Jessica and her baby; not even as big as the crowd the protest against the development had drawn, and there was no BBC crew covering it for Spotlight. More like an almost silent crowd of witnesses, there to make sure the job was done properly.

I stood with Mum and Jocasta, watching the bulldozers get to work. Tommy Devlin had (unsurprisingly) lost any desire to continue with the redevelopment of the convent and cottage hospital of St Ann's; who'd want to live there now, anyway? In buildings that had seen so much sorrow that it seemed to sit between the bricks like supernatural mortar?

At least neither building was listed or considered of great historical importance. The council had stepped in and purchased them, and there were already plans for a low-rise block of flats and a medical centre, encompassing a doctors' surgery, a pharmacy, and a dentist. All they had to do was build it, and they (the medical professionals) would come. Hopefully.

As a couple of walls slowly came down the crowd began to drift away. Maybe they'd been expecting dynamite, the buildings tumbling down dramatically like they do with tower blocks and industrial chimneys. One BOOM! and all that's left is rubble. Instead, the slow, methodical demolition of the old buildings would take at least a week, I thought.

Jocasta sighed. 'End of an era. A horrible one.'

'Yep,' I said. 'Good riddance. Let's go and have a cuppa. Mum?'

But my mum wasn't listening to us. Instead she was staring at a woman who was standing on the other side of the road, watching as the front wall of the convent was reduced to crumbled stonework. She looked to be in her mid-seventies – my mum's age – and she was accompanied by a man I estimated to be in his late fifties. He must be her son; the family resemblance was obvious.

'Mum?' I said again. But she ignored me and walked slowly over to the woman.

'Excuse me, but… are you Dot?'

The woman looked at Mum, and then her eyes widened with surprise. 'Shirley? Is that you?' After a brief pause they threw their arms around each other and hugged, hard. Mum stepped back, wiping her eyes, as the other woman – Dot – did the same. 'I didn't know you were still living here.'

'Never left,' said Mum. 'You come back to watch it come down?'

Dot nodded. 'I had to,' she said. 'Even after I got away, I had nightmares about this place. Nightmares where I never met you, and they took my baby away.' She gestured to the man with her, who stepped forward with a smile. 'Shirley, meet my son.'

THANK YOU FOR READING

THE CORNISH HALLOWEEN MURDER

IT WOULD MEAN SO MUCH IF YOU COULD LEAVE A REVIEW ON ALL YOUR PREFERRED PLATFORMS AND SOCIAL MEDIA TO HELP SPREAD THE WORD!

YOU CAN ALSO FOLLOW ME ON
INSTAGRAM @FIONALEITCHAUTHOR
AND FACEBOOK @FIONAKLEITCH

OR SIGN UP FOR MY NEWSLETTER AT
WWW.ONEMORECHAPTER.COM/NEWSLETTER
FOR ALL THE UPDATES ON MY LATEST WORKS.

KEEP READING FOR A TASTY RECIPE!

Thanks and Acknowledgements

Those of you who've been here before will know that I always write these bits to reflect the subject of the book. So, inspired by the many, *many* Halloween episodes of *The Simpsons Treehouse of Horror* I've watched, here we go…

First of all, I'd like to thank the Good Witch of the North, **(G)Lin(d)a Langlee**. Thank you for putting the 'fluence on people and getting them to give me book deals and TV contracts! You are indeed a powerful sorceress.

The next lot of thanks go to the High Priestess of One More Chapter, **Jennie Wraithwell**, and her team of busy little imps, for giving Jodie such a good home. The way you turn the fevered scribblings of a mad woman into actual books is nothing short of magical.

I couldn't let a book go by without thanking my emotional support coven, ma ghouls **Spooky Jade Boo!-khari, Cackling Carmen Radtke, Nina Kaye-of-the-Dead, Banshee Barker and Andie Eye-of-Newton**. Thank you for joining me around the (virtual) cauldron to curse, swear vengeance and occasionally celebrate by dancing around in the moonlight in the altogether (what do you mean, that's just me?). I *might* be able to do it without you, but it wouldn't be half as much fun, so I'm not even going to try.

And as always, last but NEVER least, thanks to my husband **Dominic Screech** and son **Lucas 'Fionastein's Monster'** (I made him, after all) **Bloodsucking Leech**. I love you both to the full moon and back.

Jodie's Tried and Tested Recipes #11

Pecan and Toffee Apple Cake

I'm not sure how I feel about Halloween. I mean, it's a great excuse to buy a big bag of sweets and fun size chocolate bars 'just in case trick or treaters come knocking' – they rarely do, so it means I can eat them myself – and horror films hit different when you watch them on the 31st of October. I also love a good pumpkin, but to eat rather than carve (roasted pumpkin is yummy, especially blended up with some garlic and coriander into a soup), so it's annoying when we only seem to get them in the shops here for a week in late October. I just can't be doing with all the plastic bats and skeletons.

But I *do* love Autumn and early winter, when we get days of cold, crisp sunshine, or atmospheric mists floating in from the sea (although admittedly, those get old after they've hung around for more than a couple of days, something they are wont to do in these parts). I love the 5th of November, the smell of bonfires and fireworks in the air; I love standing outside in the garden at night, watching rockets burst into the dark sky leaving trails of sparkling stars in their wake, hearing the whizzes and bangs (although not so much now I'm a dog owner). And I will always remember those days when I was a child, going round to the Penhaligons' for their bonfire night parties, eating potatoes that had been wrapped in foil and placed in the glowing embers of the fire to bake, slathered in butter and topped with a handful of cheese, and finishing off with a toffee apple for pudding.

These days, of course, I am far too sophisticated for toffee apples (and wary of my teeth – those babies are rock hard). But I still love that combination of crisp, slightly tart apple and sweet toffee. So I give you, instead, the much more grown-up delight (in other words, it's soft enough to eat without breaking your dentures) that is the Pecan and Toffee Apple Cake!

As always, I've attempted to give you both the UK ingredients and measurements and their US equivalents (in italics), but if you're not sure about the conversions look them up on Google.

1. Preheat the oven to **180°c/160°c** fan ***350°f/160°f*** and grease and line two 8" tins with baking paper. (I know, '8 inches' is imperial and all the other UK measurements are in metric, but that's just how we roll here. We still use miles instead of kilometres, and feet and inches when talking about someone's height, even though if we're measuring anything else it's in centimetres and kilometres. Anyway...)

2. Peel and chop **500g/*17 oz*** of **cooking apples** into small pieces, about 2cm big (that's like three quarters of an inch. I'm not expecting you to measure them, just make them, you know, fairly small). Put them into a bowl and sprinkle **50g/*1.5 oz*** of **light brown sugar** over them and put to one side.
3. Beat together **300g/*10.5 oz*** of **softened unsalted butter** with the same amount of **light brown sugar** until light and fluffy.
4. Beat in **300g/*10.5 oz*** of **self-raising flour,** then add **6 beaten eggs** and **1tsp ground cinnamon.**
5. Fold in the chopped apples, then divide the mixture between the two baking tins. Bake for 40-45 minutes until golden brown, and until you can insert a skewer and it comes out clean. Let the cakes cool for about ten minutes in their tins, before taking them out and leaving them to cool fully on a rack.
6. To make the frosting, cream together **200g/*7 oz*** of **softened unsalted butter** (yes, more butter! Despite this containing a lot of apples, it's not health food…) with **500g/*17.5 oz*** of **icing/*confectioners'* sugar** – make sure the butter is nice and soft, otherwise you'll end up giving your arms a rather more strenuous workout than you intended (don't ask me how I know this!). Once the frosting is nice and smooth and creamy, add **100ml/*3.5fl oz*** of **toffee sauce**. You *could*

make this yourself, but there's already a lot going on with this cake so be lazy like me and buy it. I used one of those sauces in a squeezy bottle, the sort you put on ice cream.

7. Sandwich the two cooled sponges together with frosting, then pipe or spread the rest on top of the cake. I piped swirls on rather than slathered the top with it, as it's very sweet. Then decorate it with **pecans** and a drizzle of toffee sauce. You could also use popcorn or slices of apple (although only if you're intending to eat the whole cake quickly, as the apple will go a bit brown if it's not eaten straightaway).
8. Put the kettle on, undo the top button of your trousers, and tuck in!

Have you read the rest of the Nosey Parker series?

Still spinning from the hustle and bustle of city life, Jodie 'Nosey' Parker, is glad to be back in the Cornish village she calls home. But with a missing bride on her hands, murder and mayhem lurks around every corner…

When a body turned up at her last catering gig it certainly put people off the hors d'oeuvres. With a reputation to salvage, Jodie's determined that her next job for the village's festival will go off without a hitch.

But when chaos breaks out, Jodie Parker somehow always finds herself caught up in the picture…

Can she find the killer before the village faces another brush with death?

A film company is coming to the Cornish village of Penstowan, and the whole community turn up to be cast as extras, even Jodie 'Nosey' Parker.

But right on cue, the company's caterer is sabotaged and Jodie must step up. It soon becomes clear that someone is out to spoil the filming… With actors behaving out of character and the house literally being brought down, breaking a leg is the least of their worries.

Can Jodie save the day once again, or will it be their final curtain call?

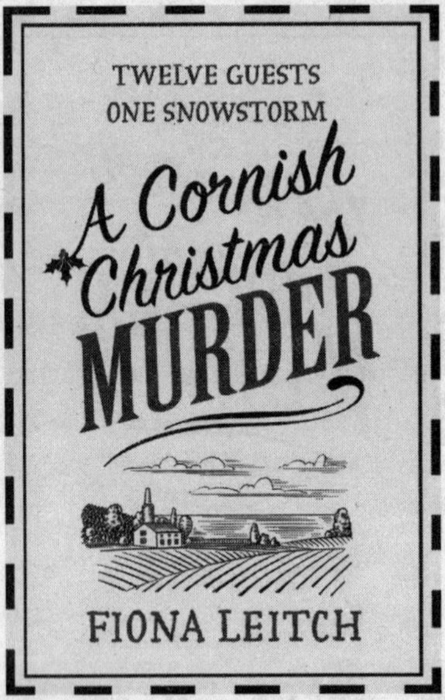

A PINCH OF PARANOIA

It's three days before Christmas, and detective-turned-chef Jodie 'Nosey' Parker is drafted in to cater an event run by a notorious millionaire at a 13th-century abbey.

A DASH OF DECEPTION

Things get more complicated when a snowstorm descends, stranding them all…

A MURDER UNDER THE MISTLETOE

Secrets mull in every corner – can Jodie solve the crime before the killer strikes again?

When 'The Best of British Baking Roadshow' rolls into town and sets up camp in the grounds of Boskern House, former police officer Jodie 'Nosey' Parker finds herself competing to represent Cornwall in the grand final.

But with a fellow contestant who will stop at nothing to win, Jodie discovers that the roadshow doesn't just have the ingredients for the perfect showstopper cake, but also for the perfect murder…

Can Jodie expose the culprit? Or will the murderer become the real showstopper?

A Siren's call… to murder

While tourists and locals alike are falling under the spell of the annual mermaid festival with its captivating legends of Sirens luring fishermen to their deaths, Jodie and Nathan fear they may have found themselves in the middle of a very real – and very dangerous – turf war.

As the casualties start to stack up, they must face the likelihood that something sinister has been going on under their noses for some time…

A campfire gathering. A circle of suspects.

Just along the coast from Penstowan, the local festival has filled the area. Former Met police officer Jodie 'Nosey' Parker has agreed to step in and help run the Pie Hard food truck, along with her reluctant fiancé, DCI Nathan Withers.

As they prepare for a weekend of camping, Jodie hadn't bargained on witnessing a fight between members of the lead band. But when the body of one of the band members is found not far from the campsite, Jodie finds it hard to believe it was an accident. Especially when the other members had so much to gain…

Could the murderer be on the guest list?

The time has finally come for former Met police officer Jodie 'Nosey' Parker to wed her fiancé DCI Nathan Withers, But their long-anticipated wedding doesn't quite go to plan…

As their guests descend on a luxurious Cornish castle for a weekend of activities, celebrations grind to a halt when they find the body of a young woman floating face down in an ornamental pond. With the champagne chilling and canapes assembled, and an old London adversary brought in to investigate, it's up to Jodie and Nathan to uncover the killer, before they strike again.

A killer waiting in the wings

It's Christmas in Penstowan, and local amateur dramatics group the Penstowan Players are putting on their annual pantomime. This year it's 'Aladdin', and half the town have been drafted in to help.

But it's not just terrible jokes, quick costume changes and backstage chaos that wait in the wings… When a corpse lying next to Aladdin's bloodstained magic lamp is found, it's time for Jodie and her partner, DCI Nathan Withers, to find the killer before the curtains close.

Everyone always says that your honeymoon should be a holiday to remember…

Ex-Metropolitan Police sergeant Jodie Parker and her new husband, DCI Nathan Withers, are honeymooning at a luxurious eco-resort on a secluded Cornish island. However, when a fierce storm traps everyone on the island, tragedy strikes – a guest is found dead in the wreckage of the boathouse, and it looks like murder…

ONE MORE CHAPTER

YOUR NUMBER ONE STOP FOR PAGETURNING BOOKS

The author and One More Chapter would like to thank everyone who contributed to the publication of this story...

Analytics
Imogen Wolstencroft

Audio
Fionnuala Barrett
Ciara Briggs

Design
Lucy Bennett
Fiona Greenway
Liane Payne
Dean Russell

Digital Sales
Laura Daley
Lydia Grainge
Hannah Lismore

eCommerce
Laura Carpenter
Madeline ODonovan
Charlotte Stevens
Christina Storey
Rachel Ward

Editorial
Rosie Best
Kara Daniel
Charlotte Ledger
Jennie Rothwell
Hana Rowlands
Tony Russell
Sofia Salazar Studer
Caroline Scott-Bowden
Helen Williams

Harper360
Emily Gerbner
Ariana Juarez
Jean Marie Kelly
Kamrun Nesa
emma sullivan
Sophia Wilhelm

International Sales
Ruth Burrow
Bethan Moore
Colleen Simpson

Inventory
Sarah Callaghan
Kirsty Norman

Marketing & Publicity
Occy Carr
Chloe Cummings
Grace Edwards
Katie Sadler

Operations
Melissa Okusanya
Vanessa Coubrough

Production
Denis Manson
Simon Moore
Francesca Tuzzeo

Rights
Ashton Mucha
Alisah Saghir
Zoe Shine
Aisling Smyth

Trade Marketing
Ben Hurd
Eleanor Slater

The HarperCollins Contracts Team

The HarperCollins Distribution Team

The HarperCollins Finance & Royalties Team

The HarperCollins Legal Team

The HarperCollins Technology Team

UK Sales
Isabel Coburn
Jay Cochrane
Leah Woods

And every other essential link in the chain from delivery drivers to booksellers to librarians and beyond!